KFIR
LUZZATTO

An Italian
Obsession

Pine Ten, LLC
205 North Michigan Avenue
Chicago, IL 60601

First publication, September 2012

ISBN: 978-1-938212-10-9

Books by Kfir Luzzatto

CROSSING THE MEADOW

THE ODYSSEY GENE

THE EVELYN PROJECT

HAVE BOOK, WILL TRAVEL
(With Yonatan Luzzatto)

AN ITALIAN OBSESSION

EXODUS '95

CHIPLESS

REWIRED (The sequel to CHIPLESS)

ONCE AWAKENED

The Tessa Extra-Sensory Agent series:
TESSA (Tessa Extra-Sensory Agent Book 1)
THE OTHERS (Tessa Extra-Sensory Agent Book 2)
HUNTER (Tessa Extra-Sensory Agent Book 3)

The DEAD & BUSY series:
#1: ACCIDENTAL LAZARUS
#2: PHANTOM LOVER
#3: MICE
#4: THE ACCOUNTANT

Contents

Dedication

To my brother, Ariel, who understands things.

CHAPTER 1

Nothing in Alex's slender figure warned me that, sooner or later, she would take me to heaven as a prelude to putting me through hell. She rose gracefully when the girls' teacher waved her ridiculous stick in the air, prompting the fifth-graders to stand up. Her full lips parted, and she looked me straight in the eyes, adding a hint of an impish smile as if to say, "I caught you staring." Then she lowered her gaze with proper modesty and joined her classmates in the singing.

Looking back, I realize that the signals she had sent me in those brief moments were way too sensual for a boy my age to handle, but right then, all I felt was a tingling in my body and the pleasant sensation that came from secretly rubbing against the choir rail.

I often wished I could recapture that elusive feeling ...

I guess that the natural thing for a boy is to turn to his closest relatives and friends when he feels lost and needs help growing up, but I didn't really have anybody to turn to. My friends had no interest in girls and no experience with them. My brother, Fabrizio, was five years old at the time and not much use to me in any respect. My father was a businessman, always involved in important talks, deals, and meetings. He used to speak at length of his affairs, but I never knew much about them despite that. Perhaps I wasn't listening, or maybe his long ramblings didn't really convey much information. I know that thermo-siphons were involved, and I'm pretty sure that at one time or another, he either sold or manufactured women stockings because he used to bring samples home to my mother, but that's more or less all I know. When he was at home, our task was to keep quiet and let him enjoy his meals, his rest, his gramophone, or his guests. My father's main concern, on the other hand, was to ensure that we would behave "properly"– an adverb that assumed different and difficult-to-grasp meanings at different times. I could almost hear him telling me that I would be old enough, soon enough, to worry about girls and that, for the time being, I should concentrate on school. This tirade would be followed by his stale anecdote about how his father, in an unusual poetic outburst, had once told him how much he would have liked him to have his first sexual experience in the same brothel where he (my grandfather) had initiated his own career.

I couldn't talk to my father about my Alessandra. And I couldn't talk to my mother either. She was–how shall I put it–a distracted woman, always busy with unimportant problems of momentous impact to her. She shut everybody else out of her world, in which perfectly simple problems turned into catastrophes of gigantic proportions, threatening to ruin her day and perhaps her whole life. I never understood how she managed to accomplish so little in so many hours at home and still get it wrong. She did perform as a mother by the book, saying all the right things and caring for us children and for my father in an outwardly fully dedicated manner, but her mind was somewhere else, often in a depressing world of her own to which we had no access.

So that narrowed my options down to the cleaning woman who came three times a week to wash the floor and to do the laundry, and to Emilia. I decided to talk to Emilia, and that, of course, was a mistake. She was an austere old woman who lived with us in a small and bare room—almost a cell—at the end of the corridor, next to the kitchen. Being devoutly religious, she prayed before every meal. To her, having fun meant going to church and, once every two weeks on Tuesdays, visiting a niece who lived nearby. (Nobody had ever seen that niece, and I heard my father once saying that he didn't believe she existed at all.) She always wore long, grey robes and a sad smile that paired well with the huge cross she kept dangling on her flattened breasts and her rosary, which she almost mechanically counted when praying on every occasion. She had a deep, man-like voice, but she spoke softly, rarely raising it. She seemed perpetually worried, like someone moving in a glass shop in continuous fear of breaking something by simply looking straight at it. But she did love us children; I knew that much.

"Why don't boys and girls have class together in school, Emilia?" I asked.

She crossed herself quickly, murmuring a few words–perhaps a prayer or an exorcism. A long, white plumage covered her upper lip, and I always had to fight with myself to keep my eyes off it.

"That's what Satan would like us to have." Her voice trembled, but not because of my question. That was her natural way of speech. "Satan always wants to lead us into temptation."

I doubted very much that Satan would be concerned at all with my doings specifically, but I knew that it was no use arguing with her about those things.

"But how does keeping us children apart help with that?" I insisted.

"That's the right thing to do. When you grow up, you'll understand the ways of the Lord."

She nodded briefly, closing her porcine eyes, which with her meant that the conversation had come to its end. But, of course, that was not the end of it. As I brushed my teeth that night, my mother walked into the bathroom and eyed me worriedly.

"Roberto ... Emilia says that you got into trouble with a girl," she announced. She stood there, looking at me accusingly and waiting for an answer.

"The old goat is imagining things," I said as soon as I washed the toothpaste from my mouth.

"You can't speak like that! I won't have you speak disrespectfully of Emilia. You're going to bed without fruit tonight."

"Mommy," I said, "we finished dinner hours ago, and I'm going to bed now."

I spoke quietly for fear of embarrassing her.

"Well, go to bed anyway," she said.

She spoke distractedly; she had taken the steps required by the book—her book, anyway—to deal with the problem with which Emilia had presented her and would be able to say to herself that she had fulfilled her maternal role. She wasn't really there with me, though, but then, she never truly was.

CHAPTER 2

I was barely sixteen when a friend introduced me to Dimitri. My parents were busy as usual with their own problems and seldom asked me about my friends, so I guess they were happily assuming that I was doing all right as long as I didn't give them trouble, and I interpreted their lack of interest as a license to hang out with bad company.

Dimitri Polansky and his twin sister, Yulia, were the offspring of an aristocratic Russian family that had managed to escape the Bolshevik revolution with all their money and obtain political asylum in Italy. Or, at least, that was the story they sold us, and they used their so-called "aristocracy" as an excuse for the fancy names. But you couldn't find anything really aristocratic about them; Dimitri, one year my senior, was better known for the wild parties he used to throw, and his sister was notoriously promiscuous. Granted, they had lots of money, which was perhaps one reason why I sought Dimitri's company so much. To me, he symbolized the free, wide world that I hadn't yet experienced. Being near him meant belonging to a circle of wild spirits who did grown-up things nonchalantly and shamelessly and made me feel important.

Take a boy of Dimitri's age without a father (his parents were divorced) and with a middle-aged mother who replaced boyfriends the way other people change socks, and you shouldn't be surprised by the result. She gave him all the money he wanted to silence her conscience and to keep him busy, and, of course, nothing good could be expected to come from the mixture. And, in fact, Dimitri's parties didn't involve only obliging girls and alcohol. As I discovered soon enough, LSD and other unnamed but equally dangerous drugs also circulated freely. I don't know how I managed to fend off the repeated offers to try it, but I never did drugs of any kind, although my abstinence made me a wimp in everybody's eyes, including my own. I know that I should've run the moment I realized that Dimitri was into drugs, but his social appeal and personality were too strong, and I didn't have the willpower to give it all up.

So you can imagine my excitement when he invited me for a long weekend to his mother's house on Lake Maggiore. The invitation, coveted by many, meant that I counted enough to be included in the small circle of close friends worthy of spending time with him. Nothing could have kept me away from it, including the two-hour-long, lonesome motorbike trip which, I'm ashamed to say, I started immediately after Emilia's funeral. The old spinster had died peacefully in her sleep, leaving this world in the same quiet and inconsequential manner in which she has lived. Her funeral had also been an unimpressive function, attended only by us, the family, and a couple of old women who, I gathered, were church acquaintances. Her only relative, the niece, didn't show up, so maybe she really never existed.

You shouldn't think me cold-hearted. I did love the old bag, in a way, and I did shed a carefully hidden tear when they put the lid to her coffin, but I was late for Dimitri's weekend party, so as soon as that coffin went into the ground, I kissed my mother, avoided my father, and jumped on my bike, my mind fixed on the treats that surely awaited me during the weekend.

And that turned out to be quite some weekend. Dimitri's mother liked to party too and had invited her own guests. As a result, she limited the number of friends that he and his sister could take to the lake. Besides myself, only Franco, his closest friend, had been invited. Yulia had also brought friends with her. The first one was Marina, a bitchy girl whom I had already met in Milan. As she introduced the other one to us, I immediately realized that we had met before, and so did she.

"Boys, meet Alessandra. Alessandra, meet Roberto and Franco. Franco is scum," she said, smiling at him and receiving a pleased smile and nod in return for the pun, "but Roberto is an okay guy."

"I know you," she said. "You went to my school, right?"

"I think so. Yes, you're right," I answered casually. Seeing her had brought back to me the old emotions in a flash, but, of course, I had to hide them. I felt strangely embarrassed at the thought that she might remember how I used to stare at her during choir practice, although it was clearly stupid of me to worry about that at a distance of years when she had probably forgotten all about it. Since we lived in the same neighborhood, I knew that this was bound to happen sooner or later, and I should have been prepared for it, but I wasn't.

"Oh, so you kids know each other. That's cool," Yulia interjected. Although she was only one year our senior, she always liked to play the role of the grown-up woman and to treat everybody else like kids. And in truth, she had the body of a mature woman, with big breasts that she made sure to show as much as possible, wearing adult designer clothes. She had fine and delicate features and long, platinum hair, which contrasted with her aggressive personality.

"Slightly," I said, hoping to make my point. I noticed that Alessandra gave me a sideways glance, but I looked away and asked Dimitri, "What's the program for today?"

"Nothing much for tonight. Tomorrow a few of our gang are coming up to the lake to stay with Marco in the nearby village, so we plan to go to the Barracuda."

"What's the Barracuda?" Marina asked.

"It's a nightclub on the lake, only twenty minutes from here. They shouldn't let you kids in," said Yulia, smiling viciously, "but the owner is a good friend of ours and won't ask questions."

"I'm going to the village for a couple of hours," said Dimitri, "I'm taking the motorboat. Are you coming along?"

"I'm coming," Marina and Franco said in unison.

"What about you, Roberto?"

"I'm beat," I said. "I'd rather rest for a while."

"Your loss," said Dimitri lightly. "I'll show you your room. And what about you, sis?"

"I promised Alessandra to go to the swimming pool with her. Besides, I'm not in the mood for shopping today."

Dimitri took me to a small but hospitable room on the second floor of the rich villa and left. I dropped my bag on the bed, and then I lay down to try to catch a nap; but whether because of the unfamiliar surroundings or the strange feeling brought about by my unexpected meeting with Alessandra, sleep didn't come. After a while, I got up and decided to explore the premises. It was a big house with extensive grounds that contained a fair-sized swimming pool, lots of grass and flower beds, as well as its own dock where they kept the speedboat.

I left the house for the garden via the kitchen and walked a narrow, cobble-stoned path delimited by a hedge on its right side. A sign with an arrow pointing down, which said "swimming pool," stood at the top of the path. I decided to check out the pool, but before I reached the bottom of the walk, I heard voices coming from the other side of the hedge, and I stopped. The voices sounded really close, and I examined the hedge to try to see where they came from. Through a small gap in the shrubbery, I saw the blue reflection of water and understood that the pool was only a few feet away. I kneeled down to see better and got a full view of the pool area. Yulia and Alessandra stood in the water, a stone's throw away from me. Alessandra wore a one-piece swimsuit, while Yulia looked stunning in a colorful two-piece bikini that accented her slim and curvy body.

"I don't mind. Try it on," she said.

"But here ...?" Alessandra hesitated.

"There's nobody here. And who cares anyway," Yulia retorted.

"Well, if you think that it's okay ..."

"Of course it's okay, you silly. Here, let me help you."

I gazed, hypnotized, as Yulia pulled the shoulder straps of Alessandra's swimsuit aside and then rolled its top down to her waist, baring her breasts. I glanced quickly at both sides of the path to make sure that nobody would catch me in my voyeurism. I don't know what I would have said if anybody caught me spying through the hedge, but I simply couldn't tear myself away. I returned my gaze to the girls and felt dizzy when I saw that Yulia was caressing Alessandra's breasts. Alessandra appeared to be ill at ease as she took a small step back, moving away from Yulia's reach.

"You have nice tits, you know?" said Yulia, apparently unperturbed by Alessandra's lack of enthusiasm. "You'll be a real peach soon. You already are, in fact. Here," she added, taking off her bikini top and offering it to the other girl, "put this on."

Alessandra took the top that Yulia offered her and put it on herself. The bikini cups looked almost empty, so much greater the size of Yulia's breasts was. I could clearly see that difference now that Yulia stood there, topless and completely uninhibited.

"It's a bit big on you," Yulia commented. "But, obviously, I'm larger than you. What do you think of my breasts?" she asked.

Alessandra, who had been looking away, lifted her gaze and stared straight at Yulia. "They're very beautiful," she said, speaking shyly, and then she averted her gaze.

"You can touch them. Here," she said, taking Alessandra's hand and placing it on her right breast, "you see, they're quite solid, don't you think?"

I saw how Yulia got closer to Alessandra until their bodies almost touched. Alessandra wore a stony, uninviting expression but didn't back up. I was totally aroused and would have paid any price to be allowed to see more, but at that moment, I heard Dimitri call my name from the house, so I got up and walked away as silently as I could, trying to maneuver in my pants to hide the painful erection, which I knew could not go unnoticed. I remember hating him for his lousy timing in coming back.

Dimitri decided that we didn't need a formal dinner that evening. Instead, someone cooked a tasty sauce, and soon a huge spaghetti dish was placed on the kitchen table. He had also sent out for pizzas, and the house was well-stocked with beer, so we took plates and went to the living room to sit around on the couch and armchairs eat. The only girl around was Marina, and even she disappeared after a couple of minutes, taking a full plate with her. A deck of cards appeared as if by magic, and we sat around a table for a game of poker. I had drunk too much, and my head felt heavy, so after losing a couple of hands, I excused myself and turned in for the night.

I fell asleep immediately, but in the small hours, I woke up with the urge to go to the bathroom and get rid of all the beer I had consumed. Feeling too lazy to dress, I left my room in my underwear, counting on the fact that nobody would be up that late to see me like that. To go to the bathroom, I had to pass by the door of Alessandra's room, and as I tiptoed noiselessly along the corridor, I heard what sounded like sobs coming from inside, and then voices.

"Stop behaving like a baby, okay?" came Yulia's voice.

"Are you mad at me?" Alessandra's crying voice asked pleadingly.

"I'm not mad. Quit whining! Stop making such a fuss about it!"

More sobbing filtered through the door, followed by footsteps and then by Yulia's approaching voice, "I'm going now. I'll see you in the morning."

I almost ran into the bathroom to avoid being caught eavesdropping. I closed the door without turning on the light, leaving a crack to avoid making noise by shutting it. Through the crack, I saw Yulia coming out from Alessandra's room, clad in milky-colored, two-piece silk pajamas; the expression on her face was serious and inscrutable.

On my way back from the bathroom, I stopped again at Alessandra's door and listened. The room was completely quiet now, and no sound came from within. I stood and listened for perhaps a full minute, and then I walked in silence back to my room.

Sleep didn't come easily that night.

CHAPTER 3

The next morning Dimitri woke us up early to go for a boat ride. I am not a boating fan, and I didn't really feel like it, but I knew that I was supposed to be sociable with my host and couldn't very well plead fatigue every time he wanted to go out. The speedboat was a big one, and the six of us had no trouble finding room in it. A long, U-shaped bench ran around the interior and provided ample seating room.

The weather was clement and cruising the lake turned out to be far more enjoyable than I had anticipated. Dimitri drove recklessly, however, speeding and turning brusquely at every opportunity, extracting squeals of fear from the girls.

I felt a little, partly from the motion and partly from my nervousness for the boat's stability, and thought it wiser to try to make him slow down.

"Skipper," I said when we got a straight patch, and the boat stopped rocking, "do you have a license to drive this thing?"

"I don't need a license; I've been driving this boat since I was eight. You need to be eighteen to drive legally in the lake, but who cares? Do you think I worry about licenses when I take my mom's car?"

"Perhaps that police boat over there will care," I said, pointing to a patrol boat that cruised not far away from us, "and they may stop you and ask questions if you keep going like this and making yourself conspicuous."

"Chicken shit," he shouted back at me. He laughed lightly, making it clear that he cared little, but nevertheless, he slowed down. I sat on the edge of the padded bench next to him and gazed at Alessandra. She sat aft, between Yulia and Franco, smiling and chatting as if nothing had happened on the previous night. Marina, who sat the farthest away from me, got up and came to sit beside me. She said something, but I couldn't make out what it was because of the strong wind and the engine's noise. "What?" I shouted.

She put her arm around my neck and pulled me close to her so that her lips almost touched my ear. I felt her hot breath on my earlobe. "So, how do you like it here?" she asked.

It was my turn to put my lips next to her ear. "It's awesome!" I answered.

"I think that Yulia likes you," she said. "How would you like her to get real with you?"

"She's very nice," I said with embarrassment.

"Oh, you're such a stiff," she laughed and patted my knee with the palm of her hand before getting up and going back to sit next to Yulia. She said something to her which, of course, I couldn't catch, and Yulia laughed.

During the rest of the ride, I stayed close to Dimitri and kept him company at the wheel, speaking with him every now and then when I thought he was about to start speeding again. Franco, on the other hand, remained aft all the time and ignored me altogether. I had little in common with him, and, anyway, it looked like he was having fun with the girls and was obviously happier without me butting in.

At noon we disembarked on a small island in the middle of the lake that was crowded with tourists. We walked through a picturesque neighborhood crammed with little shops that sold cheap souvenirs to foreigners. Twice I had to be rude to get rid of a shifty-eyed character who insisted on trying to sell me a supposedly precious gold watch for close to nothing. Finally, we reached the restaurant quarter and picked one of the many pizza houses to sit in and eat. The owner gave us a corner table with a neat white and red checkered tablecloth, and I found myself sitting in front of Alessandra. We both sat in silence, picking at our food while the others were busy merrymaking. Franco told witty stories that extracted a good laugh from Dimitri and Yulia every time, and Marina joined in with a joke that, to my taste, was far too raunchy for a girl.

Every now and then, I stole glances at Alessandra over my glass, and a couple of times, I caught her looking pensively at me. For reasons that I found difficult to explain, I felt uncomfortable talking to her, so I limited my conversation to bare essentials. She wasn't chatty either, but the others didn't seem to notice or, perhaps, simply didn't care to comment on our moody behavior.

Yulia intimidated me, and I had little use for Marina, so I was sort of happy when we got back to the house, and Dimitri cut us loose until evening. I had taken a book with me and also needed to catch up with my sleep, so I went to my room to lie down.

The Barracuda turned out to be a fine nightclub—way more sophisticated than you would have expected to find in a small village. We arrived before 10 p.m. because Dimitri wanted to be sure that we would have a good spot in the club. The host gave us a booth with a C-shaped, black leather couch in one of the darkest corners. Dimitri and Franco disappeared, returning immediately with bottles and glasses. The six of us sat on the couch, barely able to make any conversation on account of the loud music and blinded most of the time by the flashing lights that illuminated the dance floor, which at that hour was empty. If you wanted to talk, you had to get really close to the others, and I couldn't hear a word of what Dimitri and Franco were saying at the other end of the couch. Much as I tried, I couldn't come up with any topic that would sustain a conversation of more than two sentences with anybody in that room, so I kept quiet, and the same did Alessandra, who sat next to me. I drank more than I should have, to make up for the lack of conversation, but half an hour after our arrival, the place filled up with people to the point that there wasn't a free inch left on the dance floor.

Some friends of Dimitri's came to say hello and sat on the couch, which had now become really crowded. A girl sat on the floor near the couch, and another one sat on the low table before me. She said something that I didn't catch, and when I asked "What?" for the second time, she made a face at me and got up. The noise was deafening, and together with the alcohol that I had drunk, it caused an unpleasant pulsating sensation in my temples. I tried to listen without success to a conversation that was going on between a couple that I didn't recognize, who had somehow managed to sit on the few empty square inches beside me.

A weight landed on my lap, and when I turned around, I saw that Yulia had seated herself across my legs, resting her back on the shoulder of the boy who sat next to me, who shrugged and went back to his drink.

"Ouch!" I said.

"Do you mind?" she asked. She put her right hand on my left shoulder to steady herself and smiled.

"Be my guest," I said. What else could I say?

She opened her little black evening handbag and took out a pack of cigarettes and a gold DuPont lighter. It was a white pack of Muratti—women's cigarettes. I remember it well, and I can't help thinking that she, and that moment, may be responsible for my dying here. She took out a cigarette and put it in her mouth, and then she gave me the lighter. She obviously wanted me to light it for her, so I fumbled with it and managed to produce a spark and to put the flame to the end of her cigarette. She drew deep on it and turned the filter slowly clockwise, pushing it back and forth through her lips, moistening it, and then she took it out and placed it before me and close to my lips.

"Have some, take a drag," she ordered.

"I don't smoke," I said.

"Well, then it's time for you to start. Go on," she retorted imperiously, keeping the filter near my lips.

I don't know how many times I have cursed myself for giving in to her because that turned out to be the first of an endless series of cigarettes. More so, because up to that point, I had always hated cigarette smoke, which irritated my eyes and nose, and had vowed never to smoke in my life. But I never stood a chance; she was too dominating for me to turn her down. Strangely, I think it was the moist filter that broke my resistance; I found the idea of putting my own lips around it magnetically sexy. It felt as if that moist filter concentrated all the hormones that Yulia always seemed to exude in it. I had never experienced a sense of intimacy like that before, and I simply couldn't summon the willpower needed to let it pass. I know it sounds stupid, but at that moment, it felt far from it. It had gone far beyond the offer of a wet cigarette; it was an invitation to blend body and soul with her intimate self. It was flattering, arousing, and irresistible.

I hesitated, looking around to seek inspiration, and I saw Alessandra, who gazed at me disapprovingly, or so it seemed, from the edge of the booth where she now stood, observing the surroundings. I don't know why that made me feel rebellious, but my reaction was one of defiance, and I edged my head forward until my lips closed around the moist filter and sucked on it hesitantly. Right away, I blew out a little puff of smoke without taking it to my lungs first.

"Don't be a fag, take a real drag," Yulia complained. She put the cigarette back between my lips until her fingers touched them and then watched as I inhaled. Without waiting for me to exhale, she took a drag herself, and then back the cigarette went to my lips. She repeated this procedure three times before my head started to swim.

"I ... I need to go to the bathroom," I said. I felt weak and tried to get up. She shot me a quick glance and got off my lap.

"You're green. Don't you go throwing up on me, okay?" she said, speaking morosely. She held out a hand for me to grab and pulled me up. I steadied myself on my feet for a few seconds and then hurried away toward the restroom, hoping to get there in time.

You always hear people saying that something happened to make them feel so bad that they wanted to die. Until that day, I had always thought it was a stupid thing to say, but as soon as I reached the restroom and put my head above the toilet, I felt a surge of nausea like I never experienced before and which I had to stop at all costs. I trembled as cold sweat covered my forehead, and I thought that in a second, I would simply fall down, never to get up again. Then I finally vomited with uncontrollable convulsions. When the seizure that had taken control over my body stopped, I opened my eyes and saw all my spaghetti dinner, now in the form of a multitude of little white worms, resting in the toilet bowl. Slowly, I got up and put my head under the tap and let the cold water run on my face and then into my mouth until the cold stream more or less washed out the taste of vomit. Then I went back into the stall, flushed the toilet, and sat on it to rest. When I finally felt strong enough to get up, I drank some more cold water, combed my hair with my fingers, and walked guardedly out of the restroom into the corridor.

My feet didn't feel steady enough for me to go back to the club yet, so I stood in the hallway, reading an old newspaper clipping about the Barracuda, which hung on the wall in a cheap frame. My vision was still a little blurred, and as I re-read the headlines for the third time, the restroom door adjacent to the one I had been using opened, and Alessandra walked out from it. It was a narrow passage leading to the restrooms, and I took up most of its width, so she stopped before me and gave me an inquisitive look.

"Are you feeling all right?" she asked. "You're pale..."

"I'm better now, but for a while, I thought you'd have to take me back on a stretcher," I answered, trying to smile as I said it.

"If you're not used to all this, you shouldn't be doing it. Playing by their rules may be ... wrong ...," she added, clearly searching her head for words.

"What do you mean?"

"It doesn't matter," she answered evasively. She circled around me and started to walk away, but I called her name, and she stopped.

"Look ... why don't we sit at the bar and have a coke. It's much quieter there."

"Someone's waiting for me," she said, making a dismissive motion with her hand. I nodded, and she left.

I remained in the hallway for a couple of more minutes, and

then, feeling strong again, I walked back toward our booth. On my way, I passed the door that led out to a balcony facing the lake and stopped there, thinking that a breath of fresh air would do me good. But as I poked my head through the door, I saw a couple on the balcony, and I froze. I didn't recognize the boy who stood there with Alessandra, but she must have known him well because he had his arm holding possessively onto her waist. She pointed to something in the distance, and I retreated quickly; I didn't want her to catch me staring at her.

I felt anger mounting inside me, and then I grew angry at myself for it; what right did I have to react at all to what Alessandra was doing? I had been avoiding her since the moment I got there, but I now realized that my behavior had been motivated by fear of failure. I had idealized her so much since those days in elementary school that she had become an unattainable goal to me, an image to be worshipped from afar and never to be approached. Now, after seeing her with somebody else, the barrier that made her untouchable had disappeared. But, of course, it was too late. Tomorrow we would leave to go back to Milan, and I had blown my opportunity to really get acquainted with her.

Back to our booth, I let my eyes become re-adjusted to the dim lighting and scanned the area. Dimitri sat at one end, with a red-headed girl I hadn't seen before, necking. I couldn't find Franco or Marina anywhere. Some of the people had left, and the dance floor was no longer as crowded as before, but many couples still danced industriously, like puppets on strings pulled at the rhythm of the music. I narrowed my eyes to a slit and continued to scan the room until I felt a hand on my shoulder and heard Yulia's voice.

"You're back. Here, drink this," she ordered, handing me a glass that smelled unmistakably of whiskey.

"I can't drink any more alcohol," I said, shuddering at the

thought.

"You need it, believe me. If you don't drink now, tomorrow you'll feel miserable."

I took the glass and sniffed it. I, too, remembered having heard that alcohol was the cure for hangovers. I decided to follow her advice, to be on the safe side, and drained the glass to the last drop like medicine. "Good boy," she said with approval. "I want to dance now," she added, taking my hand to guide me toward the mass of dancing people. Once on the dance floor, she said, "Wait a second," and left me standing to go and talk to the disc jockey, who nodded understandingly, holding a 45 record in his hand.

"This is a new hit that I am completely sold over," she said when she returned, and the first notes of "Hey Jude" started to play.

She took my hands and put them on her waist, and then she placed her arms on my shoulders and started to move slowly. I struggled to make the right dance movements and, at the same time, to look down deep into her cleavage. After a short while, she leaned her head on my right shoulder—she was only slightly shorter than I—and got closer. God is my witness that I had never been attracted to her, but the unexpected physical contact, coupled with the effect of the alcohol, gave me a hard-on so strong that it hurt. I was grateful for the dim lighting because I am sure that I had become red in the face for the embarrassment. I pushed my butt away, which made me dance at an awkward angle and put a strain on my lower back muscles, hoping that she wouldn't notice my excitement. But notice she did, and she pushed her hands inside my jeans until I felt her long nails digging into the small of my back, just below the level of my belt, thrusting me again toward her.

"Hey Jude" plays for over seven minutes, and during all that time, we danced without speaking, her fingers maintaining an unrelenting grip inside my pants and keeping our bodies pressed firmly against one another. By the time the song ended, I had become her slave and was ready to jump through hoops at her command.

"I've had enough of this place," she said. "Let's get one more drink and go."

We moved back to our table, and Yulia filled up two glasses from the half-empty bottle of Johnnie Walker and handed one of them to me. I drank avidly; I wanted to act like a big guy, but as soon as I put the empty glass back on the table, my head started to swim again. Yulia didn't seem to notice, though, as she got hold of my hand and pulled me after her.

Outside she approached a taxi–one of the only three in the area–and said to the driver, "Back to the house." We jumped in and sat in the back for the ten-minute ride. I felt powerless as she pressed herself against me and teased me, playing with the zipper of my jeans. I don't know if she had added anything to my drink that sapped my brainpower, but I was at her mercy, unable to think or to react to anything. She bit the lobe of my left ear, and then she kissed my lips, pushing an intrusive and commanding tongue into my mouth. Her breath was heavy with alcohol and smoke, and for a moment, I thought that I would be sick.

As the taxi came to a stop at the house door, Yulia gave the driver a bill, which he took and put in his pocket without even looking at it. It belatedly occurred to me that I should probably have taken care of the fare, but she obviously didn't mind. She pulled me after her, and I followed, walking heavily in tow.

As she opened the door, we found ourselves face to face with her mother, already dressed to go out. She had one of her "friends" with her.

"Hi, Mother," said Yulia, without sounding any too pleased.

"Good evening, Mrs. Polanski," I managed to mumble. Yulia's

mother had kept her married name even after the divorce.

She ignored me altogether and said to her daughter, speaking dryly, "Try not to turn the house into a pigsty like yesterday. The cleaning woman isn't coming until Monday."

"Tell that to Dimitri," she answered curtly and pulled me inside.

We stood by the door of the living room, waiting for her mother to leave. When we heard the sound of the entrance door closing, Yulia asked me, "Do you want to go for a swim?" and then, without waiting for an answer, she added, "I need to go to the bathroom first. Wait here."

I felt dizzy, and my head hurt. I sat on the couch, and then, feeling nauseous again, I lay down. I closed my eyes and lay still until I sensed that Yulia had come to sit beside me. Then I opened my eyes and gazed at her. I had a dull ache in my stomach, and my vision was blurred. She had unbuttoned her blouse down to the middle, and through the mist of my confusion, I saw that she had taken off her bra. "Are you coming?" she asked, invitingly.

"I don't have a swimsuit here," I protested feebly.

"I don't have one either, but so what?" she asked, raising an eyebrow.

"I ..." I managed to say, and that's the last thing I remember.

I woke up at the sound of an unidentifiable noise. I was still lying on the couch, and first daylight already came in through the large windows of the sitting room. Someone I had never seen before, a man of about thirty, sat slumped in an armchair, the front of his shirt covered with vomit. He was a disgusting sight, but I kept gazing at him for a while until I reassured myself that he was breathing. Not that I particularly cared, but I reckoned that something would have to be done if he was dead. Even in my confused state, I was happy that I didn't need to worry about that.

The noise that had woken me came from the nearby ground-floor bathroom, a pretentious construction big enough to house a small family, equipped with a marble floor and gold-plated faucets. Slowly and painfully, on account of my head that ached badly, I got up and cautiously walked the short distance to the bathroom. As I opened the door, I saw Dimitri sitting on the floor, leaning against the wall in a fetal position with his head between his legs. "Make them go away," he said without looking at me as I came in. He spoke in a strange, croaking voice.

"Make who go away?" I asked, puzzled because I saw nobody in the room with us.

"The worms. The worms on the wall," he whimpered, raising his head and pointing to the wall before him with his finger.

"There are no worms on the wall," I tried to reason with him, but he started to cry, mumbling, "Make them go away, please ... On the wall ... You can see them ... Tell them to go away ... The worms on the wall ... they're big, too big ..."

Never before had I seen anybody having hallucinations, but I had heard that that was what happened to you if you overdosed on LSD. I got scared, really scared, when I realized that I could do nothing to help Dimitri through it. One thing was clear to me, though—that house was not for me. I decided, there and then, that the Polanskys and I were parting company.

I closed the door behind me, leaving a whining Dimitri to his destiny, and tiptoed to my room, making as little noise as possible. Once there, I collected my bag and left through the back door. It was cool outside at that early hour, despite the warmth of late August, and the morning air helped me clear my head. I unhooked my motor bicycle but didn't kick its engine on. Instead, I pushed it quietly until I reached a point where the house disappeared from view, then I started the engine and drove off.

That was the last time I saw Dimitri. As my bike took me away from his house and the lake, I felt relieved and thankful that I had witnessed how he had demeaned himself; without that, I would probably have continued to seek his company and that of his weird family and friends.

Yes, that had undoubtedly been a narrow escape.

CHAPTER 4

The Marchi Elementary School. That's where it all began and where the seeds of my recent fiasco with Alessandra were sown, in that high-ceilinged, cold-marbled building, toward the middle of my fifth grade. They knew how to keep us disciplined then, back in the 1960s. Italy had mostly recovered from its World War II wounds, but as far as discipline was concerned, the school hadn't heard that the war was over and the Nazis were gone. Or, at least, so it seemed to us children.

Nowadays it's different but then my school, like many others in the country, was unisex. No girls were allowed on the premises, which was fine by us boys; we were not interested ... at least I wasn't until choir practice began.

At the other end of the school's long building, as far away from us as possible, the architect had located the entrance to its all-girl counterpart. I believe that the idea was to keep us safe from temptation, but who says that temptation between sexes is a bad thing? They were right that proximity leads to temptation, though. They were so damn right ...

One day in April, we sensed that something out of the

ordinary was afoot. Teachers and secretaries conversed *sotto voce* in the corridors, a few of them wearing an excited look, and above all, too many of them walked indecorously quickly, as if new energy had been injected into their usually limp bodies. We didn't know what was going on exactly, but the announcement didn't take us by surprise: our school had been chosen for the great honor of a visit by the President of the Republic. The momentous event required preparation, and one of the items on the program was a school choir that would sing the national anthem. So the music teacher came into our class one day to select children for the choir. We were ordered to approach the teacher's desk when our name was called and to sing a song of our choice.

"Lucci Roberto," the music teacher said, reading from a list.

I lowered my gaze and studied my shoes, hoping that he would move on to the next name if I failed to respond quickly enough, but he simply read my name out louder.

"He's going to pick all the fags," Paolo whispered to me.

He was the biggest and strongest kid in our class, and his words carried weight, so I tried hard to get rejected. I picked a mountain song that my father used to sing in the car, and I timidly sang the first few bars doing my best to make my voice croak.

"Raise your voice, boy," ordered the music teacher.

I did as instructed, which to my ears sounded like a horrible and distorted imitation of my father's singing. Surely after such a hideous performance, I would be shamefully dismissed, which suited me fine.

"Good voice," said the music teacher instead. "I can work with it."

My heart sank as he nodded in approval and motioned me to join the little group of selected kids who stood unhappily in one corner of the class. Little did I know that being selected for the choir would change my whole life.

Soon after that, I realized that being in the choir wasn't such a bad thing, after all. The school had gone crazy over the presidential visit, and we were called for singing practice at all hours, legally missing geography and Roman history. In comparison with regular class, rehearsals were light work, and I began to appreciate the relative freedom and the relaxed atmosphere that reigned during those hours; the bell, calling for class, wasn't toiling for me. It gave me a sense of superiority.

The practice room was a large one located at the far end of the school building on the ground floor, in an area that I had never visited before. Two stages, built of wood, faced one another at a thirty degrees angle, and the door through which we entered led us directly onto one of them, while the other was left empty. At first, I paid little attention to it and to the door, twin to ours, which led to it, but on the fourth day, that door opened to admit thirty-odd girls, shepherded by a woman with a beaky nose, who silently took a position in front of us.

"Boys and girls," our music teacher announced pompously (being a man he, obviously, was in charge), "you have practiced your part during the last few days and are now ready to start rehearsing together. The number of rehearsals that we will need depends on you. For the first time, I'll ask each of the two groups to sing their parts separately, then we'll practice together. The girls first, please," he ordered, and, on cue, the girls started to sing.

But I wasn't listening. All my attention was riveted on the girl straight in front of me, on the second level. She was pretty, but no more than others in the choir. Nevertheless, I couldn't take my eyes off her. She had an olive-dark complexion, and her hair was straight and lustrous, of a dark chestnut color. Her eyes were black and deep. I surprised myself by taking in all those details at a glance.

Never before in my life had I noticed anything in a girl, and certainly, I had never cared what the ones I knew looked like. Girls didn't count with "the boys," and their presence at social functions, such as birthday parties, was tolerated at best. I tried hard to explain to myself why her eyes had magnetized me, and my pulse raced so fast that I feared my heartbeat would be heard above the singing. My head was light, and my hands and feet felt as if they had swelled to twice their regular size.

"Who's the girl in the middle?" I inquired of Maurizio, a boy from another class, whom I knew slightly.

"Which one?"

"The fourth from the left in the middle row."

"The redhead? I don't know her."

"No. no. The one next to her. Can't you count right?"

"Oh, I think her name is Alessandra, but I'm not sure. Why?"

"I was just curious."

"Do you think she's cute?"

"Yikes! Who cares about girls," I hastened to say.

"I don't," said Maurizio with a self-satisfied smirk, and there the matter rested.

It's difficult to describe my confusion. Throughout the rehearsal, I had derived pleasure from simply looking at a girl. I couldn't figure out why this felt so good and what this attraction meant. I was scared. I started to pay attention to groups of schoolgirls, scanning them surreptitiously, looking for Alessandra among them, and a few days later, my spying was rewarded when I saw her walking away with two friends. I followed her from afar, taking cover in the deep shadows cast by the buildings in the narrow streets and turning it all into a cloak-and-dagger adventure. My pursuit ended when she walked into a modern building in Via Stampa, a quiet street only a few minutes away from the school, which was destined to play an important role in my life through no fault of its own.

Right before the presidential visit, the school announced a "weighing day," an ordeal imposed upon us at irregular intervals, when we were instructed to come to school with clean underwear for medical inspection. I started to panic on account of a cough that had grown more cavernous in the last two days, despite what seemed to be like liters of syrup I had swallowed at Emilia's order. The last time that one of the boys had coughed like that, he had been ordered away from school for weeks on the presumption that he had to be contagious. I would normally have welcomed a forced exile from school, but not now, God, please ... not when I looked forward so much to be again in the same room with Alessandra.

That year we were taken to the basement by a grumpy janitor and ordered to strip to our underpants. I stood in line, shivering in the cold room, my body's heat drawn through my feet by the marble floor, waiting in fear for my turn. My scalp had started itching the moment the inspection had been announced a week before, causing grave concern to my mother; she was always startled into a flurry of activity the moment she saw me scratching. She had taken me to the barber's shop for a haircut the day before and had then gone through my head with a fine comb, so I felt confident that the inspection would reveal no lice. But were my underpants clean enough? I had gone to the bathroom that morning, and, despite great care, a drop of urine had fallen on them, painting a faint yellow spot on the immaculate fabric. I stood there in fear of what the nurse would say about that spot—one that could mean social shame and ruin.

That dark, cold basement always filled me with indescribable fear. The school used it primarily for medical inspections, and I hated it. Each time they took me there, I panicked, feeling unreasonably unsure that they would let me out in the end. I don't know to what use the basement had been put during the war, but an atmosphere of fear reigned in it, and desolation and despair were palpable and real as if those walls were impregnated with the suffering of countless human beings. But, of course, it could have simply been my imagination running wild.

The nurse's desk was not far away from where I stood, and I could hear her voice handing out her verdict.

"Clean. Get on the scale. Stay still! Move on."

With a sigh of relief, the boy before me stepped down from the scale and ran to the next room where we had left our clothes. "Lanatta," the nurse cried out. Piero Lanatta had been in school with me since first grade. At the end of the previous school year, our class had jumped wildly into the public swimming pool, and everybody had come out but Lanatta. They had found his body lying on the bottom of the pool. Heart failure. Standing in line in that cold basement, I felt a lump in my throat and tears forming at the corner of my eyes at the mention of his name. I can no longer remember his face now, but I recall that he had delicate, almost feminine features with a ghostly-white complexion. I remembered him as a kind and soft-spoken boy who had stood in line before me for the past four years. I missed him.

"Ma'am, Lanatta is gone," I whispered.

"Gone? What do you mean gone? He'll be punished for it. Janitor!" she yelled, "why isn't everybody here as I asked? I can't do my job in this way."

"He's dead, ma'am," I said, choking on the words.

"Oh, all right then," she said, sounding relieved that her orders were being followed, after all. "Approach!"

I stood there, feeling her gaze on me as if they were needles, while her fingers went through my hair like unkind bird claws. I practically stopped breathing to avoid coughing until I heard the magic words, "Clean. Get on the scale." I did as ordered, and she fumbled with the weights, making disapproving sounds with her tongue.

"You're too skinny, you hear me? Tell your mother that if you haven't put on some weight by the next inspection, I'll have to refer you to the Ministry of Sanity. *Capito*?"

Oh, yes, I understood. I didn't know what they did to you when they referred you to the Ministry of Sanity, but it had to be a bad thing. Most things associated with the government were bad, or so I had gathered from hearing my father talking about it at home. Perhaps I should've eaten that spinach and drunk my soup, as my mother always begged me to do. I made a mental vow to eat everything my mother put on my plate from that moment on.

The president's visit turned out to be sort of a letdown. We expected to feel the mighty power of The Republic unleashed by the presence of its leader; instead, we got a nice, little old man, who walked into our class and asked a few automatic questions, gazing at us with an uninterested eye.

The choir was a success, though, and it surprised me how proud I felt at being a part of it. In the confusion that followed, I somehow managed to get close to Alessandra in the line that waited, armed with little tricolor flags, for the president to walk out of the school. That was the closest I had ever gotten to her, and my legs felt a little shaky. I stood one step behind her and a little aside, feigning to look at the door from which we expected the president to emerge but, instead, inhaling the inebriating scent of cleanliness coming from her hair.

"I forgot the words," the girl next to Alessandra whispered to her with anguish. "Do you think they noticed?"

I realized that I had been handed a perfect opportunity to talk to them. I tried to work up the courage to intervene in the conversation and reassure her that nobody could have noticed, but before I managed to speak, Alessandra shook her head, brushing my face lightly with the back of her long hair, and said, "Don't be silly!" I remained silent, enjoying the intimacy of the casual contact with her.

Our music teacher had handed out musical scores with the words of the songs on them. I had left mine behind, but Alessandra held hers in her hand. She must have sensed my presence—perhaps she felt my gaze on her—and turned her head a little, giving me a quick side glance. Then she dropped her musical score, and I hastened to pick it up and give it back to her. The smile that rewarded me kept me awake for nights afterward. I could have kicked myself, thinking how I had missed the opportunity to start a conversation when I returned the pages to her without a word. Surely she had noticed how intensely I had been gazing at her for days and had dropped them on purpose, to give me a hint and a chance to speak to her. But I had blown it, and I tortured myself, convinced that she must be thinking me a dummy.

I have often wondered what could have been if, instead of chickening out, I had taken the hint and spoken to her. Perhaps all my future would have been different. Or maybe not. Getting to know each other as children doesn't necessarily mean that passion cannot erupt years later, or does it? In a sense, it is better not to know; maybe we're not really the masters of our destiny, after all.

But I'm rambling...

The president's visit also marked the end of the school year and the beginning of the summer vacations. Elementary school would be over in a few days, and I had to get ready for middle school. Milan in July was a tough place for a boy my age, however. I could find little occupation outside of hanging out with other kids and trying to stay out of trouble. And trouble always chased me, one way or another. A gang of kids from another school decided to turn our neighborhood into its own territory, which made me join a rival group. At the time, it seemed only natural to go out and buy a switchblade knife to be ready for these ruthless kids who thought nothing of teaching you a lesson with the chain of a bicycle if you incurred their displeasure. Perhaps it was the heat, but nobody seemed to need a real reason to pick a fight; sometimes, even just gazing at someone was considered an offense.

My first fight didn't turn out to be quite what I thought, though. Despite all preparations, when a kid a head taller than I decided to make me his target, I lost my nerve and left the knife and knuckle-duster in my pocket. All I got out of joining my gang, besides ruining my self-esteem, was a good beating that left me with a puffed eye and miscellaneous bruises and cuts. That, in turn, earned me a long and painful lecture at home.

After that experience, I decided that I would be better off alone than in bad company. That started a happier period during which my bike became my best companion. I roamed the streets of Milan, riding over cobble-stoned streets, through narrow alleys, and in its open gardens, until one day I found myself in Via Stampa, perhaps subconsciously driven there by constant memory flashes in which Alessandra's image seemed determined to haunt me. Day after day, I rode my bicycle in front of her building, hoping to catch a glimpse of her but not really knowing what I would do if I did. Luckily, I never saw her, and for all I knew, she had gone away for the summer.

I also spent time on the bench of nearby Piazza Vetra, reading and re-reading the sign that marked the spot where, in the seventeenth century, witches and those accused of spreading the plague were hung, burned on the stake, and tortured in many other creative ways. Sitting there and enjoying the freedom, I alternated between images of those tortures and dreams of Alessandra, there with me on that bench, holding hands.

But I was lonely.

My family didn't interfere, as long as I respected meal times and made no noise in the house. My few friends had already left for the summer, and the city felt empty; its pulse slowed down to an urban coma.

Mercifully, July came to an end, and my parents decided that the time had come to take us to the country for "a change of air" because I'm not sure that I could have endured my self-inflicted torment much longer.

CHAPTER 5

My weekend with the Polanskys had left me all keyed up for a real romantic adventure, but the one I picked turned up to be much more than that, for better and for worse. The instrument of my loss of innocence was Lillian, a mulatto girl whose exotic looks I found simply irresistible. I recall the day I met her as vividly as if it had happened yesterday. I had gone to the used schoolbooks market, not so much to find used books to buy for school, but to show off my new motorbike, which I had finally paid for and picked up the day before, using all the money collected for two years, together with an unusually generous sum given by my parents for my last birthday. The bike I had before was such a sorry-looking thing that I had preferred not to be seen in public with it. But this one was flashy and cool...

She stood there, under one of the two big tents that housed rows of long tables packed with books of every description, behind a desk that sold Latin books. I had already bought my books at another stand, but as I saw her, I hid them quickly in my bag and approached her.

"Hi! Do you have a good copy of the *De Bello Gallico*? "I asked. That was the best I could come up with to start a conversation. Pathetic, isn't it?

"Certainly," she said, pushing a copy at me. "It's five hundred Liras," she added in a businesslike tone.

She had deep, black eyes and naturally moist, sensuous lips that jumped at you above her plump figure like a flashing neon sign. A tomboyish haircut framed her face. When she smiled an inquisitive smile, I realized with embarrassment that I had been gaping at her. I knew that if I paid for the book and left, my opportunity would be gone, so I decided to be daring. "Five hundred is big money," I said. "Would you take a bike ride instead?"

She studied me intently for a few seconds, looking amused, then she said, "It depends on the bike."

"It's an awesome motorbike and a brand-new one," I lied. "Would you like to take a look? It's on the corner, just outside."

"Show me," she said.

She followed me out of the tent, and I couldn't believe my luck: she had actually taken the bite.

Although my motorbike was a mere 50 c.c., the one I had bought second-hand looked like the real thing, painted in red and silver and fully accessorized. The law forbade small motorbike owners to take passengers, but the fine for transgressing didn't stop anybody. And nothing short of a death sentence could have stopped me from getting Lillian behind me on the saddle.

"This is it," I said.

I proudly patted my motorbike on the gas tank.

"It doesn't look like much," she said, smiling broadly, "but if you're a good driver, I'll take a ride and ice cream instead of payment."

"Deal," I said, perhaps too quickly.

I kicked the engine alive, trying hard to do it like a pro. She sat behind me, and I drove off. The touch of her soft body on my back worked like a drug on me, and I was sorry when we reached the ice cream place and had to stop. We got off the bike and stood in line. Fearing an awkward silence, I started babbling about the ride, the bike, and the book fair. One thing really puzzled me, though.

"Can you just take off like that without telling anybody?" I asked.

"I can do whatever I please. I was only helping a neighbor, but he knows me and won't be surprised to see that I'm gone. I come and go as I please," she added, making it almost sound as a warning. "What's your name, by the way?"

"I'm Roberto. And you are ..."

"I'm Lillian," she said, putting out her hand mockingly. "I like pistachio and chocolate," she added, turning to business now that the couple before us had moved aside, giving us room to order.

I got us ice cream and leaned against my motorbike to eat it. She ate it hungrily, like, as I later learned, she did everything. Lillian lived a hungry life.

"Do you mind taking me home now? I'm fed up with the market, and I don't feel like going back."

"That's okay. I'm done with that too."

"Oh, and here's your book," she said, handing it to me.

"I don't really need it," I said, smiling, "I already have a copy." I wanted her to know how smart and daring I had been.

"You're cute," she said, and then she mounted on the saddle behind me.

As I drove her home, following her directions, I did my best to alternate sprints and brakes, each time feeling how she tightened her hold of me and how the warmth of her body passed exciting vibrations onto my own. When we reached her address, I started to panic. I didn't know what to say or do, and I realized that all my "cool" behavior had been no more than a façade; circumstances were now calling my bluff, and I was helpless. I cut the engine and parked beside her door. She dismounted and gave me a long, silent stare while I locked it.

"You're not coming up, in case you were wondering," she said point-blank. "Give me your hand," she then ordered before I managed to think of some repartee.

Too confused to argue, I gave it to her, and she took a pen from her pocket and scribbled on its back.

"That's my phone number. You can call me if you want."

I nodded, trying to appear only mildly interested, but my heart was pounding. She walked into the building without giving me another look, and I drove away, my mind in turmoil. I was lucky to get home in one piece, driving mindlessly as I did, thinking only of Lillian and trying to figure what her parting words meant. It didn't take me long to find the courage to define to myself what had taken place that afternoon: love at first sight, that's what it amounted to. I had no doubt.

I waited for two days before dialing her number. That was all I could stand. When she picked up, I realized that I didn't know how to start a conversation with her.

"Hi, it's Roberto," I managed to say.

"Hi, Roberto. Want to come over?" she asked, quite simply.

Want to come over? I positively ached to see her, but of course, I didn't tell her that.

"Yeah, I'm not busy this afternoon," I condescended.

"Then come at five. My apartment is on the third floor. See you then," she concluded, and then she hung up.

I must have brushed my teeth five times that afternoon, and I recall washing my hair for the first time in a week. I took my motorbike out of my building's garage at four o'clock, although it took only a ten-minute ride to get to her place. I got there early, of course, and drove around the neighborhood to kill time. At five sharp, I knocked on her door. I wore a smart leather jacket over a pair of fashionably worn-out blue jeans.

She opened the door wearing a simple white T-shirt over blue jeans, pretty much like mine, and motioned me to come in. We passed through a small living room filled with heavy furniture in bad taste. An old, dark-skinned and heavily wrinkled woman sat on the sofa and didn't even give us a glance. A short corridor led to a door with a sign pasted on it that said, "Lillian's room—Mood: Dangerous. Keep out!" She pushed the door open and made an inviting gesture with her hand. "Come into my palace," she said, and I thought I heard bitterness in her voice.

Her bedroom was small, with a narrow sofa that doubled as a bed, a tiny closet, and a little table. A gramophone with an empty turntable that turned idly made an annoying screeching noise. She sat on the sofa and pulled my hand, so I sat beside her. She gazed straight into my eyes for a full minute without speaking, as if to dare me to look away. When I didn't, she finally spoke and ordered, "Kiss me!"

I was petrified and also a little frightened by her sudden directness. Her lips got closer and closer to mine, and I pushed my head forward the last inch, to the inevitable end. Her mouth tasted of almond, orange, and chocolate. Her skin released a heavenly scent that worked as an aphrodisiac on me. My brain had stopped functioning under the overload of sensations, and I felt like drowning in a sweet pond smelling of tantalizing perfume and soothing honey.

When the tip of her tongue touched the side of mine, I was

puzzled for a moment by the foreign sensation. Then I realized what it was and what it meant and timidly moved the tip of my tongue, trying to match her own movements, in the hope that I was doing it right.

"You're a good kisser," she whispered.

She moved back a little after what felt both like an eternity and too short a moment. I felt elated; that had been my first real French kiss, and I hadn't given myself away for the novice I was. I had become now no lesser a man than any of my friends, with all their alleged experience with girls.

"You're not bad yourself," I said, trying to sound nonchalant.

"Shhh ..." she admonished me.

She lay down on the sofa and placed an LP record on the gramophone, then she pulled me onto her by my shirt. We spent the next two hours kissing and caressing, learning each other's scents and tastes. Each time the gramophone needle reached the end, and the music stopped, she took it back to the beginning of the record, but once we got so carried away in our kissing that the music stopped for a few minutes without us noticing. I was jerked out of my inebriated state when Lillian suddenly pushed me away and jumped to a sitting position. The record turned silently, with the needle caught in an endless loop and making a light scratching noise. The sound of heavy steps supported by a walking stick approached the door. Lillian quickly picked up the gramophone head and dropped the needle in the middle of the first song, bringing the music out again with a screeching sound that made me shiver. The steps stopped, and after a few seconds, they resumed, but this time walking away from us.

"What was that?" I asked.

"My grandmother," she answered, still sitting without touching me. "She leaves me alone as long as she hears music coming from my room, but if it gets silent, she always comes to see what's going on. We're okay if we don't forget to keep the music playing."

I sat beside her, my hands in my lap. Somehow I sensed that she didn't want me to touch her.

"Does she live here with your parents and you?"

"It's only my father and me. Mom died three years ago, and that's why my dad decided to come back from Argentina. He went to Argentina before the war, and there he met my mother."

I kept quiet, surprised by her willingness to talk about personal things with someone she barely knew, but sensing that she needed to tell me. Seeing that I was listening, she went on.

"Grandma doesn't speak Italian at all, so she stays at home all day. She sits on that sofa, and I'm the only one she can talk to—my dad is away at work until late every evening—and she drives me crazy."

I hopelessly searched for something to say, but nothing seemed to fit the moment, so I kept quiet but took hold of her hand. She let me take it, but it felt limp, lifeless, in striking contrast with the purposefulness she had shown before. She kept her gaze fixed on an indefinite point on the wall, her naturally lively expression gone.

"Time to go now," she said, apparently addressing the wall.

She stood up without looking at me. I got up too and stood there, feeling stupid because I didn't know what she expected me to do. Should I kiss her goodbye? Did she expect me to say words of affection? My embarrassment was soon relieved, to be replaced by puzzlement. She took my hand and walked me through the sitting room to the door, then she opened it and waited, clearly expecting me to go.

"Don't pay attention to my moods. They mean nothing. It's just the way it is," she said.

She spoke quietly, and I felt as if a wide gap had opened between us.

"I..." I began to say, but she put her index finger to my lips and silenced me.

"Come again tomorrow," she simply said.

I gazed at her, trying to fathom what thoughts she hid behind her distanced expression, but to no avail. Her grandmother sat on the sofa in a ridiculous-looking flowery dress, her walking stick between her legs, gazing fixedly at a dead TV set.

I nodded, and Lillian closed the door.

If asked to define Lillian with a single adjective, I would have chosen "soft." Her full body was soft wherever you touched it; her hair was soft, and so was her sweet perfume. She had no rough corners in her behavior as if all bad things in the world left her unruffled. She was soft-spoken and somehow managed to make everything she said sound pleasant, even when she meant to be mean to you.

After all that softness and warmth, I didn't expect to have to pay a heavy price for my first two hours of innocent pleasure with a girl. Emilia would probably have rated it as a "divine retribution for my sins," which manifested itself as an almost unbearable pain in my testicles. It started at Lillian's door and grew stronger as I sat on my motorbike. By the time I got home, I could no longer stand erect, and I ran to my room, pleading a strong headache to fend my mother's "how was your afternoon" usual question. Lying down eased the pain a little, and I lay in the dark and threw my mind back to that afternoon, replaying every moment and each movement in my head. I had no doubt in my mind that becoming lost in my temporary heaven had been worth every second of pain, and if God wanted to punish me for that, I was more than willing to pay the price.

The next day was more or less a repetition of the previous one, with the exception that I didn't need to be ordered to kiss her; I had been waiting so hungrily for the moment when she would close the door behind us and turn on the music, that as soon as she sat on her bed, I leaned over her and kissed her without any preamble.

Kissing was great, but I feared monotony, and the thought that she perhaps expected me to be more daring put me under great pressure. Realizing that I had to make some progress, one way or another, after some cuddling, I sent my right hand up her back, trying to find the clip of her bra under her shirt. I finally found it, but it wouldn't open and, after I fumbled with it unsuccessfully for a while, she pushed my hand away and unclasped it herself. Together we rolled up her T-shirt, exposing her round, full breasts.

I had never been that close to a girl's breasts before, and, in fact, all I knew about these things came from magazine photographs and comics that circulated clandestinely at school. I knew that I was expected to fondle them, though, so I rubbed them lightly until her nipples stood erect, then I started to massage them more aggressively, taking the full cups into my hands and squeezing with my fingers.

"You're hurting me," she complained after a while, and I stopped kneading her flesh, murmuring words of apology. She pulled her shirt down, and we kissed some more, but it didn't feel the same, so a few minutes later, I left.

I had been careful this time, and gentler in rubbing my body against her, so my testicle ache seemed more bearable.

We repeated this routine three or four times a week, and in the third week, she agreed to come out with me. I took her to a movie that I knew some of my friends were going to see.

"Have you 'done her' yet?" asked one of them.

"Of course," I answered, not fully knowing what he meant.

"She's quite a piece," he said. He sounded appreciative, and I felt very proud.

Lillian and I had been going out for two months on the last day I saw her. I had adjusted myself to her somewhat misanthropic way of life and to her preference for the long hours on the couch, apparently absorbing the warmth that I was more than willing to give her. She seemed to be in continuous need of physical contact— so much so that sometimes she behaved wildly, almost savagely. Still, I managed to convince her to go out with me every now and then for pizza or ice cream, and my social circle considered her my "girlfriend" because of that.

"You always pay for me," she explained one day when I tried to argue against her refusal to come to the movies. "I don't have much money; otherwise, I would come and pay for myself, but I can't have you pay for me all the time."

"I don't mind," I said, and I meant it. The cost of a movie ticket seemed to me a more than reasonable price to pay for the privilege of being seen holding hands with her in public.

"But I do mind," she said, and then she kissed me, biting my lower lip teasingly and putting an end to the argument.

She was not actually poor, but everything around her was economical. The neighborhood where she lived was a good one, but her apartment building wasn't elegant and had no keeper to guard the door. Her own apartment had been fitted out with cheap furniture, of the kind you could buy at the cheaper department stores, and everything in it spelled working-class level. Even Lillian's clothes looked somewhat outdated.

I didn't care. I wouldn't have minded it if she had slept in a hut and dressed in rags, but she was a proud soul, and I understood her desire to avoid going where her outfit might not measure up to that of other girls.

That's why I was so happy when she agreed to come with me to a party, one Saturday night. We were to meet there as soon as I could manage to get away from the dinner table, but by the time I got to the party, it was past 11 p.m., and the atmosphere wasn't particularly merry. Three or four people stood outside the entrance door, smoking and conversing in low voices. Others sat on couches, glasses in their hands, and only a few people moved around in an almost completely dark room, illuminated only by faint blue and red-colored bulbs. Five or so couples danced in various sensual grips, no doubt fueled by the many semi-empty bottles of liquor that filled a nearby table. I scanned the room for Lillian, but she wasn't sitting anywhere. I was disappointed that, apparently, she had decided not to come and had not bothered telling me, but I decided to sit down for a while, on the off-chance that she might still show up. The music stopped, and someone switched on some lights; I blinked to adjust my eyes to the sudden brightness and gazed at the couple standing straight before me and kissing hotly. I knew the boy; he was three years my senior and lived in my neighborhood, so I was mildly interested and kept watching to see who the girl was. Her hair looked familiar to me, and her silhouette ... my eyes saw, but my brain refused to register. A new song started to play, and the couple resumed dancing, turning around until the girl faced in my direction. Lillian's face showed above the boy's shoulder; she gazed at me dully, without surprise, remorse, or embarrassment. She was totally expressionless and detached and seeing that made something snap inside me. I could perhaps have found some consolation had she acted startled or ashamed, but her complete lack of emotion was too much for me.

You know, they say that a girl can literally break your heart.

She shattered mine to pieces, and it felt as if an icy hand had taken it, squeezed it to make it stop beating, and torn it away from my body. I walked out in a trance and somehow found myself at a tramcar stop where I sat until one came along. I boarded it without knowing or caring where it headed to. Despite the chilly night, I didn't feel the cold, so much colder I felt inside. I don't remember how I got home or what I did during the next few days.

I never heard from Lillian or saw her again. I don't know if she meant to hurt me or simply didn't care. I couldn't figure out what I had done to deserve what she did to me, and I waited uselessly for a sign from her, a phone call, a note ... for an explanation that never came. That added one more unresolved issue to my list; who knows what role that played in making me what I turned out to be ...

CHAPTER 6

My experience with Lillian turned me into a misanthrope for a while. I stayed at home most of the time, reading a lot, avoiding the company of people I knew, and particularly not willing to be questioned about her. My parents seemed happy at my change for the better and never asked any questions. They didn't know about my smoking vice, though. On the day of my return from the weekend at the lake, I had bought a pack of cigarettes of the same brand that Yulia had smoked, and slowly, but surely, I had become addicted to tobacco. I tried hard not to smoke in the apartment for fear of being caught, and only once or twice at night, when I couldn't resist the urge, I pocked my head out of the bathroom window and smoked, mindless of the fierce autumn wind that froze my face. To keep my parents from finding out, I brushed my teeth after every cigarette and always kept spearmint in my pocket, but I lived in perpetual fear of exposure, sniffing my clothes after every cigarette to reassure myself that the smell of smoke hadn't stuck to them.

I had gotten into the habit of taking long, aimless walks, me and my cigarettes, and sure enough, whether by chance or by a device of my subconscious, I found myself one afternoon in Via Stampa again. As soon as I realized where I had ended up, the street attracted me like a magnet, and I walked in circles around the neighborhood. It took me five rounds before I saw Alessandra coming out of her apartment building. She walked quickly to the grocery store, and through the window, I saw her standing at the food counter, buying a few items. After a moment of hesitation, I followed her inside. The store was licensed to sell tobacco, and I walked straight to the cashier, acting as if I hadn't seen her, and bought a pack of "Nationals"—probably the worst and the cheapest cigarettes on the market. I kept track of her from the corner of my eye, and I timed my departure from the cashier with her movements, so I got ready to turn around to face her as she came to pay.

"Hi!" I greeted her, hoping to sound surprised.

"What are you doing here?" she asked curtly.

"I'm buying cigarettes," I said, showing them to her.

"So you smoke regularly now," she stated as a fact. She sounded accusing.

"Sort of," I said. I spoke defensively; I had expected her to take me more seriously when she saw that I was a grown-up who smoked, but her attitude was clearly hostile as if she took my smoking as a personal offense.

"But you don't live around here, right?"

"I was just passing by," I said, feeling uncomfortable that she questioned me, "but since you're here, why don't we go for an ice cream?"

She gave me a strange look and then said simply, "I need to go."

"Some other time, then?" I asked, hopefully.

"Mmm ... maybe," she said, but she sounded as if she didn't

really mean it.

"Look," I said, "why don't you give me your phone number, and I'll give you a call one of these days?"

"My mother doesn't like it when people she doesn't know call me at home," she said, and then she added, "Bye," and left, cutting our conversation short.

Alessandra's attitude should have discouraged me, but my obsession with her, sparked again by our meeting, only grew daily. The fact that she cold-shouldered me even increased my attraction to her. During the most boring parts of Latin class, I would close my eyes and conjure up her picture with Yulia in the swimming pool. I would lie in bed at night and recall her pleading voice, as I had heard it coming from her room that night on the lake, and would try to imagine what Yulia could have done to her to make her cry. I made up different stories, each one of them more exciting than the other, all of them culminating in the exchange I had heard to give it a link to reality. I simply couldn't get her out of my head, day or night.

So I started to haunt her neighborhood, until a week after our first encounter, I saw her walking toward the park. She wore a light black overcoat and had gathered her hair in a ponytail. I quickened my steps and caught up with her.

"Hey, Alessandra, can I speak with you for a moment?"

"If you insist," she said, shrugging uninvitingly.

I stood there before her and realized that I had no intelligent roundabout way to tell her what I wanted to say. I had to be direct. "Look here," I said, sounding openly unhappy, "I don't know what I've done to you to make you mad at me, but I only wanted to be nice and buy you an ice cream ..."

"Well, I'm not interested," she retorted snappily. "Why don't you go and spend your ice-cream money on Yulia?"

"Yulia? Why would I buy her anything? I'm not in touch with her. In fact, I'm pretty sure that she hates my guts."

"It certainly didn't look like that on the lake ..."

"Yes, I know that she made passes at me, but I wasn't ... how shall I say ... cooperative."

"So you two aren't going out?" she asked, for the first time looking animated. "She didn't send you to talk to me? Tell me the truth!"

"I haven't seen her since that evening at the nightclub, and I don't expect to see her in the future. Not if I have a vote. Why did that bother you?"

"You don't know her," she said, avoiding giving me a direct answer. "If you did, you wouldn't want to have anything to do with any of her friends either."

"Well, I'm not one of her friends. So can I buy you that ice cream?"

"Yes, I think so," she said, smiling now, and my heart leaped up.

My courtship–because that's what it really was, an old-fashioned, pre-war style courtship–proceeded slowly. Alessandra was still enigmatic to me, although her misunderstanding of my relationship with Yulia had been cleared up, so I behaved guardedly, fearing that I was walking on thin ice without being able to tell where it might break. At first, it was pizza, then a movie, and then another one. During the second movie, she leaned on me and put her head on my shoulder, so I dared take her hand, and she let me hold it. When I took her home, it had already become dark and cold, but she suggested sitting on the bench in the Piazza Vetra garden.

"It's cold," she said right after we sat there. "My hands are frozen. Come closer and keep me warm."

I did as she asked, taking her hands and rubbing them to keep them warm. "You're peeling my hands away." She smiled, looking straight into my eyes, and I stopped. I knew with clarity that the time had come, and it felt right, so I put my arm around her shoulder; she edged closer, and we kissed.

"It took you a long time to do that," she whispered when our lips parted. I kissed her again without answering. She was right, and I had to make up for the lost time.

We no longer felt the cold outside and sat there for a long time, or so it seemed, and when she murmured that she had to go back home, we walked together, hand in hand, cutting through the cold night in a warm bubble of our own, from which all the bad things of the world were shut out. The two-minute walk to her door felt like a beginning, not an end of that evening.

Those were, no doubt, the happiest days of my life. For the first time, I understood what loving and being loved meant. It wasn't a boyish infatuation like the one I had felt for Lillian, and it wasn't my ongoing discovery of the pleasures of sex that caused it. I was in love, and my love was returned; I found it easy to say, "I love you" to her, and so did she to me. And with love came the will to give pleasure. Since then, I have had many women, but never again have I felt that fusion of body and soul that Alessandra and I reached together.

But loving each other on the physical plane was no easy task when we didn't have a safe place to do it in. My apartment and hers were out of the question, so we had to rely on moments stolen in unfamiliar rooms at other people's houses, during parties often populated by people we barely knew. We always felt apprehensive lest someone might walk in on us unexpectedly, so we never took off our clothes, contenting ourselves with exploring each other's bodies stealthily and noiselessly underneath their layers.

Until Alice's parents went to Japan.

Alice was Alessandra's best friend, and we often took her out with us for pizzas and movies to take her mind off the boyfriend who had dumped her. She was an only child and almost seventeen years old then, and her parents trusted her enough to leave her alone when they had to travel to Japan. Alessandra looked radiant when she gave me the news.

"Alice's parents are going away for two weeks, and she's going to let us use her apartment as much as we like," she announced. Her eyes shone bright with excitement.

"That's awesome!" I said, already excited at the prospect of being left alone with Alessandra without having to worry about interruptions.

"She's made it a condition that we leave no trace behind because the cleaning woman comes every morning, and Alice's mother has instructed her to report anything unusual that goes on in the house." I nodded in assent, and she continued, "and, of course, I promised to tell her everything you and I do."

"What do you mean?" I asked with puzzlement. "What business is it of hers what we do when we're alone?"

She hugged me, and then she looked up into my face, laying her chin on my chest and smiling coquettishly. "Why ... you know that we girls tell each other everything. She's naturally curious ..."

"But that makes me feel uncomfortable," I complained.

"Well, you shouldn't be," she answered, and there the matter rested.

Our first meeting at Alice's apartment turned out to be all I had dreamt of and more. We decided not to use one of the bedrooms when we realized that the living room was comfortable enough with its soft couch and long-haired rug. Besides, we felt less inhibited in an environment not so personal as other people's bedrooms. We closed the Venetian blinds, leaving the room in semi-darkness, and then we sat on the rug at the feet of the couch and kissed at length, nurturing our growing excitement.

"Undress," she ordered softly at last and started to unbutton her blouse. I couldn't take my clothes off quickly enough, despite my natural shyness at baring myself so completely for the first time before her. I turned aside a little; not looking at her undressing gave me comfort, as if she wasn't gazing at me either, and the room's poor lighting also helped me overcome my inhibition. I tossed my last piece of underwear onto the floor and turned slowly. I sat on the floor, and she stood there, with nothing on, astonishingly beautiful, her right hand forward inviting me to get up. I took it, and she pulled lightly, helping me to my feet. I stood there, too happy to move, and then she burst out laughing.

"What's so funny?" I asked, feeling hurt at the thought that my body had in some way fallen short of her expectation.

"You ..." she almost choked on her laughter, "you've kept your socks on."

I looked down and saw that she was right; I joined her in her laughter, and then I took a step forward, for the first time feeling her whole, warm and silky skin against my own body.

We spent the hours that followed exploring each other's bodies, without reservations and without fear, each trusting the other completely and unreservedly.

"I want to keep my virginity," she had said at the outset, "for my husband when I choose one. As my gift to him," she had explained quietly.

I wasn't disappointed; I loved her so much that I would have done anything for her, and no sacrifice was too great to make her happy. And respecting her virginity wasn't really a sacrifice; in fact, it only enhanced our creativity in pleasuring each other in endlessly evolving and ever new ways.

But her resolve to remain a virgin couldn't last. I didn't pressure her, and that perhaps helped to make it all so perfect. On the third day, as I lay above her, our hearts pounding, I froze as she started guiding me inside her.

"Are you sure?" I asked, almost in a panic.

"Yes, yes!"

"Won't you regret it?"

"No. Stop talking!" she rebuked me impatiently.

"Wait a second," I said, reaching for my pants where I prudently kept a pack of condoms that had cost me much blushing at the pharmacy. I took one out and showed it to her.

"It's a safe day," she said, brushing it aside.

"Are you sure?" I asked doubtfully.

"I'm sure. Not today. We don't need it."

So we did go all the way, clumsily at first, but soon we reached a perfect, almost holy fusion of bodies and souls.

During those two magic weeks, I learned every sweet taste and inebriating scent of her body; I explored its topography, impressing its valleys and mountains into my mind from every angle; I tuned my movements to the rhythm of her breath until the two of us became one and the world outside her eyes ceased to exist. Our intimacy grew so perfect that no act seemed improper or dirty as, together, we explored the many facets of pleasure and discovered new erotic games and spots to be used in them.

We didn't do drugs, and we didn't drink in excess. In fact, the only liquor I brought with me to the apartment was a bottle of *Grand Marnier*. I remember pouring a few drops of the thick, sweet liquor on each of her nipples and then licking it off her while she arched her back in pleasure. I can still see that picture vividly before my eyes. Her perfect body was standing out against the narrow strips of light that penetrated the Venetian blinds and painted her breasts with ever-changing shapes. Her unblemished skin looked so perfect and smooth that it had the character of unreality and made me wonder if I was awake or in a dream.

We drank Coke to extinguish our thirst and rehydrate our sweaty bodies and fed on pickles, peanuts, and love.

Alessandra had a peculiar birthmark, four fingers below her navel, in the shape of a caravel, complete with masts and sails. I liked to kiss it, and I called it my little *Niña*, after Columbus' smallest ship. She laughed every time I did it, giggling like a little girl so I would do it again and again.

One afternoon when we lay embraced on the couch, satiated from our lovemaking, I finally found the courage to ask her about that night on the lake.

"What happened that first night at the Polanskys?" I asked.

"What do you mean?" she asked guardedly.

"You know ... What passed between you and Yulia in your room ..."

"What did she tell you?" She now sounded coldly distant.

"She didn't tell me anything. I heard you talking to her as I passed near your door on my way to the bathroom. You sounded really upset ..."

"I don't care to talk about it," she said dryly.

"You can tell me," I said.

"I don't want to," she answered, and I panicked, seeing that tears had appeared at the corners of her eyes. I held her tight and kissed her eyes, wiping away the tears. She shivered a little but said nothing.

I never dared to ask her again.

She kept silent for a long time, and then she said in a barely audible voice, "Love me."

"I love you," I said.

"Show me how much," she whispered.

And show her I did. In each and every way I could think of, until she embraced me frantically, panting and moaning as never before. And then I heard someone else moan and pant in unison with her and discovered that it was me or, rather, us–in perfect communion of body and soul.

When our heartbeats returned to normal, and our sweaty bodies lay entwined in a new and glorious stillness, moments before sleep reclaimed us for its own, she opened her eyes for a moment and said simply, "I love you."

Those were indeed two happy weeks. Perhaps the only two weeks of real, perfect happiness that I can recall. So I wonder, is that all that Life had to give me?

CHAPTER 7

Things got difficult again once Alice's parents returned from Japan, and we found ourselves shut out of our little, private Garden of Eden. Our friends always complained that being so busy as a couple, we weren't fun anymore. But we couldn't help it; we didn't seem to be able to keep our hands off each other and took every opportunity to kiss and caress, even in public places. In fact, unbuttoning and caressing in public lent an additional, adventurous spark to it. One of our favorite spots was the "witches' bench," in the park of Piazza Vetra, where years before I had sat, lost in a twisted dream, thinking of medieval tortures and of Alessandra; necking on that bench was my own personal dream come true.

I became nervous when Alessandra announced one day that her mother wanted to meet me. "She knows that we've been going out and wants to make sure that you're a regular guy. Nothing to be nervous about," she reassured me. And, in fact, her mother was quite nice to me. She offered me a hot chocolate, making me feel like a little boy, which under the circumstances suited me fine. As long as she treated me like a child, there would be no awkward questions asked. Having completed the chocolate ceremony, she only asked me a few questions about school. She seemed particularly interested in hearing about my parents and, finally, she inquired about the movie that we planned to see that day. My unreasonable fear that she might ask me if I was having sex with her daughter never materialized. To her, so it seemed, Alessandra was an innocent little girl, and sex was not at all an issue. I smiled to myself when this thought occurred to me. Had she only known...

But other parts of my life weren't going so well. I was so busy coping with my hormones that I had lost interest in my studies, and my grades clearly showed it. So when the dreaded day arrived, and our teacher handed out our mid-term report cards, mine brought with it a well-deserved shock in the shape of five Fs. My own shock, however, was nothing compared with my father's.

"Five effs? Five!" he kept repeating in disbelief. "What have you been doing with yourself? This is a disaster. Selling oranges is all that you'll be able to do if you go on like this. Selling oranges. What have I done to deserve it?" he asked himself bitterly. It was typical of my father to look upon everything from the point of view of how it affected him. It wasn't so much that he worried about my future as an orange seller; he was concerned that people would attribute his son's failure to him and that it would reflect negatively on his image.

"You can forget about that motorcycle of yours until your grades improve. Go get me the keys to the garage. And I'm suspending your allowance. Not a penny will you see from me until you start to behave."

And so my "dry" period began, in which I had to scavenge all the armchairs in the house for coins fallen out of people's pockets and buried under the cushion and to be alert and quick to pick up any little money left lying around. Luckily, I managed to convince my mother to give me small sums behind my father's back, every now and then, but that was not enough to keep me going. I had many expenses: besides the need to take Alessandra out, I had to buy cigarettes. Until then, I had always bought my cigarettes at the tobacconists, but tobacco sold legally was subject to heavy duty, and I could no longer afford it. I saw only one solution–I would have to buy my cigarettes from the smugglers, who bought them cheaply in Switzerland and sold them at half the official price.

A few inquiries with knowledgeable boys at my school produced the name of a reliable smuggler, Mrs. Masi, and an address in the neighborhood within walking distance. Right after school, I went to look for her and found myself in a street I had never visited before, standing before the main entrance to a shabby building that emanated a strong stench of urine. Inside, an almost illegible sign beside a wooden door had the name "Masi" on it. I knocked lightly, and an ancient man in slippers opened the door and gazed at me malevolently.

"What do you want?" he asked impolitely.

"I'm looking for Mrs. Masi," I said, taken aback by his appearance and by his lack of enthusiasm for my call.

He poked his head out a little, gazed to the right and to the left, and then took a step back and motioned to me to come in. I took a step inside, a little nervous on account of the strange appearance and behavior of the old man, and the first thing that got my attention was a strong smell of cabbage that emanated from every corner of the hallway. It was an old apartment, with a badly repaired tiled floor that had been recently waxed and was deeply cold, as only a place that is never heated can be.

Two steps took us to a door that opened into a small, dark room occupied by the fattest woman I have ever seen. She looked about fifty years old and sat in an upholstered armchair that had seen better days, beside one of those big radios they used to make before the war when they thought it had to be the most impressive piece of furniture in the house. It looked like a small cupboard, with a base on which towered the radio itself, looking intimidating with all its dials and knobs. The woman raised her head from the knitting on her lap and scrutinized me.

"Who sent you to me?" she asked, gazing at me intently.

"Giovanni from my school told me that I can buy from you at a good price," I said, almost apologetically. Giovanni had cautioned me that she would be suspicious because of the many rats who would go squealing to the *Finanza*, the finance police, about anybody who tried to make an honest living ... well, perhaps not so honest, but those were difficult days, and people should have had more compassion. Because of the flourishing of the smuggling business, the police had made several successful raids, arresting and putting out of business many smugglers, and that was why every new client was viewed with suspicion and treated as a potential police decoy.

"Giovanni with the black hair and the cauliflower ear?" she trick-questioned me.

"No, Giovanni the redhead."

"All right, I believe you. Now, what kind of cigarettes do you want? I have everything—Rothmans', Marlborough, Gauloise, Turkish ... what would you like?"

"I'll take the Rothmans'," I said. I had never tried them, but a boy in school had a pack of them, and I had admired the beautiful and rich-looking appearance of the box, with its blue and gold logo embossed on its face. I fancied myself showing off to the boys with it.

"A carton or two? If you take two, I'll give you a good discount."

"I don't have the money for a carton ... I wish I had. I can only afford two packs."

"Oh, all right, but two packs are hardly worth the hassle," she complained. She got up, sighing, and placed her knitting neatly on the armchair. She went to the radio, turned a knob, and lifted the top, exposing stacks and stacks of cigarettes of different brands. Each stack reached deep down into the basis of the radio that had been gutted to make room for them. Money changed hands, and I was the proud owner of two serious-looking packs of foreign cigarettes.

"Thank you very much," I said. I made an effort to sound polite; I wanted to ingratiate myself with this source of inexpensive smoke.

"Wait a moment," she said, gazing intently at me. "You look like a good kid to me. How would you like having a free supply of cigarettes?"

A free supply? I was certain she was kidding me, but nevertheless, I said, "I'd give an eyeball for it!"

"There is no need for *that*," she said, smiling broadly. "I can use a bright boy like you to bring in clients. I'll make a deal with you: for every two cartons bought by someone you bring in, I'll give you a pack of cigarettes of your choice. How do you like that?"

I couldn't believe my luck. My prayers had been answered, and I would have a little bit more cash to spend on Alessandra without having to give up smoking.

"It's a deal!" I said. "I'll be back."

The old man followed me to the door and let me out. It's strange, but although I saw him many times in the following weeks, I never learned his name, so I decided to call him Mr. Owl because he resembled one. I didn't call him so to his face, of course. He always opened the door, repeating his look-left-look-right routine every time. He was too old to be Mrs. Masi's husband and too young to be her father, so I labeled him a brother. He was really skinny, in fact merely a sack of bones, and his demeanor imposed a very depressing atmosphere on the apartment. Left alone, I would have had nothing to do with him, but the appeal of the free American cigarettes was too strong for me to give up.

I discovered that I had a knack for spotting potential clients. Mrs. Masi's neighborhood turned out to be crowded with competition, and I soon learned that a man who walked hesitantly, scanning his surroundings timidly, had to be a first-timer looking for a reliable smuggler to buy cigarettes from. It was my task to approach him and to deliver him to Mrs. Masi, who would then charm him into becoming a regular customer. My innocent appearance and youth were my working tools, allowing me to approach even the most shy prospects. I became so successful that at one point, I didn't know where to stash all the packs that I had earned. Mrs. Masi was ecstatic, and I had become her pet.

I was three weeks into "the business," as I had taken to thinking of it, and out for reconnaissance, when I saw a man about forty years old, in a worn-out jacket and battered hat, who walked with uncertain steps a couple of streets away from Mrs. Masi's. He smoked a cigarette without a filter that looked like it had been hand-rolled and peered timidly into the main entrances of the buildings he passed on his way. His dark complexion betrayed his southern origin, and he had the unmistakable look of a newcomer seeking to buy cheap cigarettes.

"Hey, mister!" I called, walking up to him. "Can I help you with something?"

"Who's ya?" he asked, giving me a puzzled look.

Instead of answering his direct question, I embarked on my usual sales speech, "I'm sure you wouldn't mind it if I arranged a present for you; would you say no to a free pack of American cigarettes?"

"Why do you want to give me anything? You don't know me."

"I don't know you, but I think I know what you need ..."

"Yeah? And what is that?"

"I think you need cigarettes, and that's why I want to fix you up with the gift of a free pack." This guy was being obtuse and starting to get on my nerves. Two weeks before, I would have given him up as one too stupid for his own good, but by then, I had grown too greedy and cocky to let him go.

Still, he didn't seem to be taking the hint and said, "I don't believe that you want to give me something for free."

"Look here, mister," I said, now really annoyed, "I see that you're new at this, but if you come to my employer and buy three cartons, she will give you a bonus pack for free. Capish?"

"Oh, I see what you mean now. Yes, I need to buy cigarettes. I hope your employer is not far from here."

"No, it's close by. I'll lead you," I said, relieved that he was finally catching up, and headed for Mrs. Masi's address, followed by my newly-hooked customer. When we reached the main entrance, I stopped outside. "Wait here until I call you," I ordered. That was standard procedure; I always knocked on the door and went inside to report to my employer about the new customer and what he wanted. Then she would send me out again to bring him in when she was ready with a little assortment of merchandise. Since my first encounter with her, she had become more careful and avoided showing customers where she kept her stock. Word was that a colleague of hers—a nice old woman—had been robbed and savagely beaten by one of her customers.

"This one doesn't seem to be rich, but I think he's good for three cartons of Marlborough," I announced, knowledgeably.

"Good, wait a second, and ..."

Right then, all hell broke loose. The sound of wailing sirens coming from all directions bombarded our ears. The house had a back entrance but judging from the noise coming from that direction, that had been clearly blocked too. Someone started hammering on the main door and yelling, "Open up. Police!"

Mrs. Masi looked at me in disbelief and then at the old man. "He brought the finance police here. Stupid idiot!" she said in resigned despair.

It's lucky that eyes can't kill; otherwise, I wouldn't be here to tell the story.

I don't know if I felt more humiliated at been taken into custody by the police or by the fact that they didn't take me seriously enough to handcuff me, as they did to Mrs. Masi and to Mr. Owl. They took us from the house so quickly that we didn't have the time to understand what was happening to us, and then they brought us to the police station in separate cars. My fake customer, who later turned out to be Inspector Carmana, of the finance police, commanded the operation.

The trip to the police station took about fifteen minutes, which I passed in a stupor, sitting in the back of the police car between two uniformed policemen, looking enviously through the window at the people outside. For the first time in my life, I understood what it meant to be free to walk in the street as you pleased. I watched as a boy pushed his bicycle beside the police car and projected my mind into his body, imagining the feeling of the cold air on his face. I caught a glimpse of a waiter who served coffee to a table in a little café at the corner of a business street and resented him his freedom. For the first time in my life, I grasped the meaning of liberty, that which had been taken away from me.

The car stopped outside a gray and characterless building, recognizable as a police station only by the emblem that towered above the entrance, next to the flag. Once inside, one of the guards took me to a small room and left me there. The room was bare, with only a metal table and two wooden chairs in it. I sat in one of the chairs and, for want of better things to do, I ran my gaze over the walls and read and reread the many inscriptions left by prisoners over the ages. The walls were dirty and clearly had not been painted over for decades, so that they still bore anachronistic inscriptions like "Death to the fascists" and "Long live the King," which had been painstakingly scratched into the thick coat of paint. I know it's stupid to feel better because you know that someone, somewhere, is always in a worse situation than you, but on many occasions, that helped me keep my spirits up even when in a real fix, and I had never been in a worse one. I started to wonder who wrote the first of those inscriptions and what must have happened to him. He surely was a partisan who boldly stood up to the dictators; I could imagine the interrogation, conducted no doubt with torture, that he must have endured. I tried to visualize his face and was surprised at the ease with which I conjured him up, sitting in the chair in front of me and gazing at the door in fear of what would come through it. I hadn't heard the click of the door being locked when the policeman had left me, but I didn't dare to get up and check; after all, what would I do if I found it unlocked? I couldn't simply walk out of the police station...or could I?

The room was cold, and the little electric heater that the policeman had turned on before leaving didn't seem to help at all. It was also unnaturally silent. The longer I sat there, the more the tension mounted in me, and I guess that I had been left there to stew over on purpose. The cracked walls were closing in on me for the first time in my life, making me claustrophobic. I felt relieved when Inspector Carmana walked into the room and sat in the chair before me. Without speaking, he took a pack of cigarettes from his pocket and offered it to me. The awful "National" brand tasted like wet cardboard, but I took one gratefully and put it in my mouth. He lit it for me and watched me as I sucked avidly on it, then he leaned forward and looked me straight in the eyes. "So," he said. It wasn't a question, simply a statement, but it seemed to require some comment from me.

"Am I in trouble?" I asked, immediately sounding stupid to my own ears.

"In big trouble, I would say. But I can help...if you help me."

"How?"

"You're a minor, and inducing minors to engage in illegal activities is a serious crime. We want your full testimony regarding your connection with these people; we want to know all you know about them, and we need you to tell us how you came to become involved with them."

"What will happen to them?"

"That's a matter for the magistrates to decide, not for me. But, for sure, they're looking at a long stretch in jail."

I considered it; I had no particular affection for Mrs. Masi, who, after all, had gotten me into this trouble. To me, she was no more than an employer, but still, the thought of becoming a snitch to the police didn't feel right. I thought of Mr. Owl, who looked so old that he would surely die in jail. "And what if I don't help you?" I asked.

"Then you'll walk out of here with a criminal record. I don't think that would be smart of you; that's no way to begin your life, and you're so young..."

He seemed sincere in his concern and, besides, I really owed those people nothing. "I'll tell you everything," I said, for the first time finding the courage to look him in the eyes. He smiled at me and nodded. He had regular, white teeth, which monopolized your attention when he flashed them in the midst of his dark complexion. He made me think of a predator; I only hoped he had already satiated his hunger.

Taking my statement turned out to be a long process. First, Inspector Carmana left promising to be back soon, but with the police "soon" appeared to have an indefinite meaning because it took more than an hour before a young, uniformed policeman came into the room with paper and pens, which he put on the table without saying a word or looking at me, and then went away. I had started to feel more claustrophobic than before and yearned to be allowed to leave; I also worried that my family would have realized by then that I had disappeared and no doubt they would be looking for me. Eventually, however, Inspector Carmana returned with the same policeman who had brought the paper and pen, and, prompted by him, I started to tell my story from the beginning, which took the best part of the following three hours. The young policeman scribbled incessantly, summarizing what I said, and when the inspector pronounced himself finally satisfied that I had nothing more to relate, he submitted the sheaf of papers to me to read and sign. I was in such a hurry to get out of there that I only read a few words from each page and then signed at the end.

"Can I go now?"

"You'll have to wait outside until someone comes to pick you up. We have called your home, and they're on their way."

They made me sit on a bench in the corridor outside a row of offices. The clacking of several typewriters resounded from there and created a strange concert. To while away the time, I invented a tune to go with it and hummed it in my head. Many uniformed and plainclothes policemen went to and fro, but nobody paid any attention to me.

Eventually, Inspector Carmana's voice calling, "Roberto," startled me out of my mentally detached state, and as I lifted my gaze, which I had kept fixed to the floor most of the time, I saw my father walking along the corridor alongside the inspector. Inspector Carmana made a vague gesture in my direction with his hand and said to my father, "You can take him," and then he left, leaving us alone in an embarrassed micro-cosmos created by my father's presence.

"Dad," I said, getting up from the wooden bench, hoping for the consoling fatherly hug that I needed so sorely. The unexpected slap to my face hurt, therefore, so much more.

"Criminal! Idiot! You're the ruin of the family!" he threw at me, slapping me again on the other side of the face. He pinched my earlobe so hard that I thought my ear would come off and dragged me by it through the whole corridor, to the entrance to the police station, and out to his car that he had parked outside. He pushed me into the passenger's seat, started the engine, and drove jumpily and nervously away. He didn't speak a word to me, and when we reached our apartment building, he parked the car in the backyard and motioned me imperiously to get out. He didn't look at me in the elevator and kept his hands in his pockets, playing nervously with a few coins. He breathed heavily as if about to blow flames from his nostrils.

My mother opened the door for us before we even touched it. Clearly, she had been waiting behind it for the noise of the elevator's door to tell her that we had come home. Inside, in the hallway, my father finally burst out all his pent-up anger. "This is your criminal son, who goes and gets himself involved with the underworld. Take a good look at him," he said with a frightening calm, and then he slapped me again.

"I..." I tried to say, but another slap silenced me. The blow had been administered with strength this time, and I fell, dazed, to a sitting position on the floor. My mother brought her hand to her mouth to stifle a little cry but said nothing. I watched as my father unbuckled his belt and slowly pulled it out of his pants, turning it into his hand to get a good grip.

"This is what you deserve," he said, and as he spoke, he lifted the belt up in the air.

"Please..." my mother tried to say, but my father silenced her with a single glance.

I knew that I deserved a good beating for what I had done, and, in truth, the punishment that my father administered didn't hurt too much—at least not physically. The humiliation of the treatment and the lack of compassion that my parents showed me really hurt. I knew that I had screwed up, but I thought that my parents' love for me would make them understand that I had made a boyish mistake, which I regretted, but that I didn't really mean to do anything bad. I knew that I could make them understand how much I loved them and how sorry I was that I had let them down, but I never got a chance to say anything.

After a few lashes, my father ran out of steam and ordered me to go to my room and not dare coming out unless instructed. I closed the door behind me and threw myself on the bed, curling up as much as I could, and for the first time in years, I wept, tears coming from a dull and hollow pain inside. But I did it silently, sharing my pain only with my pillow; I didn't give them the satisfaction of hearing me cry.

CHAPTER 8

Time passes slowly when you're cooped up in a small room with little to do, so I took to reading again, which I had neglected in the previous years. I got reacquainted with *Moby Dick* and *The Last of the Mohicans*, and in the intervals between reading, I took up drawing again. In school, I had always hated the drawing lessons during which we wasted time drawing useless parts of old Roman buildings, but secretly I liked the power given to me by the pencil to make a three-dimensional object appear out of nowhere on a white piece of paper. In my drawing block, I found a page with the first lines of a Corinthian capital that I should have submitted as homework months ago and started to work on its finer details. For long minutes at a time, with the pencil in my hand, I forgot all my troubles.

I went to the bathroom several times a day—that was implicitly allowed, and it helped me feel less of a prisoner. Other than that, I stayed in my room as ordered, alone and almost completely ignored by the rest of the household.

On the late morning of the day after my imprisonment, my

mother came into the room with a tray, carrying a meal that didn't look like much. A bowl covered with a saucer contained some sort of soup, and beside it rested a bread roll; a sad-looking whitish chicken breast lay in the middle of a plate, surrounded by green peas, next to a glass of water.

"I'm not hungry," I said without looking at my mother. It had just occurred to me that a hunger strike would have been the right way to retaliate for the treatment they had given me.

"You must eat something," she said, also avoiding looking straight at me. The previous day's beating had left us both embarrassed, each for his or her own reasons.

"Yeah…" I mumbled, still not gazing at her as she put the tray down on the table.

"Your father and I…" she paused, obviously searching for words to describe my evil deeds, "it…you did a very bad thing," she finally managed to say. I said nothing, and she gazed at me sadly for a few moments and then left.

I felt sorry for her. She had woken up one morning, the mother of a juvenile delinquent. That must surely have spoiled her day. I bet she worried herself sick at the thought that the neighbors might find out. And what would Mr. Danieli, the austere grocer, think? Would he give her a cut of beef of lesser quality next time, on account of her reduced social status? Or, perhaps, he would simply wait for my mother to leave the store before exchanging commiserating glances with other customers.

Little wonder that she was miserable.

My starvation resolve didn't hold for long. I ate everything on the tray and still felt hungry, so I fished in my drawer and came up with white chocolate that served me as dessert. As a growing-up boy, the craving for food attacked me at all times, so I always kept bars of chocolate in my room against night hunger. I finished up all the chocolate and, feeling a little more optimistic, I went back to reading *Moby Dick*.

It was a Saturday, and I remember thinking how true it is that there are always two sides to a coin: being punished had also meant legally missing school that morning, which looked to me as self-defeating behavior for parents who wanted to educate their son. As the day passed, I started wondering how long they would keep that punishment up.

Toward evening the food tray ceremony repeated itself. "Alessandra has called," my mother said as she put the tray down. I had completely shut her out of my mind, so wrapped up in my misery I was. "What did she say?" I asked, feeling apprehensive.

"She wanted to speak with you, and I told her that you're in detention and can't come to the phone. She asked me to tell you to call her when you can." I felt relieved; at least Alessandra knew I hadn't simply disappeared and would wait for my call.

"Who's Alessandra?" My mother then asked. She was obviously simply trying to make conversation, but without any real interest.

"A friend," I said.

"She sounds very nice." She spoke absentmindedly as if we were having a pleasant mother-and-son chat instead of her being the warden and I the jailbird. I gazed ostentatiously down at my book without responding and, after a few seconds, she left.

Sunday morning, I woke up at the sound of the early morning bells calling the believers to church. I had never woken up that early on Sundays, although, obviously, the bells must have sounded the same every time. I wondered how I always managed to sleep through the racket they made. I opened the window, avidly inhaling the fresh morning air; despite the thick smog, it carried a smell of liberty, and I was only now learning to value freedom, which I had always taken for granted. I went to the bathroom, making as much noise as possible, as a signal to my mother that I was up and about and, I hoped she'd understand, hungry. I might also be able to ruin my father's morning sleep, which he held so dear, and the thought gave me satisfaction. I finished brushing my teeth and went back to bed with my book, waiting for something to stir. It wasn't until noon that the door of my room opened, however. To my surprise, my father walked in without closing the door behind him. I lifted my head from the book and gazed at him interrogatively.

"I wanted you to know that I have sold your motor bicycle," he said, and I felt a pang of pain, knowing that I would never ride it again. I had a lump in my throat, and my eyes became wet.

"Why?" was all I managed to say before I choked on my words. I fought back my tears, knowing that seeing me cry would give him pleasure. He was being needlessly cruel, and I couldn't let him see how much he had hurt me.

"Why? Ha!" he said, shaking his head. He managed an expression of sorrow as if to imply that it hurt him more than it hurt me, and, without another word, he retreated, closing the door behind him. Left alone, I allowed my grief to take control; tears came flowing down my cheeks, finding their way to the corners of my mouth where they announced their presence with a strong salty taste. I pressed my mouth to my shirt sleeve to silence the sobs and sat there, feeling empty, for a long time. Later, when my mother came in with her usual tray, I gave my back to her and waited until she left the room. She, too, had betrayed me; she alone could have stood up for me, but she hadn't bothered. I no longer felt sorry for her, and I hoped that the grocer would publicly snub her.

That evening I was summoned to the sitting room. My father sat in his beloved upholstered armchair, and my mother, who had come to fetch me, went and stood beside him. My father waited theatrically for her to take position beside him, and then he addressed me. "You can leave your room now, for the remaining time," he said. I didn't understand what "the remaining time" meant but was happy that detention had come to an end.

"That's good. I've got to go find someone to lend me his Latin exercise book for the test tomorrow," I said. That was a story I had made up on the spur of the moment as an excuse to go out and run to Alessandra. However, my father shook his head and said, "You're not going to school tomorrow."

"What do you mean? I've got a test, and if I don't go, I'll flunk Latin."

"You're not going to your school anymore. We are withdrawing you from school," said my father.

I started to panic. Something very wrong—and very bad—was going on there.

"I don't understand. You wanted me so much to do well in school, and now you want me to drop out? And what will I do?"

"Oh, you'll do well. You'll do very well, but not here," he answered, almost savagely. "A good friend of mine has recommended a boarding school to us, one where they know how to deal with boys like you. I have already spoken with the principal, and we will have the paperwork ready by the end of next week. You'll start there the next Monday."

I was dumbfounded. They were sending me away. They had decided to get rid of me, just like that, without any show of regret. And what would happen to Alessandra and me? A hundred questions popped up in my head all together, and my brain felt like a hornet's nest. I forgot where I was, and my face must have shown my emotion because my mother spoke for the first time. "It's for your own good," she said, apparently expecting that stupid sentence to put everything right. That really set me off. At that moment, I hated them both and no longer looked upon them as my flesh and blood. I was no longer a child who could rely on his mother and father to keep him safe and happy. I had always deluded myself that, no matter what could go wrong, my parents would find a way to put it right for me. No more. Faith in the ones you love is hard to die, but mine was now officially dead and buried for good.

CHAPTER 9

At least they left me alone for a few days before my exile began. I don't know if they had run out of other ways to torment me or if they had simply lost interest in me. Whatever the reason for it, I was happy to stay out of their way; I had enough to deal with, trying to come to terms with my bitter destiny, to worry about anything else. I didn't know how to break the news to Alessandra. Right after the announcement of my exile, I found myself in no shape for anything, and surely I wasn't up to telling her. My session with Father and Mother had ended in awkward silence, with me trying to process what I had heard and my father waiting for an emotional reaction. It must have taken a full minute before he realized that there wasn't going to be one.

"That's it," he said.

"That's it?" I echoed.

"Yes," he confirmed.

I have often wondered whether I should have begged them. Perhaps that was what they were after—begging and tears. Maybe that could have changed everything, but they never gave me a hint that pleading might make a difference or even that circumstances could exist in which they might consider calling my exile off. And it never occurred to me that I might, or should beg. Perhaps the shock or the hatred that I felt growing inside took control of me, but I simply turned around without another word and walked away.

They didn't try to stop me.

Back in my room, I sat in my desk chair for a long time. I kept my gaze fixed on the wall while my brain strived to put a real-life meaning to what I had just been told. I found myself examining little imperfections of the wall and wondering about small details of a picture frame that I had barely noticed before. My mind raced aimlessly between irrelevant questions until I started wondering whether I had lost it.

Hours later, I woke up in the chair with an aching back and dragged myself to my bed, where I relinquished my consciousness to the silent night.

The next morning I waited until my father left the apartment, and then I sneaked out before anybody could think of stopping me. I waited for Alessandra at the exit of her school. It was cold outside on that early February day, and I walked back and forth to keep my feet from freezing until I spotted her coming out surrounded by a small group of girls.

"Roberto!" she cried in surprise. "What's the matter? Your mother said..."

"I'll explain." I gave her friends an unhappy glance. They stood there, so obviously waiting for juicy details, that I found it annoying. "Let's walk," I said.

"Bye, girls," she said, and then she tucked her hand into the pocket of my coat and interlaced her fingers with mine. "You're freezing!" she exclaimed. Well, I had worse problems than that.

Perhaps freezing to death wouldn't be such a bad solution to them, I thought bitterly.

"Now, tell me," she demanded.

"Let's go and sit down," I said.

She gave me a worried glance but said nothing. As we walked in a frozen silence toward her home, I realized that I had to be honest with her and let her have the full truth.

"I got myself into real trouble," I said as we sat on the bench in the park that we had come to consider our own, feeling that I had to give it to her in stages. After all, admitting to having been arrested by the finance police wasn't half as bad as what I would tell her later. So I told her everything about being taken into custody and what preceded it, in full detail, including the most painful ones; that helped me delay giving her the really bad news. As my narration proceeded, her expression became darker and darker, but when I came to the point where my father came to pick me up, her face softened, and her hand squeezed my arm in a spontaneous gesture of sympathy.

"You're really nuts!" she said, at last, shaking her head in disbelief. "What were you thinking, getting involved with those people? Little wonder that your father hit the ceiling. So, have your parents calmed down by now? They must have if they let you out."

So here came the tough part. She was smart and didn't need to hear much to understand what I was trying to tell her. Long before I reached the end of my tale, tears formed in her eyes, and she buried her head in the hollow of my shoulder. "My poor baby," she kept murmuring, stroking my back all the while. That brought tears to my eyes too, which I dried surreptitiously with the back of my hand. I stroked the back of her neck to comfort her, although I was the one in greater need of comfort.

"What shall we do?" she asked after a while.

I knew what she meant; I, too, had wondered whether our love would survive the separation and how often we would manage to meet. I didn't have the answers, but I knew that I had to be optimistic. "We'll manage, somehow," I said, but I didn't sound convincing even to my own ears.

"How?"

"I don't know right now, but we'll find a way. I'm sure that I'll be coming home at least every other weekend, and then you have the holidays..." I said, increasing the pressure of my hug to emphasize my statement. She felt limp in my arms, though, as if she had lost her power to give me strength. And she didn't argue with me, which for some reason increased my dispiritedness.

I went to my school that Tuesday, during the lunch break. I didn't feel like simply disappearing without telling anybody; if I had to leave, I wanted to go in style, letting everybody know what a dangerous character they had gone to school with. I also wanted to show off my contempt for my teachers, the so-called "professors," now that I was beyond punishment. My classmates had already heard rumors of my run-in with the police and greeted me with manifestations of respect and with a chorus of questions.

"Hey, Lucci!" one of the boys, Alfredo, called out to me. "How come you're not in jail? We heard you stole a car and got pinched by the police."

"No, he stabbed a policeman," a second boy whose name I forgot added, helpfully.

"So what's the real story, Lucci?" a third boy by the name of Renato demanded to know, speaking with a supercilious smirk. This Renato was a classmate I particularly disliked, so I seized the moment, got up close to him, and speaking between clenched teeth, I said, threateningly, "Both, Renato. And I'll be waiting for you outside..." The startled look on his face brought a smile of satisfaction to mine, but I had to turn away before I burst out laughing.

"What's all this?" a voice thundered behind me. I didn't need to look to know who the voice belonged to—it had the unmistakable timbre of the much-hated vice-principal, Professor Marchetti, the sadistic pig who enjoyed inventing new punishments for every minor infraction. He seemed to love writing venomous reports to the student's parents at the slightest provocation. Running into him was a bonus for me, seeing my state of mind that day.

"Ah, Marchetti. What can I do for you, my good man?" I asked, trying to sound majestic. The boys around me turned their heads, covered their mouths with their hands, and did all kinds of contortions to stop themselves from laughing. The vice-principal turned a beautiful purple and started to stutter. He always stuttered when he got really angry, and I had counted on it.

"Wha ... wha ... who do you think you are, Lucci? I'll show you. You're sus ... sus ... suspended. I'll write a strong note to your parents. A strong note!"

"You can't suspend me, Marchetti," I answered seraphically, smiling a broad smile.

"I ca ... ca ... can't, can't I? I'll show you what I can do. I'll get you ex ... ex ... expelled from this school. From this school. My school!"

"You can't expel me from your little, pathetic school, Marchetti. I'm withdrawing from it. I find that it's a sub-standard establishment, and I'm moving on to one more suited for quality people. Be well, my good man," I said, and, thinking this a good line on which to exit, I waved goodbye to my audience, which still bravely fought the need to laugh. I gave my back to the vice-principal who seemed to have lost speech altogether and walked calmly down the stairs and out.

My farewell visit to the school had left me in a good mood, and once in the street, I considered who else I needed to say goodbye to. There was only one more person I really wanted to see—the old lady from the pen and paper shop. I got my notebooks and writing implements in her little shop not far from the school, which was slightly bigger than a telephone booth. I liked to go there, partly because I loved the smell of paper which impregnated the air—the little volume of air that filled the tiny shop and appeared never to be refreshed—and partly because the old lady always seemed to have time for me. She enjoyed answering my endless questions about beautiful and expensive pens, which she knew I would never buy, and most of the time, I was her only customer, and luckily so because two people in that little space were a crowd. I couldn't leave without telling her because she would wonder what had happened to me. Besides, she was well over eighty and might not be alive on my next visit home from the boarding school.

So I walked the short distance from the school to her shop but was dismayed to find it locked. A sign on the door said, "I'll be back soon," but I was too fretful to wait, so I moved on.

I regretted my impatience all my life. I never saw the old lady again, and the next time I passed by her door, years later, it had turned into a pizza place. I always felt bad, knowing that she must have thought it inconsiderate of me to leave without a word to her. And, to be honest with myself, inconsiderate it was.

Throughout the week, I did my best not to think of what would happen next. I tried to kid myself that those days would go on forever, like Lillian's record that played in repeat, again and again.

Being cynical helped a little, so I played the role of the one who doesn't care, forcing myself to look upon everybody as less fortunate than I, having to remain stuck in their old, unchanging world. That's how I handled my fear of leaving the familiar places where I had lived all my life, heading for an unknown future.

I managed to avoid my parents almost entirely. The few times that I saw my father, I looked away and moved on; he didn't show any interest in talking to me either, so that was easy. I don't know what they had told my brother, but he avoided me too, with elaborate showings designed to convince me that he wasn't, making me feel like a dead man walking. On the other hand, my mother tried to behave as if nothing had happened, but she only got "yes" and "no" answers from me. I was angrier at her than I would admit, and I didn't mind letting the world know. I felt cheated because my childhood had ended so abruptly and I hadn't been consulted about it; I felt betrayed by my parents who, instead of looking out for me and paving my way into the cruel world, behaved like my enemies; and I was mad at the world in general, because nobody came to my aid, to show me the way out of the mess into which I had gotten myself.

But the last day eventually arrived, inevitably and mercilessly. My belongings had already been packed, including a jacket that looked like a prisoner's uniform, which my mother had bought for me and which apparently was required by my new school. I had said my goodbyes to the few people that mattered to me and now had to deal with the hard task of parting from Alessandra. We had been talking a lot during that week, stealing every free moment she had, to be together, but our sentences had become increasingly shorter and spoken more and more in undertones as the days went by. Other than repeating to ourselves the reassuring words already exchanged over and over again during the week, confirming the strength of our love and its ability to see us through these difficult times, little remained to be said.

"Giorgio is giving a party tonight," she said that Sunday morning.

Giorgio was her cousin, three years her senior. I had met him a couple of times, and I liked him, but I didn't feel like spending my last night at his party.

"Oh, I don't know…I'd rather you and I went somewhere together alone…"

"We will be alone. He's letting us use his room. My uncle will be back very late, so it's okay."

She gave me a meaningful glance which I found difficult to interpret. Our relationship was so open that we spoke about everything and never resorted much to hints and glances. Anyway, all that counted to me was to spend my last hours with Alessandra, undisturbed. When I was away from her, I felt so hollow inside that I couldn't imagine passing a day without seeing her.

It never occurred to me that my parents might object to my going out on my last evening, but of course, as I prepared to walk out through the front door, my father stood in the way.

"Where are you going?" he asked as if he cared.

"Out," I answered curtly.

"Tomorrow morning, we must make an early start. We are leaving at seven, so it's not a good idea to go out now."

"I have a book that I lent to a friend, which I want to take with me. I'll fetch it, and I'll be back." I spoke dully, hoping that my tone wouldn't give away how important going out was to me. I simply had to spend the last few hours with Alessandra and pack them into a memory to take with me. I knew for sure that, had he known, my father would have enjoyed taking that last little consolation away from me.

"All right, but be back by nine," he condescended.

I nodded in assent, and he smiled satisfied, certainly convincing himself that he had already broken my spirit and turned me into the meek son I was supposed to be. He would be bursting with fury when I didn't return at the appointed time, but I didn't care. What could he do to me that he hadn't done already? He couldn't send me away twice, I reflected.

Alessandra waited for me at Giorgio's door, and as I stepped inside, she took my hand without speaking and guided me through the crowd. The living room was full of people with glasses in their hands, talking, and a few danced. We moved slowly through them, careful not to bump into anybody and spill their drinks until we reached Giorgio's room and closed its door behind us. A key was in the lock, and Alessandra turned it. Then she took off her blouse and hung it on the handle, covering the lock with it. "So nobody can peep through the keyhole," she answered my unspoken question.

She stood there in her bra, waiting for me to take the next step, so I got close, hugged her, and started kissing her. In a moment, we found ourselves on the bed, kissing and caressing hungrily. The only light in the room came from a small night lamp with a red bulb, which gave a surrealistic feeling to the whole scene. I searched my head for things to say in a sudden surge of panic brought about by the now unavoidable realization that time was running out and that anything left unsaid between us would be missing. But speech seemed to be entrapped in my chest and unable to fight its way out.

Slowly, softly, she unbuttoned my shirt and then unzipped my jeans.

"I want you," she whispered.

My heart started to beat hard as I saw tears running down her cheeks. She pulled my head toward her and gave me a long, sweet kiss mixed with salty tears. I found myself crying too and, this time, I didn't try to hide it.

We made love intensely, with animal passion, and then again, tenderly and quietly. We didn't speak; we had no need for words, and none could help anyway.

A knock on the door woke me up. We had fallen asleep in each other's arms and now woke up in a silent house, the party obviously over.

"Get your act together, Cinderella," came Giorgio's muffled voice from the other side of the door, "my parents will be home soon."

We dressed in silence; nothing had been left unsaid. It was past midnight, and I walked her home, hugging her so hard that it must have hurt, but she didn't complain. At her door, we kissed for the last time, exchanging futile words that wanted to sound like plans for the future. Tears ran again down her cheeks and seemed to be in endless supply.

"Go now," I said, "before I cry too."

She nodded, kissed me quickly again, and then ran into the building. I took a few steps back and leaned against a parked car, feeling too weak to move. I must have stood there for a long time, my head empty and my heart heavy. A stray cat approached guardedly, sat in the middle of the road a few paces from me, and gazed up at me with mocking eyes. I don't know why, but that cat's stare was the last straw, so I tore myself away from her door and walked home with a bowed head.

CHAPTER 10

The St. Anna College, just outside Pavia, was the place chosen for my exile. They called it a boarding school, but in reality, it was a private prison. On that Monday morning, my father brought the car to a halt in front of a long, gray building that looked unwelcoming with its gloomy smog-stained facade. We reached it just before noon and much later than planned because, of course, he had gotten lost reading the roadmap, and we had to circle around Pavia several times before he agreed to ask for directions. No matter how many times he got lost before, misinterpreting the map and turning each one of our trips into a much longer undertaking than needed, my father would always claim to know best and refuse other people's help. This always started endless bickering with my mother, who wanted him to admit that he was lost. But this time, she kept silent while he drove around almost empty roads, muttering to himself details from the map he held in his left hand, which added to the already heavy atmosphere of gloom and doom that reigned in the car.

The empty and silent street added to my surrealistic feeling—

almost an out-of-body experience—that I was witnessing something happening to somebody else. We got out of the car without speaking as I gazed at the impersonal façade of my new home. The sun shone brightly over it, in an almost cloudless sky, but the air was cold and damp, in good harmony with the place itself. My father put on his hat and faced the building. My mother stood a step behind me and out of my sight. I picked up one of my two suitcases and walked pointedly up the stairs that led to the large entrance door to the building, in a show of defiance, as if to say, "That's fine by me." My father followed, carrying the other suitcase, and my mother closed our little procession, somehow managing to look busy while doing nothing.

As soon as we walked past the cyclopean door, a thick smell of minestrone greeted us. It seemed to be everywhere in the building, and it hit my nostrils. It took me days to get used to it and to stop smelling it all day long. Nobody was in sight, and we walked along the high-ceilinged corridor, our steps resounding like those of a military march until we reached a door with the sign "office" on it. A long wooden bench stood in front of it, and my father motioned to me to sit there. He knocked lightly on the frosted-glass insert of the door and walked in without waiting for an invitation, followed by my mother. They left me sitting on that bench with my two suitcases, one on each side of me. I sat there for what felt like a very long time before that door opened again, and my father's bent forefinger summoned me inside. All I possessed in the whole world and cared about I kept in those two suitcases, which I felt would be unwise to leave unguarded, but they were too heavy for me to lift together, so I dragged them across the corridor and through the door. I still remember vividly how my father simply stood there, watching me struggle with the weight, not even considering to help me; I didn't know that I could hate him more than I already did, but that small, perhaps insignificant accident, showed me how little he cared for me. In the years to come, the recollection of that moment has often come back to me as the turning point of my relationship with my family and has helped me strengthen my lack of remorse and guilt.

In the room, I saw a huge desk flanked by two shelves full of serious-looking books. Behind the desk stood a man of about fifty, impeccably dressed in a gray suit with a sober tie that seemed to grow out of a wine-red cardigan that he kept buttoned all the way up. He had gray hair and wore horn-rimmed spectacles above a large and beaky nose. He wasn't smiling.

My mother sat in a small armchair, one of the pair placed before the desk, and my father went to stand beside her. I dropped my suitcases and looked inquisitively at the group.

"Stand straight!" The man behind the desk commanded; then, turning to my parents, he explained, "Discipline must be taught from the very beginning; otherwise, they won't learn."

I felt outraged by this unwelcoming introduction and gazed at my parents as if to say, "What kind of place is this?" but my father looked appreciatively at the man while my mother was busy studying the design of the carpet, and they both avoided meeting my gaze. For the first time in years, I behaved smartly, and instead of reacting defiantly, I decided to go along with it, at least until I learned the rules of what I already understood was a damned place. I straightened myself up and said, "Yes, sir."

My father gave me a strange, surprised glance. I knew what he was thinking: I had given this stranger the deference he had always expected from me and could never get, and he struggled to figure out what he had been doing wrong all these years. That made me smile.

"I am Professor Renato Fasulo, the director of this school," said the man. "You will only speak to me to answer a question or when invited to speak. Is that clear?"

"Yes, professor."

"Good. If we are clear on that, we can proceed. From this moment on, you are a pupil of this institute—one of the oldest and best in Italy, with a tradition that dates back to the seventeen-hundreds. You will respond to me and to the staff of the Institute only. Now go and wait outside until summoned."

I turned around without a word, opened the door, and painstakingly dragged my suitcases out again. A few minutes later, the door reopened, and they came into the corridor.

"Don't worry. We will make an exemplary student of him," said the professor, talking to my parents as if I wasn't there.

My father thanked him, and they shook hands. My mother hugged me dutifully but without conveying any real warmth and said her stupid line for the last time. "It's for your own good," she murmured absentmindedly. I stood there, frozen, and didn't return the hug.

"You'll behave yourself, you hear me?" was my father's last warning, administered with a meaningful nod obviously meant to impress upon me that terrible things would happen to me if I didn't. Quite superfluous, as I had already realized that.

Having completed their function, they turned and left. I watched them as they walked quickly along the corridor, clearly in haste to get out of there, until they reached the door and left hurriedly through it. They didn't turn back to look at me, to take a last memory of me with them for the road or, as perhaps I had secretly hoped, to have a last-moment change of heart, unable to stand the thought of the separation and to take me back home with them. I kept looking. I needed that reality check to rid myself of all illusions.

"Your personal instructor will be here soon to take you to your quarters," said the voice of the professor behind me. Lost in my thoughts, I had almost forgotten that he existed. He didn't wait for an answer from me and closed the door, so I sat down on the hard bench again to wait.

Waiting seemed to have become an integral part of my life.

My instructor, Mr. Paolini, was tall, thin, and curt in dealings with the pupils. Nevertheless, I soon learned that he was the kindest among the gang that ran the St. Anna boarding school–or rather, to tell it like it is, the St. Anna reformatory. He appeared out of nowhere, introduced himself briefly, and picked up one of my suitcases, ordering me to follow him. Up one flight of stairs, he led me to a huge room where I counted forty-two beds arranged in two rows and walked me along the narrow space between them, finally stopping at the foot of one bed located toward the end of the dormitory. Adjacent to each bed, they had placed a tall and narrow metal cabinet locked with a padlock.

"This is your bed," he said. "Here is the key to your cabinet lock. All your belongings must go into the cabinet, which must be locked at all times. You can stow your suitcases under the bed, but they must be empty. The school accepts no responsibility for items stolen or lost. Everybody else is in class now, but in one hour it will be lunchtime. When you hear the bell, you must rush to the dining room at the entrance level. Go down the staircase we took coming up and turn right at the bottom. You'll recognize the dining room because everyone is going there when they hear the lunch bell. After lunch, follow everybody to the main hall where you'll be given this week's program and other relevant information. At five p.m. I will talk to you and give you specific instructions. Search me out. Any questions?"

I didn't have any. I might have asked how I would recognize the lunch bell, not having heard it before, or how and where I should "search him out," but I was in no state to ask questions. I had always had my own room to myself; I had always cherished my privacy and taken it for granted, and now here I was, apparently going to share my private moments with some forty-odd strangers. The thought was mind-boggling, but I realized that the sooner I came to terms with it, the better.

He left quickly, without asking any personal questions or saying anything to ease my initial shock. Everybody seemed to wish to get away quickly from me that morning. I sat on the bed, unable to think and unwilling to unpack. After a while, I took out my notebook and started writing my first letter to Alessandra. I needed to write to be able to throw my mind back to her and forget for a moment that I was in a hostile place, far away from her. My lines came out confused and unclear, but I didn't care; I wasn't going to mail that letter anyway.

A bell rang in the background. I assumed it was the lunch bell, but I wasn't hungry. I didn't want to eat. I didn't want to be there. An idea occurred to me: perhaps if I got myself into a state of starvation, they would have to send me back home.

The door of the dormitory opened, and a boy came in. He was almost a head shorter than I and stocky. He studied me for a moment. "Hi!" he then said, walking up to me. "You're the new boy. You're out of luck; they gave you the bed next to Stinky Johnny. I am Fabrizio," he said, putting out a plump hand for me to shake.

I warmed to him. For the first time that day, someone seemed happy to see me and welcomed me. I got up from the bed and shook his hand.

"I'm Roberto, and I just got here. Who's Stinky Johnny?" I

inquired.

"You'll find out, but now we must rush if we don't want to miss lunch. I just came to pick up something. He went to a bed in the facing row, five spaces from my own, and opened his cabinet with a key that he kept on a chain around his neck. He took something from a box inside, closed the door, and clicked the padlock locked. Then he turned to me. "Let's go," he said.

All of a sudden, I no longer felt like staying in the dormitory to starve. It looked like I had found a friend, and that made a world of difference.

CHAPTER 11

Life at the St. Anna revolved around discipline and, for someone like me who had never been regimented before, the first days resembled a surreal nightmare. The morning started with the ring of a loud bell that startled you out of your sleep and wits and, if you weren't quick enough to get out of bed, the instructor yelled at you with the accompaniment of miscellaneous threats. On the morning after my first night, most of which I passed tossing from side to side on the hard mattress, I was jerked out of bed by such a sudden clangor that my body started to shake, and it took me the best part of five minutes to regain my composure.

It was another unpleasant feature of the school that you never simply walked from one place to another. Unless you were excused to go on your own on some personal errand, we always had to keep ranks. When leaving the room, we had to form a double line and were then marched to our next destination in a silly-looking martial drill, at the orders of one of the pupils, usually chosen on the basis of his vocal virtues.

Unfortunately, loudness was not always matched by a sense of rhythm, which often entailed dire consequences. We marched in that fashion to the dining room in the morning and from the dining room to our class and then, again, to the dining room for lunch. After a brief recreation period, we marched again to our class, then to dinner, and finally to the dormitory. This routine repeated itself every day, but sometimes we had little and always welcome variations. Even a boring lecture by some over-zealous priest who took full advantage of his captive audience counted as a diversion.

For the first few days, I joined the ranks as if in a dream, refusing to believe that I would become a member of that ant colony, but after a while, the routine got the upper hand, and I realized that repetition brings acceptance. I was past caring sooner than I had imagined.

The school had strict timetables for everything; we had forty-five minutes for lunch and dinner and fifteen minutes for the morning ablutions. Mornings were the worst times for me. Not only was my bed hard and the room cold, so that I always woke up stiff and aching, but I had to wash my face and brush my teeth in a hurry, together with my roommates, in an endless line before a sink that looked like a pig trough, equipped with parsimonious faucets that only agreed to dispense recalcitrant droplets of icy water.

And then I had to deal with the shower problem.

On that first night, I went to sleep after a long and confusing lecture by Mr. Paolini. I sat on the bed, debating whether to undress or simply kick off my shoes and crash out in my clothes. The instructor had kept me long after dinner as a punishment for my forgetting to seek him out at 5 p.m. as instructed, and by the time I reached my bed, I found the dormitory already shrouded in darkness. Most of the pupils were asleep, and only a few sat on the bed, writing letters or reading at the faint light of small candles. As I threw myself on my bed, too tired to undress, the boy next to me got up and faced me. "Hey, there," he said in a friendly way. "I'm Johnny; what's your name?"

"I'm Roberto," I answered. I spoke guardedly because I had already been warned that this Johnny didn't have all his marbles and that I should be careful before getting too close to him.

"New here." He stated a fact, asking no question, so he obviously expected no answer, and an awkward silence followed. After a minute during which he kept gaping at me—or at least, so I thought, but I couldn't tell with certainty in the dark—I felt the need to break the silence.

"How long have you been here?" I asked.

"This is my second year. And how long are you going to stay with us?"

Up to that point, I had avoided thinking about that question, and I was sorry that he had brought it up.

"Oh, I don't know. I'll see how I like it here, and then I'll decide."

"That bad, ah?" he said. He sounded sympathetic.

"That bad and then some," I conceded. "Tell me," I asked, feeling that now that the ice had been broken, it wasn't impolite of me to ask questions, "why do they call you 'Stinky Johnny'?"

"I don't wash," he answered. He stated it simply, almost as an obvious point. "At least, not during weekdays. I shower on Sunday morning ... some weeks."

Like many other kids my age, I had never been a stickler for cleanliness before Alessandra came into my life, but I had become an obsessive washer as soon as I started dating her. With no girls in that place, it meant that I could now happily relapse into my previous indifference to hygiene. Even so, however, washing only on Sundays, and even not every Sunday, seemed a bit extreme to me.

"But why's that? Don't you itch all over?"

"Sometimes I do, but I prefer that. If you're smart, you'll do the same, at least at first."

"But why should I…"

I didn't get to finish my question because the boy three beds away from me raised his voice to silence us. "Will you shut the fuck up?" he said testily.

"Sorry, I didn't mean to disturb…"

"I don't give a shit; shut your trap!"

It wouldn't have been wise to get into an argument on my first night, so I lay down, and Johnny did the same. I had been given a coarse and itchy blanket, but I was so tired that, by itself, the unfriendly fabric wouldn't have kept me awake. I had trouble finding sleep, nevertheless. I had too many things on my mind that I hadn't had the time to process yet.

During my first three days at the St. Anna, I moved around as if in a dream, more or less refusing to admit that I was there in the flesh. I took small, strange rules, such as the one banning drinking water while eating soup, as a confirmation that I was, in fact, dreaming. That was one of the strange rules invented by Mrs. Fasulo, wife of the headmaster and proprietor, and a sadist in her own merit. On my second day, we had chicken soup at dinner—or at least some sort of dish-washing water, which they wanted us to believe was soup. To mask the dreadful taste of the mixture, the cook had added a liberal amount of salt to it so that as my first spoonful went down, I felt a terrible thirst. I quickly poured water into my glass from a pitcher next to my plate and brought it to my lips. But I didn't manage to sip from it because a hand coming from behind me took hold of my glass and forcefully pushed my arm back onto the table. Surprised by this unexpected interference, I turned around to find myself face-to-face with the gray-haired, bony face of Mrs. Fasulo.

"What do you think you're doing?" she asked icily.

"Drinking water, ma'am," I answered, surprised that she couldn't see that for herself.

"You don't drink water before everybody has finished drinking soup. That's the rule!"

"But I'm thirsty," I protested, "there is too much salt in the soup."

"You have all the water you need in the soup. Nobody drinks water while drinking soup. You'll be allowed to drink water after the last boy finishes his soup; until then, no water," she said and left without giving me an opportunity to argue.

I was hungry, but I wasn't going to drink that soup without water. I looked around; all the other boys were drinking their soup avidly. I wondered bitterly if I would become a housebroken, pre-programmed pupil and behave submissively like them. I decided that I wouldn't and pushed the bowl away. Mrs. Fasulo gave me a nasty look, and for a moment, I thought that she might force the concoction down my throat, but she apparently decided that I wasn't worth it and turned away. My belly ached from its emptiness, but bending my pride could hurt more.

It took me three days to reach the conclusion that even if I wasn't going to come to terms with the fact that I had to stay in that prison, the time had come that I had to wash. We were allowed time to shower before bedtime, and, every evening, small groups of my roommates hastened to the showers as soon as the free time started to shower before the hot water ran out. I had used public showers before, but I always hated having to bare myself in front of a bunch of strangers, and, somehow, I felt uncomfortable at the thought of showering before my classmates whom I had met only three days before. So on that evening, I waited for everybody else to come back from the showers, and then I went alone, happy to have the place all to myself, even if it meant having to shower with lukewarm water.

I opened the door of my cabinet and took out a piece of soap and a small towel. I saw Stinky Johnny gazing at me as I locked the door, and I looked inquisitively back at him. He opened his mouth as if to speak, but then he closed it again, shook his head as if to get rid of some thought, and then turned his back to me. I had already labeled him for a weirdo by then, so I paid little attention to him.

The water in the shower was still hot, and I stood under the jet, lathering my body leisurely and enjoying the feeling of the hot stream running over my body. The shower room was badly lit, which is why it took me a long time to realize that the shadow that had appeared in the dirty, milky shower curtain was a man. Startled, I moved the curtain aside, and my surprise was complete when I saw Professor Fasulo standing there, his back to the wall and his body leaning slightly forward. His right hand was inside his trousers, and I realized with horror that he was playing with himself.

"Professor!" was all I managed to utter.

"It's all right, my boy," he said. I don't know if it was the idiotic expression of gratification on his face or his calm, ingratiating manner of speech that freaked me out, but I took a step back deeper into the shower, turning half around to hide my nudity without losing sight of him. My heart beat so fast that my throat hurt. He moved away from the wall, coming closer, and I stepped further back, trying to put the barrier of the shower jet between him and me. The hot water supply had run out, and cold streaks, mixed with a tepid stream, hit my back and made me shiver, but I didn't mind—I would have frozen to death rather than let him come close to me. He looked puzzled and hurt as he gazed down at the droplets of water that wetted his shoes. "You're very athletic," he said. "What sports do you practice?"

I couldn't believe it; he tried to make small talk while I was on the verge of hysterics. I couldn't find anything to say or the strength to answer him at all. I simply stood there, shaking my head, and he went on.

"You know, I could make your stay here much more pleasant and comfortable if we were to become friends…"

He continued to play with himself as he spoke. I wanted to look away but feared that he might jump into the shower and grab me, so I kept staring at him, but I fixed my gaze on a point above his shoulder. He seemed disappointed and shook his head.

"Well…if you change your mind, I'll always be there for you. Remember, I can be a good friend."

I nodded. That seemed the best thing to do to make him go away. "May I go now?" I whispered although I had nowhere to go as long as he remained there.

"Yes, but don't forget that we never had this conversation. You understand? It would be very unpleasant for you if you decided to talk to people and tell all kinds of lies about our little chat."

I nodded again, and he nodded back, smiling a satanically satisfied smile, then he simply left. I remained under the water in the shower, I don't know for how long, but it must've been a long time because I found myself shivering at the touch of the icy water coming from above my head. I cut the water and dried myself hastily, and when I got into my pajamas, they felt damp. But I didn't care; I only wanted to get back to the safety of my overcrowded dormitory. I grabbed my clothes, soap, and towel and dashed out of the empty shower room that resonated with the sound of my feet. The empty corridor amplified the sound of my steps so much that you could have thought they were those of a beast chasing me. I ran through the empty corridors until I reached the dormitory and threw myself on the bed, hoping that nobody would speak to me. As I tossed on the bed, trying to release some of my tension and frustration, I caught a glimpse of Johnny gazing intently at me; I may have been wrong, but I believe that he was smirking.

I learned a lot during the first week in that inferno. Fabrizio, the boy who had greeted me when I first came to the dormitory, kept close to me most of the time, giving me useful tips and hints on how to behave and what to expect. I admired him at first because he always seemed to be in control; he always dressed neatly and somehow managed to obtain extra rations of whatever little good stuff they gave us on occasions, which he often shared with me. Then, one day, I understood what a "more pleasant and comfortable stay" meant.

An ingrown toenail had been torturing me for a couple days, and my instructor had finally arranged for me to go to the infirmary after hours to take care of it. The infirmary was two doors next to the management office, and, as I opened the door to leave after a painful treatment, I saw Fabrizio coming out of Fasulo's room. On an impulse, I retreated quickly into the darkness of the hall leading to the infirmary, where he couldn't see me. He stood in the corridor for a moment, and I thought he wiped a tear from his cheek with his sleeve, then he walked toward the dormitory. He had a little paper bag in his hand, from which later that night he offered me a candy bar. I took it as I always did before, but this time I couldn't eat it.

I'm not judgmental, I've never been, and I'm sure that Fabrizio had gone through tough times, perhaps unbearable ones, before allowing himself to become a plaything for that revolting, fake professor. But I had lost my respect for him, and there was nothing he or I could do to restore it. Fabrizio must have felt that something had changed because he gradually let go of me, and we drifted apart. So I was left without a close friend. I was on my own.

CHAPTER 12

I often wondered whether things might have gone differently if all this had happened nowadays when we have cellular phones to keep in touch with each other. Not only cellular phones had not been invented then, but even using a landline wasn't so easy. The St. Anna housed over 120 boys in three separate wings, and it only had one public telephone, which we were allowed to use every third Sunday. Telephone lines were so rare then that that phone had a ridiculously short number. But even on that one Sunday, we only had ten minutes to use the phone, provided we paid in full for the call beforehand—no refunds given if the call failed—to a supercilious secretary who seemed to hold us personally responsible that she had to spend time on Sundays at the institute.

My class' turn to make phone calls wasn't until the second Sunday after my arrival, so my only means of communication with the outside world was by letter. On my second evening in that cold, unfriendly place, I spent all my free time writing a letter to Alessandra. I tried not to sound desperate or complaining and concentrated all my writing energy on conveying how much I missed her. Her reply came only five days later, and I sat on my bed at night, reading avidly through it. It was a wonderful letter, and it is the only one I have kept all these years. I'll read it to you, and then I'll destroy it; it feels like sacrilege to let the paper fall into unfriendly hands because it embodies the essence of Alessandra's soul, and over the years, it has become impregnated with my own. So it will go where I'm going—into nothingness. Here it is:

10 March 1969
Dearest Roberto,

Only today I received your letter, which made me immensely happy. I feared a scribbled page and, instead, your letter was a poem that revealed an altogether different Roberto to me. I don't know if you can call what I feel for you "being in love" because it is a feeling much deeper and less ephemeral than love. It is a friendship of a kind that I have never experienced before. I would do anything for you, and, without a doubt, I would overcome all my egoism to help you through your difficult times and to see you happy.

I wish I were there with you, at the St. Anna, to share every minute of your day, to have fun with you, to be bored, to speak, to keep silent—sharing that silence in which you and I express ourselves better than with words. I know you won't be disappointed by my words and that you will see that they confirm all my love for you.

I don't know what you will make of my confused thoughts—it is certainly easier to speak, and to communicate through silence than to write; you know that a look, or a smile, would be enough for us to understand what we mean, more than words can tell.

I'm dying to see you...
Your Alessandra

I read and reread it, looking for the hidden meaning behind the words, for the first time trying to understand her without being able to touch her, smell her and integrate her words into the multicolor picture created by all my senses. Was she saying that she didn't really love me? No, she specifically said she did. But then, why did she doubt being "in love." I examined her words a hundred times, each time going from the peak of happiness to the depth of desperation and back up again. I fell asleep with her letter in my hand. That way, I felt her closer to me.

At last, my turn to use the telephone arrived. We had a list of names posted on the door of the little telephone booth, each with the allocated time of his ten minutes written beside it. My time was at five minutes to twelve, and as soon as I got hold of the phone, I dialed Alessandra's number. I knew that number by heart and still do. Here, I'll prove it to you: 86.39.72. See?

It took eight rings before someone picked up, and I almost despaired that they would. Alessandra's mother's voice sounded in my ear. You can imagine my disappointment; I had hoped that Alessandra would pick up and I would hear her voice right away.

"Yes?" was the curt answer.

"Good morning. May I speak with Alessandra, please? This is Roberto."

"She's not at home; I'm sorry."

I panicked. That was my only chance to speak with her.

"Can you tell me where she is? Can I call her there?"

"I'm sorry. No. I don't know. Shall I tell her anything?"

"Yes, please. Tell her that I called and won't be able to call again for the next three weeks. I'll try, but I think I won't be able to. Will you tell her that, please?"

"Yes. I'll tell her. Goodbye."

She hung up, and I looked at my watch. I still had five minutes of my turn, so I dialed home, hoping that my father wouldn't be the one to answer the phone. I was lucky, and I got my mother's voice at the other end of the line.

"Hello?"

"Mommy," I said, feeling that my eyes had filled with tears at the sound of the familiar voice.

"Oh, hi, sweetie," she said, as if everything was as usual, "how are you?" She had a knack for avoiding thorny issues and dealing with appearances as if they were the only thing that mattered, so she made it sound as if I was calling from some ski resort.

"Mommy ... you need to take me out of here. This place is terrible ..." my voice broke, and I pushed the mouthpiece aside so she wouldn't hear me sobbing.

"Oh, I'm sure it's not that bad. You simply need to get used to it. I'm certain you'll be all right."

"No!" I almost yelled, "I won't be all right. Nothing is all right here. When are you coming to see me? I need to tell you what's going on here. I can't do that by phone. Please come," I was begging, and I hated myself for it, but I couldn't stop.

"Soon, honey. We'll see you soon. Don't worry. Everything will be all right."

That was exactly what I needed. At that moment, I asked for my mother's reassurance like a small child, and for once, she delivered. I would have gone on seeking comfort, but the boy in line behind me opened the door and asked, "Are you done?" so I signaled to him to give me another moment and, as soon as he closed the door again, I said, "Just come soon, please. I can't stand it anymore. I have to go now, but please come next weekend." I hung up and took a moment to compose myself and wipe my eyes dry. I felt strangely strengthened; my parents would come to see me, and surely they wouldn't let me rot in that place once they heard what was going on there.

But, of course, they didn't come the next week, or the one after that, or the next one. After a while, I realized that I had been forgotten there and that I no longer existed for them. Every two weeks or so, a package arrived, with my name written on it in my mother's neat handwriting, containing assorted items and a little money. Not much, but enough to buy cigarettes. We had to buy our cigarettes at almost twice the regular price from one of the cooks who had made quite a nice business out of it, so any money I got was earmarked for that. Everybody knew about the cook's racket, including Management, but they didn't seem to care. Perhaps they got a cut of the profits. Anyway, they didn't interfere as long as we only smoked during our free time.

Sometimes my mother would send chocolate and, on other occasions, wafers, but she always included in it socks and some piece of underwear. That's how she kept a clear conscience; she always bought us stuff we didn't need and traded it for our love. It had worked for her in the past, but with me, it wasn't working anymore.

One of those packages had a note from my brother in it that made me cry. I had never really been close to him, and, in fact, I pointedly ignored his existence altogether. I had never given a thought to him since my exile, and here, in his childish handwriting, the note said, "Dear Roberto, I miss you, and I hope you're well. Your brother, Maurizio."

I didn't cry because I missed him—I didn't know him well enough to care. I cried because I realized that he was at home where I longed to be, getting all of my parents' attention, safe in our warm apartment, with the nice clothes and the good food, while I had been sent to that jail and turned into a non-person. I cried because I had thrown all that away with my own hands, but although I recognized my own mistakes, it was unfair that I had never been given a second chance.

After a while, Alessandra's daily letters became shorter. I couldn't complain, however, because mine had become telegraphic. But what did I have to tell her? My days passed monotonously, and the little accidents that we, the inmates, amplified out of proportion as a diversion from the boredom of our everyday routine sounded trivial and uninteresting when put on paper. Assuring her of my love only took a paragraph, and the rest of the letter consisted of mere fillers, so my own writing became more and more concise with every letter.

Alessandra, on the other hand, coped with the problem of filling the pages by telling me all about her friends, her school, and a million little details of no importance to me, but which I read avidly because the words in her handwriting worked the magic of linking me to her.

Then the letters stopped coming. I guess I had been expecting it—that was the inevitable outcome of the evolution of the chain of messages, in which the invisible thread that linked our souls had become thinner and thinner until in her last few letters, as well as in mine, it had vanished altogether. I had come to accept what I couldn't change, and in fact, I had become too numb by then to feel anger at the thought that I had been abandoned by her too. I hadn't stopped loving her, but she had become an ephemeral being, unreal in too many ways and so far away that sometimes I wondered whether she had existed at all. Often at night, I would wake up doubting my own sanity of mind and sweating at the thought that, perhaps, she was only a figment of my imagination.

That was when I got a fever. I woke up in the middle of the night sweating, my throat dry and my head aching. I didn't know where I was, and I moaned and groaned so much that Mr. Paolini, who slept behind a curtain at the end of the dormitory, got up and approached my bed. He felt my forehead and looked worried.

"We need to wait till morning," he said. "I'll get the medic in the morning."

He got me some water that I drank avidly, and then he went back to bed. The medic came and gave me some medicines in the morning, but I couldn't remember what I was supposed to take and when. My temperature wouldn't go back to normal, and, on and off, I became delirious. Whether because of my natural strength or perhaps thanks to the medicines, which I took only when, occasionally, Mr. Paolini came to see how I was doing, three days later I woke up without a fever; but I was too weak to get up and stayed in bed for two more days. Nobody in the management seemed to be concerned or worried over my situation, and I could have easily died there unnoticed.

In one of my delirious moments, I dreamt that I was back in middle school. I never felt happy in that school; I hated my teachers and, for the major part, also my schoolmates. It was an old building, cold in appearance and temperature, much like my primary teacher's heart. She was an elegant and statuesque woman of middle age, of the kind that would have fitted well as the companion of a fascist bureaucrat. And in fact, her behavior was unforgiving, rigid, and unfriendly. For whatever reason, she had taken a dislike to me from the first day, and nothing I could do seemed to change that.

In comparison, my elementary school had been a friendly place where I had managed to stay out of trouble simply by being nice and polite. But there, they wanted me to study Latin, to submit papers, and, above all, to keep abreast with lessons. So, of course, I got the mumps right after my first month in school and by the time I returned, trying to catch up was hopeless.

With little to do, lying all alone in my bed, in and out of fever dreams, I started to reminisce about those days. Moving to my new school, I had lost sight of Alessandra, and despite my conviction, acquired during choir practice, that I had given her my heart forever, I soon forgot that she existed. Other factors contributed to that; not only did I have a hard time finding my place in school, but also my parents went through a rough patch, accompanied by loud arguments that often stretched into the night. They apparently settled their differences after a few months because the arguments stopped, and the atmosphere at the dinner table became less icy. They never told us children anything, always keeping appearances as a lifeline. Of course, we never asked; we would never have gotten a straight answer anyway. Besides, I positively didn't want one.

My birthday falls in July, so I could only dream of a decent birthday party because my friends were never around to give me one. For my twelfth birthday, my parents bought me an inflatable mattress and promised that I would soon be able to try it out. They made good on their word, and a few days later, they took us kids to the seaside to escape the excruciating heat of the city summer. The place, however, was a letdown to me, and I complained about it to my mother on the third day.

"This hotel is a mortuary," I said. "There are no kids around."

"Well, you should go to the beach and make friends there," she retorted.

She spent most of her time sitting in an easy chair on the veranda of the hotel's bar, a bottle of *S. Pellegrino* before her, sipping her eternal mineral water. My father had gone away on one of his business trips, and on those occasions, my mother always seemed to be in some kind of suspended animation, no real activity allowed, until his return.

Our hotel was one of a long row, and I had seen with envy how bunches of kids my age played in the yards of more modern-looking ones. So I took her advice and went to pick up the mattress that I had left in our beach cabin. The hotel rented beach cabins for guests to go and change in, and ours was the last of the row. I knew that the one next to ours belonged to the only other family with children that stayed at our hotel—or rather, in the old-people home that passed for a hotel with my parents. I had seen a mother and a girl my age sitting at a nearby table in the hotel restaurant, but I had never had any reason to speak with her. I knew that her name was Carla because of her mother's annoying habit of crying "Carla!" at her every movement. If she sprinkled too much salt on her dish, she would cry "Carla!" and so she would do if her daughter asked the waiter to bring her a second helping of something. On the other hand, Carla was a depressed-looking kid with a freckled nose and short brown hair. Altogether, they were not my type.

The beach cabins were made of rough planks of wood, painted in blue and white, and seemed to have been put together in haste by a not-particularly-meticulous carpenter. As soon as I stepped into my cabin, a play of light from the one next to me exposed a crack in one of the slabs in the communicating wall. Instinctively I put an eye to the crack, and my heart skipped a beat when I saw that Carla was in there, undressing. She had taken off her top, baring a small, rounded breast. I gazed at her hypnotized as she moved slowly, taking off her skirt and pants and then tantalizingly putting on her one-piece swimming suit in slow motion. Then she left, and I sat on the narrow wooden bench of the cabin, breathing heavily and waiting for my excitement to subside and the bulge in my swim brief to disappear. It took a while, but as soon as it felt safe enough to go out, I ran to the waterline, saw Carla sitting in the shallow water, and dropped my mattress next to her.

"Hey!" she complained, "you're splashing on me."

"No big deal," I said, dismissing the complaint. "You're

staying at the hotel, right?"

"Yes. And you're there too, with the little boy."

"That's my brother," I said, happy that the conversation was moving along. "Would you like to float with me on my mattress?"

"But not too deep, okay? I'm afraid of going too deep."

"All right, grab your side of the mattress, and I'll grab mine. That way, we will be balanced."

Holding the floating mattress, we ventured a little farther into the sea until Carla begged me to go back. I turned the mattress slowly, trying to take command of an erection that was the simple reflex of the accidental touch of her hand on my arm, coupled with the sudden recollection of her involuntary striptease. When we reached the shallow water, I sat on the wet sand, keeping the mattress above my waist and praying for the cold water to end my embarrassment. I had never had such an uncontrollable reaction before and didn't know how to cope with it.

"Hey, do you like to play cards?" she asked.

She liked to say "hey" a lot, I noticed.

"Depends ..." I said.

"I have a deck of cards in my room. Would you like to come and play with me after dinner?"

"Don't you have to go to sleep early?"

"Yes, but not tonight. I don't want to. My mother always turns in early. After dinner, you can come, and I'll teach you a new game. What do you say?"

"Maybe," I said.

I didn't know what she was really up to or whether I wanted to go along with whatever she wanted. She clearly liked me, to invite me like that. I felt no attraction to her—not at all in the way that I had felt attraction for Alessandra during choir practice. But I was tickled by the thought that she didn't know that I had seen her naked, and it felt as if I had power over her because of it. I toyed with the idea of hinting something to her, and I turned my head to hide a smile.

"I'll wait for you," she pressed me.

"Oh, all right. Don't push me."

"But come, okay?"

Without waiting for an answer, she got out of the water and ran barefooted on the hot sand toward the hotel.

Soon after dinner, Carla's mother sent her to bed, and then, for the first time since our arrival at the hotel, she sat on the porch beside us and engaged my mother in conversation. I guess that she was as bored as my mother was. Her husband, if she had one, wasn't there either, and the solitude of the semi-deserted lobby, almost entirely silent after the old people had vanished to digest their dinner elsewhere, must have been too much for her. In any case, it had been enough to make her renounce the protective shield of her usual aloofness. My eyes were beginning to feel heavy, so I stood beside them, trying to be noticed until my mother stopped her chatter to ask me what I wanted.

"I'm going to bed, Mommy."

"Yes, yes. Go," she said without even looking at me.

It was lucky that my father had to go back to Milan; during the first two days at the beach, he had made a point of spending "quality time" with me, his version of which meant cornering me on the balcony, away from anybody else, and engaging in long and winding monologues meant to glorify him, his many qualities and any of the many accomplishments that he cared to describe to me in great and boring detail on that particular occasion.

As soon as I rapped on Carla's door, she opened it and motioned me to come in.

"You can sit on the bed," she said.

She fished a deck of cards from the drawer of her bedside table.

"We must be quiet because Mother has the room next to mine, and if she finds you here, there will be trouble."

"I don't want any trouble," I said.

Carla's mother looked scary enough to me when she wasn't mad, and I certainly didn't want to have to confront her when she was angry, particularly when burdened with an unclean conscience. I felt uncomfortable, although I reasoned that she couldn't know that I had been peeping at her daughter in the cabin because I knew that it would have imparted a far more sinister meaning to my being alone with her in her room at night.

"Why don't we do this tomorrow morning?" I suggested.

A veil of sadness suddenly appeared on her face.

"Tomorrow we're leaving," she said.

So that was it. My plans had gone sour. I had hoped for a few more peeping sessions in my cabin to alleviate the boredom of the place, but there would be no more peeping for me, and I had one full week to go in that mortuary, all by myself. I saw little point in spending time with Carla now and started searching my brain for a good excuse to go while she earnestly shuffled her deck of cards. An imperious knock on the door, followed by the words, "Open up, Carla!" checked my mental efforts and her shuffling.

"Quick," Carla whispered to me. "Get into the closet."

That was probably the dumbest thing that I'd ever done, but in the grip of a strong panic, I let her push me into the closet and close the door on me. It was dark and stuffy in there, and after ten seconds, I decided that I would die of suffocation among a bunch of girl's clothes. However, ten seconds was all it took Carla's mother to open the closet door again and to hiss, "Get out" at me. Her eyes were icy cold and entirely lacking in sympathy.

"We were doing nothing wrong, ma'am," I said.

I spoke apologetically, but I didn't expect her to soften, which was lucky because she didn't.

"Shut up and get out," she said. "I'll tell your mother."

She spoke in an undertone, and that spooked me. I would rather have had her yell at me, but she simply towered over me, her finger pointing to the door. I stole a quick glance at Carla. She stood in silence with downcast eyes, looking resigned and quiet as if she had been through all this before. She didn't return my gaze.

Back in my room, I learned one of my first lessons in dealing with girls: you always want what you can't get. As I sat on my bed, I felt how my desire for Carla's presence mounted in me—an amorphous desire and an immature one, but no less aching for that. A strong, painful feeling of loss overwhelmed me, and I was scared by my unexpected ability to feel strange, new emotion in such bizarre circumstances.

I sat on the bed waiting for the door to open, a herald to my well-deserved punishment. However, nobody turned the handle, and time passed, so I fell asleep without undressing, exhausted by the tension.

When I got up for breakfast the next morning, Carla and her mother were gone. My mother never mentioned the incident to me, and no punishment was ever administered. After all these years, I still wonder whether she knew about my misconduct at all. I also wonder what caused Carla's mother's quiet reaction; was it because Carla had behaved "improperly" with boys before? And if so, did she know that I had watched her as she undressed in her cabin? Could it be that she had been playing with me? I know that these are entirely unimportant questions, certainly not the kind that a sane person would ask himself on his deathbed. However, I torture myself knowing that I will never have the answers to them.

CHAPTER 13

As far back as I can remember, I have always tried to look for the bright side, even when one didn't actually exist, knowing that finding a positive angle was my lifeline to sanity. At the St. Anna, the mechanic shop counted as the bright spot. The school worked under the assumption that we, its pupils, were lost causes to society and should not be expected to reach any position of real prominence in life. As a result, in addition to our regular studies, we had to take practical courses so that when they kicked us out of school, we would at least be able to earn a living in a humble profession. We had a choice between wood crafting and mechanics, and given my allergy to sawdust, I had little choice. Besides, I had always liked cars and enjoyed learning about them and working on them.

You shouldn't think that the sole purpose of our practical studies was to educate us. I believe that, in reality, the Fasulos had devised a bright scheme to make more money out of us. The woodwork, unsophisticated as it was, produced tables and other furniture that the school sold, allegedly to keep the shop furnished.

In my shop, on the other hand, we fixed minor mechanical faults and did maintenance work, such as filter and oil replacements, mainly for people in the rural area, who sought cheap alternatives to the extravagant prices that mechanics charged in the city. I didn't mind that the school made a profit on my back; I enjoyed working on different vehicles, so I tried to be assigned to passenger cars and volunteered to work on tractors and other heavy machinery. Somehow, working in the mechanic shop helped me chase away my thoughts, and sometimes I surprised myself by feeling happy at the end of the day.

In addition to doing practical work, in which we engaged under the supervision of three experienced mechanics, we had frontal lectures given by our instructor, Mr. Paolini, who, besides his dormitory and general duties, managed the mechanic shop. He was a decent sort of chap who took pride in his profession, and since I quickly grew enthusiastic about my work there, an invisible but strong bond began to form between us.

"You have skillful hands," he said to me one day, nodding appreciatively after he saw me changing a recalcitrant gasket. "If you take this seriously, you may become a good mechanic."

"I like this work. A lot. I never did anything like this before, and the feeling that you have when you put the pieces together and the machine runs smoothly..."

"I know, I know. I can see that you have passion. Keep on like that."

It didn't take long before Mr. Paolini allowed me to do complex jobs on my own. I spent all my free time there, studying old and oily manuals and disassembling and assembling machine parts. Those were my only peaceful hours and the only times when I could be found smiling again.

One day, after class, I remained in the shop to clean up and organize my tools. I worked so intensely that I didn't notice that Mr. Paolini hadn't left and watched me until he spoke.

"Lucci," he called, startling me out of my solitary concentration.

"Mr. Paolini..." I said, trying to figure out whether I had done anything wrong. He approached me and sat on the side of a small tractor that stood, partially dismantled, next to me. Without speaking, he took a pack of cigarettes from his shirt pocket, pulled one out, and offered it to me. His gesture surprised me—it was an offer of intimacy unheard of at the St. Anna—and after a moment of hesitation, I stepped forward and took the cigarette he offered.

"It's forbidden to smoke in the shop," I commented as if he needed me to tell him.

He shrugged. "It's after hours," he said, lighting a match and putting it to my cigarette and then lighting his own. We smoked in silence for a minute before he spoke again.

"So, what's with you, Lucci?" he asked, speaking in a friendly voice.

"I'm all right," I answered guardedly.

"That's not what I meant. I meant, how is it that a nice boy like you gets sent to this place?"

It was as if he had opened a dam. I needed someone to confide in so much—someone mature, a father's figure—that I started talking torrentially, holding nothing back. I told him about my family, my girlfriend, my brush-off with the law, everything. He listened without trying to stop me and without asking questions. He gave me more cigarettes. I don't know how many because I stood there, babbling, for a long time. At times my eyes filled with tears, and I had to stop talking to wipe them away. When I did, Mr. Paolini always found something to busy himself with—a cigarette, a shoelace—feigning not to notice my emotion. I loved him for it.

When I finished telling all I had in me, he eyed me with his usual serious expression. "It's tough on you, but you'll get over it," he said. "You're tough; I'm not worried. But whenever you feel like talking, come to me, okay?"

He spoke shyly, but his words sounded heartfelt. I swallowed and nodded, too grateful to speak. Mr. Paolini stood up from the tractor and walked away but stopped at the door, as in an afterthought. "Don't tell anybody that you smoked in here," he said with a smile and left.

I felt better and lighter than I had been since my arrival. And I was grateful to him. Very grateful.

Easter was finally upon us. The principal gathered us in the lecture hall Sunday morning during Lent to tell us that the school would close for Easter week. Our families had been notified that we would have to leave the school the next Thursday and be home for Good Friday. My heart started to beat fast at the thought that soon I would be back home, even if only for a few days. I didn't want to admit it to myself, but hope had been reborn that the damage could be undone. Surely my parents had missed me, I reasoned and would take the opportunity to bring me back into the family. I anticipated long rebukes from my father, certainly mixed with endless lectures about my lack of virtue and abounding in comparisons with his own spotless conscience and behavior when he was my age, but I was ready to take anything so long as I didn't have to go back to the St. Anna.

I barely slept during all that week, so great was my excitement, planning my words of apology for my unforgivable behavior, and even going to the length of writing down an apologetic speech. In my mind, I rehearsed the scene during which I would tell my parents all about the unbearable days at the St. Anna, as a result of which they would break down and vow never to send me back to that unspeakable place again.

I had one unresolved issue, though—Alessandra. I don't think I wanted anything more in the whole world than to see her, but her letters had stopped coming, and I didn't know how she would react, seeing me. I didn't want to think of the possibility that she had a new boyfriend. Imagining her with someone else was too painful, and I would rather be left with the uncertainty than having to face the knowledge that she belonged to somebody else. But I had little choice; I needed to see her so much that it hurt.

I decided to write her a letter telling her that I was coming home for Easter and needed to see her. It was a masterfully crafted letter in which, once again, I expressed all my love for her. I made it clear to her that I longed for her more than I needed air to breathe; I left no doubt that she had been on my mind constantly and that the thought of her had kept me going during the weeks of our separation. I hinted that I understood that some kind of *force majeure* had kept her from writing, or perhaps her letters or mine had been intercepted. I did all I could to impress on her that I had no complaints and that she had nothing to explain or to apologize about.

I posted the letter in the big, rusty postal box next to the entrance, giving it a few unspoken words of encouragement, as one would do when speeding an ambassador on a difficult diplomatic task, and then I switched my brain off to keep it from overloading with the expectation of the coming Friday.

"Lucci!" the much-expected call finally came from the dormitory's door. I got up quickly from my bed, picking up the satchel in which I had put a few items that I didn't want to leave behind, and walked quickly to the door. "To the Secretariat," Mr. Paolini almost inaudibly said to me as I passed through the door, giving me a strange glance. I could make nothing of his behavior, but he sometimes acted strangely for no apparent reason, so I merely shrugged off the thought and walked away.

I quickened my pace, unable to contain my expectation and my anxiety. How should I behave if both my parents had come? And how if only my father showed up? On second thought, it could be that my mother had come with the driver that my father sometimes hired to take her out of town. Perhaps he was still too mad at me to come in person to pick me up. On the other hand, if he had come together with my mother, wouldn't that mean he was seeking a reconciliation? The corridor seemed to stretch endlessly.

The place that passed by the grand name of "Secretariat" was no more than a tiny ante-room that separated a small area between the corridor and the principal's office, in which a secretary sometimes sat, looking important and annoyed. My heart beat fast as I pushed the door while my embarrassment toward the upcoming reunion mounted quickly.

I could've spared myself the anxiety; the person in the room was not my father.

"Uncle Dan..." I murmured with astonishment. I hadn't seen him for a year now, and I couldn't figure out what he was doing there. He wasn't really my uncle, after all. He was my mother's uncle, but he was only a couple of years older than she, so she called him "Dan," and I called him "uncle"; I guess that "granduncle" sounded too pompous. Uncle Dan lived in Rome but always spent a week or so of the summer holidays with us, and once, I had stayed at his home in Rome for two nights.

"Roberto...how are you?"

We stood there, two paces away from each other, each frozen in his embarrassment. The males of our family didn't hug or otherwise display affection. It wasn't done. Although nothing specific had ever been said about it, showing familiarity was considered unmanly and inappropriate. I couldn't tell you how my father managed to instill that and other precepts in us merely by lifting eyebrows and gazing askew at us at various times, but there was no doubt that he had succeeded at least in that inglorious part of our education.

"Where are my parents?"

"They thought...they asked me to come in their stead."

"Are you coming to us for Easter?"

"Roberto," he said, stepping forward and getting hold of my arm. I gazed into his face, and his compassionate expression told me the story.

"I'm not going home, am I? They're leaving me here, right?"

"Of course not! They wouldn't leave you here, even if it were possible. I'm taking you to Rome with me. Come, I have a taxi waiting for us outside to drive us to the station. The train leaves in an hour."

"Why I'm not going home? Why can't I go back to Milan?"

I choked on my words and no longer managed to hold back the tears that had replaced my joy at the expectation of a reunion with my family. Uncle Dan put his arm around my shoulder and spoke in a low, unconvinced voice. "Your parents think that you should stay away for a while. I think it's tougher on them than it is on you, but they're doing it for your sake. They have consulted with psychologists—more than one—and they are all unanimous that a period of separation is necessary to put things right, so as much as they're sad missing seeing you, they have decided to follow their advice."

"So I'm the only one they didn't consult," I said. I spoke bitterly and saw the pain in his eyes.

"It's not too bad being with me. We'll have fun together, you'll see, and I'm happy to have you."

I appreciated his attempt to lighten up the atmosphere, but it wasn't working. I picked up my bag and walked heavily out. I felt relieved, at least to some extent, though; I was leaving the St. Anna behind, even if only for a few days, and that amounted to something—a small mercy, but something. Uncle Dan followed me in silence, and we both climbed in the back of the taxi that waited outside.

On the train, I sat moodily by the window of our second-class cabin, brooding on my situation and trying to find the bright angle, but this time there wasn't one. Uncle Dan escaped from my oppressive company by falling asleep and snoring through most of the six-hour train trip. I couldn't sleep, dazzled by the scenery that ran before my eyes, conscious of the freedom enjoyed by everyone else in the world outside but denied to me.

CHAPTER 14

Uncle Dan was a good person, kind and gentle. He lived alone, and we were his only family. He had been married once, but his wife had not been quick enough coming home with the coffee and sugar that she had bought for him on the black market, and the 1944 German curfew had caught her unprepared in the street where she had been shot by a passing patrol. I had heard my mother telling stories about her, and she came across as a friendly but absent-minded person. She was a stickler for good manners, and everybody loved her. That didn't impress the Nazis, however. People who had witnessed the incident, watching from behind closed windows, had said that she had looked surprised as she died—almost as if thinking it bad form on the Germans' part to shoot her. Uncle Dan never spoke about her, and the only time he told me the story, it was clear that he blamed himself. So he was a sad man and not much fun being with, but I think I had him on my side and he disapproved of what went on in my family and, without betraying my parents' trust, he did his best to make it up to me for what they were putting me through.

It was evening by the time we reached his apartment, and I had only one thing on my mind—to call Alessandra before the hour got too late.

"May I make a phone call, Uncle?"

"You're not going to call your parents, right?"

"No. I just need to speak with a friend. It's important..."

"Go ahead; the phone is by the entrance door. You need to dial 02 before the number..." I knew that, of course, and he knew I did, but by acting helpful, he tried to show me that he was on my side, and I appreciated it. Such little acts are sometimes worth so much more than a verbal assurance.

The small hall by the entrance door was semi-dark, which I found reassuring, feeling more sheltered and readier for an intimate conversation in that atmosphere. I picked up the phone and dialed the number I knew by heart. At the other end, the phone rang five, ten, fifteen times before the ring turned into the disconnected toot-toot-toot sound I dreaded. I dialed again and let the phone ring until I had to accept that nobody would pick up.

I searched my head for Alice's phone number; it had been a long time since I last dialed it but, by some miracle, or perhaps because it was my last hope and my brain summoned all its resources, I managed to retrieve it from my memory. At the third ring, Alice answered.

"Yes?"

"Alice, this is Roberto. I need...how are you?" I asked in a belated show of courtesy.

"Roberto?" She sounded more surprised than I would have expected, almost as if I had returned from the dead.

"Yes. Listen, I need to ask you something. I have tried to call Alessandra, but there is no answer at her home. Do you know where she is?"

"They've gone away for Easter."

"Can you give me her phone number—where she is now, I mean?"

"No, I don't know it. Sorry."

She sounded evasive to me, and I didn't believe her. She was her best friend, and Alessandra wouldn't go away without telling her where she was going or without giving her a way to keep in touch.

"I need to speak with her, please..." I no longer minded sounding pleading. I was desperate by then.

"Listen, you should leave her alone. You've caused enough trouble for her already."

"I haven't done anything," I protested. I honestly didn't understand what she meant.

"If you want to know, once her parents found out that she had become involved with you, after what you'd done, with the police and all that, they made her life miserable." I detected resentment in her voice as if I had any control over what had happened while I was away.

"But how did that happen? I thought they knew nothing."

"Her mother found one of your letters, and she called your father. He told her everything. And when you wrote that you were coming home for Easter, they took her away to keep her from you. She's miserable on account of you and if she means anything to you, just leave her alone. I have to go now."

I panicked. Alice was my last link to Alessandra, and I had to get her help. "Wait a second! I know you care for her, and you know she would want you to help me. I need you to tell her that I called and that I love her. Will you do that for me, please?"

"To be honest with you, no, I won't. I worry about her, and I really think you should leave her alone. I need to go now," she said and hung up before I could protest.

My feet refused to go on supporting me, and I sank to the floor, the receiver in my hand. It felt as if the whole world had turned against me, and I had been left without a friend to rely on. I found some consolation in the thought that she hadn't stopped writing to me because she didn't care, but very likely, the mail had been stopped by her mother. But for all it mattered, we might have been on different planets, so slight were my chances of seeing her or talking to her in the near future.

I don't know for how long I sat there, in the semi-darkness, feeling miserable and on the verge of crying, but when my uncle's voice called me to the kitchen, I knew I had to pull myself together and keep going. I had only myself to count on now, and I couldn't afford the luxury of wading in self-pity.

After a cold dinner, which we ate in silence on the tiny Formica table in the kitchen, I threw myself onto the bed in the small bedroom that Uncle Dan had prepared for me, feeling exhausted. I fell asleep almost immediately and slept until the early morning light coming in through the thin curtains woke me up. Finding myself the next morning in Uncle Dan's two-bedroom apartment, I felt strangely rested. I lay on my back with eyes open, my head empty, and my body relaxed. I hadn't felt like that in the morning for a long time, and I relished the sensation, avoiding any movement for fear of chasing it away. After a while, the sound of dishes handled in the kitchen alerted me to a void in my stomach; I had eaten sparingly and without pleasure the night before.

I got up and crossed the corridor to brush my teeth in the cold bathroom, and, after returning my toothbrush and toothpaste to my bag, I walked into the kitchen. Uncle Dan was handling a frying pan, and an inviting smell of eggs and coffee reached my nostrils. On the chair by the table in which I had sat the night before stood a huge Easter egg, enclosed in a blue and silver wrapping held together by a beautiful golden tape.

Hearing me coming in, Uncle Dan smiled. "It's for you, in case you were wondering," he said.

I felt tears coming to my eyes. I had forgotten the feeling it gives you when people care about you and think of little acts of kindness to make you happy, and the stupid egg that Uncle Dan had bought for me had brought all that back to me in a flash. Without a word, I went over and hugged him. It felt good to break the rules—the idiotic rules that felt even more oppressive because they were never spoken.

We sat there in the kitchen eating fried eggs and my chocolate egg, and, more than once, I found myself smiling. I realized that I was doing that when I saw that Uncle Dan was smiling too.

My ten days with Uncle Dan passed quickly. He spent most of his time at work—he sold fine fabric to tailors and the general public in a little shop with a huge basement in central Rome. He wasn't rich, but his business kept him going well and allowed him to save a little. He lived a Spartan life, which he religiously kept free from pleasure almost as a self-inflicted punishment, spending most of his time at work. I went with him to the shop on the first day of the week, all geared up to help him out, but he took me aside after a couple of hours and pushed some money at me. "Go out and enjoy yourself," he said, speaking quite seriously. "There is so much going on in the city right now that it's a sin to stay inside."

"It's okay, Uncle," I protested feebly. "I don't mind helping you."

"Don't take this the wrong way, but you can't really help me. Go, have fun!"

So I wandered the streets of Rome, filling my eyes with the

multicolor sights of the street markets, eating sugary stuff, and stopping to listen to every street musician I came across. Once, I gave a coin from my little treasure to an old man who played the violin with horrible screeching sounds. The violin case lay open and empty at his feet, and I figured that nobody would give him money as a reward for his music unless I did it first.

But all good things have to come to an end, and so did my holiday. Uncle Dan put me on the train on Monday morning, counting on my solemn promise to go straight to the St. Anna. After he saw me safely settled in a second-class car and examined the other passengers to make sure that no dubious character sat among them, he stood straight before me and said for the last time, eyeing me seriously, "I'll come with you all the way if you don't promise me to be a good boy and report at the school on time."

"I won't make any trouble, Uncle," I said, meaning it. I wouldn't have let him down for anything in the world.

"Good. Don't forget that. I'm responsible for you."

"I won't forget. And, Uncle..." I hesitated.

"Yes?"

"Thank you for everything."

"I should be the one to thank you; it has been nice having you around. I had forgotten how good it is to have company. Take care of yourself," he concluded. He gave me some more money and then stepped down from the train and stood on the platform until the car moved. He took off his hat and waved to me with it. I pushed my face onto the glass of the window, waving back to him and swallowing quickly to keep myself from crying.

CHAPTER 15

The last months of that school year came and went surprisingly quickly as if it was all happening to somebody else. I came back from Rome a changed person; I had grown in a manner that I found difficult to define. I became quieter and kept more to myself. I invested in my studies the minimum needed to be left alone, netting a string of average grades that never warranted an interview with the principal, to be either scolded or commended. The only exception was my mechanics shop, where I always was at the top of the class.

The beginning of July saw the dormitory gradually emptying as boys were taken home by their respective families after the final exams. My birthday came and went, ignored by all, and although I had prepared myself for it, I couldn't help being moody when no letter or package came for me on that day, not even from Uncle Dan. When August came, our dormitory emptied except for me and Giannini, a dark-skinned little boy from Naples who spoke with a funny accent that we liked to mock. And, of course, Mr. Paolini, whose only duty at that time of the year was to look after the two of us. Because school had ended, I had a lot of time to spend in the mechanic shop, and the rest of the time I killed reading and playing ball all alone in the backyard.

"Why don't you come and play ball with me, Giannini?" I asked him one day as I was about to go out. He was sitting on his bed at the other end of the dormitory, sulking as usual.

"Doesn't it bother you that you're still here?" he asked me in a subdued tone. "You know that the St. Anna will close in two weeks, and we're the only ones left. I asked Mr. Paolini what is gonna happen if nobody comes for me, but he wouldn't say."

"Oh, I wouldn't worry about that. I'm sure they'll come around soon. They can't just leave you here. Anyway, try not to think about it. I know it sucks, but what good does it do to you to sit here all day by yourself?"

"It's easy for you to say," he said, looking at the tips of his shoes. I got a good view of his soles, which were worn out, with a hole clearly visible in the middle of the right one. His clothes always looked old and used, sometimes with patches or badly hidden stitches.

I didn't know why he should think that I was better off than he, and his self-pity irritated me. Being among the last ones to leave for the vacations was hard, but I knew they had to come for me before the school closed, so I tried to be patient.

"Well, suit yourself. I'm going out. I'm sick and tired of sitting around here on my fanny."

A day after this conversation, Mr. Paolini walked into the dormitory and motioned to me to approach. "Your parents will be here tomorrow to pick you up, Lucci. Get ready with all your stuff."

"Mr. Paolini?" came the unspoken question from Giannini.

Mr. Paolini shook his head sadly. "I'm sorry," he said. "We haven't heard from your family yet, but I'm sure that we'll hear from them soon."

Giannini lowered his head and said nothing.

The next morning I woke up and packed my suitcases, emptying the cabinet and preparing to return the padlock to Mr. Paolini. I tried to be as quiet as possible and avoided looking in Giannini's direction. I saw him from the corner of my eye, sitting on his bed, as usual, his head bent forward. He rocked slowly in a back and forth movement, like a slow-paced horse rider.

I was summoned to the entrance a little after 10 a.m., and I left the dormitory without saying goodbye to Giannini; I didn't want to rub it in. I walked slowly, dragging my bags after me. Midway along the corridor, Mr. Paolini caught up with me and took one of the bags from me without saying anything.

My father waited at the door and, as I saw him, my pulse accelerated, but it wasn't out of happiness. I had learned to expect anything from him, and I wouldn't have put it past him to tell me that I wasn't coming home and that he would send me to some other place. This time, however, my fears didn't materialize.

"Hello, Roberto," he said, speaking coldly. "I hear from your instructor that you're doing well, particularly in the machine shop. You've always been gifted for manual work."

I didn't tell him that he was talking rubbish. I had never done manual work of any kind before, and this was the first he had heard of my knack. But I wasn't looking for trouble, so I merely said, "Yes, Father."

"Come, your mother and brother are looking forward to seeing you. We have taken rooms that overlook the sea, this time. You'll enjoy it."

I turned to Mr. Paolini and said politely, "Goodbye, Mr. Paolini. Enjoy your vacation."

He put a hand on my shoulder and squeezed lightly, in a

gesture of friendship that warmed my heart. "You enjoy yours," he said, good-humoredly, and walked away, soon to be swallowed again by the dark corridor. My father hadn't touched me and, after Mr. Paolini's farewell, he would have seemed pathetic to me had he tried.

In the car, I sat beside him in silence. I wasn't in a chatty mood and, besides, I didn't have anything to say. He drove silently, and it gave me satisfaction to note that he, too, seemed embarrassed. Twice along the road he tried to make conversation, but I clammed up and pretended to fall asleep to discourage any further attempts. Three hours later, he brought the car to a standstill outside the hotel, which like me, had known happier times. The Adriatic Sea was only a stone's throw away, and the area was nice. Under different circumstances, I would have been happy to be there.

"You have a room with your brother. Here's the key," my father said, handing me a heavy key holder with a number on it. I nodded and picked up one of my bags. "I'll come back for the other later," I said.

To go up to my room on the second floor, I had to pass through the lobby, and there sat my mother, as usual, in her chair with her endless glass of sparkling water before her. As she saw me, she jumped to her feet and ran to me. "Sweetie!" she said, hugging me lightly and kissing me on the cheek.

"You promised to come," was all I managed to say to her. "You promised." I made it sound accusing, hoping for an apology, but I should've known better.

"You don't understand," she said. Of course, I never understood anything—or so they wanted to believe, to shrug away their faults. "It's all for your sake, all for the best. You'll see that, eventually."

I didn't feel like arguing, so I merely nodded and moved on

with my bag. Up in the room, I found my brother reading comics. I almost didn't recognize him; he had grown so much in such a short time, and he seemed like a stranger to me.

"Hey, brother," he said as I came in. "How's everything?" He asked that without any real interest and went back to his comics before I had time to respond.

"Everything's fine," I said. I spoke curtly. I didn't plan to take him into my confidence.

I had a plan, a simple and effective one—I would behave myself. I would be pleasant and never lose my temper; I would never tell them how much I hated them for what they did to me, and I would be a model son. At the end of that vacation, they would be begging me to come back with them. I behaved politely at the dinner table. I let my father corner me and bore me with his self-glorifying stories. I kept my mother company on the balcony without disturbing her moody silences. I was even civil to my brother and took him to the beach with me more than once.

By the end of August, I started to worry. School was only ten days away, and not a word had been spoken about my coming home. It was a Sunday, and my father was about to drive back to Milan for a business trip, to return only three days later, when I resolved to take up the matter with him. I went to knock on his door, but nobody answered, so I went down to the lobby and found him in an agitated discussion with my mother.

"It's a disaster! What will I do? The concierge says that it will be impossible to find a mechanic before tomorrow morning. What have I done to have this happening to me?" He waved his hands in the air as if to attract God's attention.

I stood there, ignored by them, trying to understand what the commotion was about. The word "mechanic" had aroused my interest. If my father needed a mechanic, here I was, the dutiful, model son.

"Is there a mechanical problem?" I asked, importantly.

"Oh, yes! I didn't think of it. You have learned a lot about cars in school, so your instructor told me. And he said you're pretty good. Would you know how to fix the clutch? Somehow the cable has become slackened, and half of the time, I can't shift gear."

"That's not a problem. I know the Lancia Flavia. I fixed one just like yours last month, and I don't need any special equipment for that. The toolbox that you have in the car will do."

"That's good news. Let's go and do it now. I should've been on my way already."

We walked together to the car park, and, eager to make myself useful, I took the toolbox, lifted one side of the car using the hydraulic jack, and got under it lying on my back. Fixing the cable was a matter of a moment, but when I finished, I continued to fumble with the tools, making professional-sounding noises. I was biding my time, but I realized that there couldn't be a better moment to ask my father about my future.

"Dad," I started to say—I hadn't called him "dad" for a long time now. "I was thinking, you know...I think I've learned my lesson, and you've made your point, so now it would be time for me to come back home, don't you think so?"

"No, definitely not!" he said. "Did you think that you could get off lightly after all you've done? After all the shame and sorrow that you brought upon your mother and me? You can't imagine...Perhaps in a year or so...but not so fast. You know, your mother and I can't help loving you, and because of that, no matter how difficult it is for us, we must make sure that you learn your lesson. For your future."

You will think that I'm a monster. I did think so myself for a while, but you must understand all my frustration and my pent-up hatred for my father and his sadistic ways. And I think that Fate also played a role in it, not God—He didn't have anything to do with that. But just as my father spoke to me and about me with ill-concealed hatred, my gaze fell on the reservoir of hydraulic oil next to the brakes. I have revisited those moments in my mind a thousand times since then, trying to remember what really happened, to distinguish between reality and imagination—but in vain. I would like to be able to tell you what I was thinking then and whether I had a clear understanding of the consequences of my acts, but quite frankly, I can't. All I know is that an inner voice ordered me to tamper with the brake system. The brakes have a sealing cap next to each hydraulic reservoir, and I tried to open the one near me, but it had been screwed on tightly at the factory and wouldn't turn. I took a key and a hammer and worked on the oil sealing cap, loosening it and then turning it until it unscrewed almost completely and became so loose that I could turn it with my fingers. Then I screwed it back a little with my hand until my fingers encountered a little resistance.

I lay there, looking at the sealing cap and wondering what I had just done. It was one thing to wish my father dead and an altogether different one to do something about it. The sensation of power that had sent electric pulses through my body was gone, and I fixed my gaze on that cap, unable to believe that I had actually unscrewed it. It had clearly been a moment of temporary insanity, I realized, but now that I had returned to my senses, I had to fix it. I fumbled in the toolbox for the key that I had put back in, and then my father's inpatient voice reached me as if from a great distance. "Are you going to take all day with that? I have to drive to Milan, you know?"

It was hearing his voice that made me snap. I threw the key that I had just retrieved back into the toolbox, slammed its lid shut, and got out from under the car. "I have just finished; you can go," I said.

I lowered the car back to the ground, then I threw the jack into the trunk with the toolbox and turned away without looking back. When I heard the noise of the engine and the car driving away, I thought that perhaps I should've looked back. That might have been the last time I saw my father.

Three days later, I got to see him again when he came back from his business meeting. Since my last conversation with him, I had withdrawn into myself, refusing to go on playing the role of the loving son. I had barely spoken a word with my mother and none with my brother, who didn't care anyway. One night I went to sleep on the beach after long hours spent debating whether to drown myself. But I knew I wouldn't do it—I wouldn't give them that satisfaction.

And what about the car brakes, you will ask. Well, I hadn't given any thought to it when my father was away, and, eventually, I had come to the conclusion that I hadn't done real harm to the brake system. The whole episode became somewhat blurred in my mind and, after a while, I convinced myself that I hadn't really done anything of consequence. It all seemed to me like a dream in which, for a while, I had kidded myself that I had the guts and the power to get even with my father. It didn't take me long to convince myself that nothing really happened, that it had all been a dream—nothing more than wishful thinking. I even felt bad about it, thinking how helpless I was and how spineless that I hadn't taken advantage of a good opportunity. It never occurred to me that loosening that cap might bear dire consequences. And, in fact, I don't know for sure even to this day that it did. Perhaps, after all, I am not responsible for what happened later.

Two days after my father's return, we packed up and left the hotel, my family to go back to their cozy apartment, and I back to the St. Anna. Strangely enough, I felt relieved when they left me with my two bags on the steps and drove away.

CHAPTER 16

The dormitory resembled a noisy beehive when I got there. Almost everybody had already returned from vacation, and the boys exchanged pleasant memories and jokes. It surprised me that I was happy to see them, but, somehow, it felt like home, and they had become a much closer family to me than my own flesh and blood. At least, they shared my predicament.

I dropped my bags on the bed and stood still to watch the commotion in the dormitory, trying to gather pieces of information from snatched bits of conversation shouted across the room or whispered privately. Everybody seemed to know what was going on but me, and I felt excluded.

"Have you heard?" The question came from Fabrizio; his face was flushed with excitement. He looked at me expectantly, obviously hoping to be the one to tell me the tale.

"Heard what?"

"That Mr. Paolini is gone. On account of Giannini."

"I don't know what you're talking about. Gone where? And what about Giannini?"

"So you don't know," he said. Now, of course, he would take his time telling me about it, enjoying every moment of his superior knowledge. "Giannini and Mr. Paolini were the last two in the school before it closed for the holidays. Mr. Paolini was supposed to look after him, so when he climbed up to the roof and jumped, they held him responsible."

I furrowed my brow. I understood the words, but they weren't registering. Who climbed and who was held responsible—and for what? "Do you mean to say that Giannini jumped from the roof? And what happened to him? Is he okay?"

"Yeah, he's okay like a piece of butter spread on a slice of bread. They had to scrape him off the floor," he said.

He spoke morbidly, smiling as he savored his own words. I felt rage mounting in me, and I pushed him on the chest with both hands. He lost his balance and fell backward on the bed behind him. I panicked, feeling responsible because my leaving had obviously meant Giannini felt completely alone, so much so that he had simply given up.

I wasn't really to be blamed, I knew; what could I have done? Perhaps I should've talked to him more, making him feel more accepted, but how could I know that he would take his own life?

I also felt sorry for Mr. Paolini, who was paying for it, I didn't know what price; and for me, because I had been deprived of the only decent soul in that inferno, the only one who cared enough about me.

Fabrizio got up and stood before me, shaking his fist. His round figure, knees bent and red in the face, was pathetic. "What did you do that for? What for?" he shouted hysterically.

"Get off my face, you little fag," I said. I spoke quietly and dangerously, with hate. He looked at me in disbelief, gaping for a moment during which I thought he would burst into tears, and then he simply walked away.

Life wasn't quite the same after the summer break, and I worked myself into a state of apathy. I did as little as I could, trying not to be noticed. I was past caring with no prospects for the immediate future and little interest in what happened around me.

And then, one day, during history class, a secretary came in and said that I was wanted in the principal's office. I hadn't done anything wrong, at least not in the last week or so, and I searched my head in vain for possible reasons for this summons. I opened the door of the Secretariat, and since the anteroom was empty, I knocked lightly on Professor Fasulo's door. No answer came, and, instead, the door was opened by the stern-faced professor.

"Come in, Lucci," he said in an undertone. I did as instructed and, to my surprise, as I walked in, I saw that the man who stood by the desk was none other than Uncle Dan. He gazed at me without speaking, with a strange look on his face.

"Uncle Dan...what...?" I asked, surprised. He took a step toward me, opening his arms in an inviting gesture, and then I saw his eyes. They were red, with black circles under them. His open arms attracted me like a magnet, and I hastened to find refuge in them.

As he hugged me forcefully, he whispered in my ears, "You must be strong, Roberto. You must be strong." He repeated this sentence until he choked on his words and remained silent. I panicked. I didn't know what was going on, but surely it had to be something really bad. Was I going to jail, after all?

"What happened, Uncle? What is it? Please, tell me!"

"There has been an accident. A terrible accident. Your family was involved. You must be strong..."

I extracted myself from his arms and took a step back, gazing at him. His words reached my ears, but not my brain. "What are you saying? What happened to them?"

Uncle Dan stood there, shaking his head, unable to speak. I felt a hand on my shoulder, and I turned around to see Professor Fasulo's face close to mine. "They are dead, my boy. I'm sorry."

I froze, trying to find an alternative meaning to those words; the plain one was too unreal to accept. "But what happens now?" I asked, refuting the notion and trying with the power of my words to change the reality that those adults were forcing on me. That was too much for Uncle Dan, who no longer managed to contain his tears. He came close to me again and hugged me, seeking to draw strength from our physical contact. "It's us, now. It's the two of us. I'm with you. I'll always be with you," he mumbled, again and again. I stood there, petrified, captured in his embrace and unable to take any consolation from him or to give any back.

I don't remember much from the funeral. I do remember standing there, though, inside the Monumental Cemetery, embalmed in a suit which I had outgrown and which felt like a winding sheet, listening to people talking around me.

"A terrible accident..."

"They say he drove right into that building as if he never tried to stop..."

"...human mistake. He hadn't been drinking..."

"I gather the car was so badly burned that the police couldn't tell what caused the accident."

"...poor boy, left all alone in the word..."

"...I always said that these modern cars are dangerous..."

Uncle Dan stood by me, in a black suit, his hand on my shoulder. Strange females, some of them vaguely familiar, came to kiss me, murmuring useless words of consolation. Grave-faced men with dark ties shook my hand, treating me like the adult that I had been forced to become. I couldn't tell you who all these people were or what they said to me through the mist that enveloped me and swallowed every word and meaning, but I was glad that a little crowd had come to see my family off. It was kind of sad, though, that no children had come to accompany my brother to his resting place. It wasn't fair, I thought, quite incongruously, that we children always came last, even when burial was concerned.

My father, well-organized and punctilious to the last, owned a family grave—a little marble mausoleum that had room for five. I remember how bitterly he complained that he had been forced "to host" an aunt of his in the family grave for two years while a suitable alternative burial place was being located for her. Well, nobody would take up the space he needed for himself, now.

I found myself looking all the time toward the entrance, and I realized with embarrassment that I hoped that Alessandra would show up. I was sure that she would come to console me if only she had heard about the accident. My mind kept drifting to her and remembering our moments of intimacy—the picture of her nude, with strips of light from the Venetian blinds playing on her body...the two of us kissing on the bench in the park...

Startled by my impure thoughts, I forced my mind back to the cemetery, the grave, and to my family that lay in it. But my gaze kept going back to the entrance, and my mind kept drifting away, imagining her walking up to me, although I knew that she wouldn't come.

Several people gave me strange looks during the funeral, and I wondered what they meant. After a while, I started worrying that, perhaps, they knew that I had been tampering with the brake system of my father's car—but then, no, I was sure that nobody knew and nobody could know. A police officer had come earlier in the day to talk to me. He had spoken kindly but formally.

"I'm very sorry," he had said, managing to sound really sad. "We investigated this tragic accident, but there is little I can tell you because the car was badly burnt."

"Did you..." I had started to say but had to stop to swallow. "Did you find the cause?"

"Nothing points to anything but a driver's error. No other car was involved."

"But, the car itself, was it in good repair?"

"As far as we can tell now, it was."

"And the brakes," I had pressed him, almost on the verge of confessing my crime to him, "tell me about the brakes."

"There is nothing much I can tell..."

"Officer," Uncle Dan had intervened, giving him a significant glance.

The officer had nodded and got up. "I'm sorry," he had said again before taking his hat and leaving.

"Time to go, Roberto," Uncle Dan had said. I don't know what would have happened if Uncle Dan hadn't been there to steer the conversation away from the car brakes. I could've gone to jail for the crime that I may have committed, but perhaps I didn't, after sparking a serious investigation with the confession that I had almost made. But perhaps that would have been better than living without knowing the truth.

At the funeral, I heard one of the females saying, "He's so quiet. He's not even crying," to which another woman answered, "Poor thing, he's in shock. He'll have to face it soon enough..."

That was really weird. I couldn't bring myself to cry, and God knows that I tried, but tears wouldn't come. I think I would've felt a hypocrite, crying for those who had repudiated me and abandoned me. Besides, I had cried enough for them—or for the ones in the past I mistakenly thought they were—and for myself, during my first weeks at the St. Anna. I felt that my mourning duty had been fulfilled beforehand. Even when we opened the door of my family's apartment, which was still impregnated with their presence, all I felt was emptiness. I walked through the rooms, taking mental pictures of snippets of the life that was no more. A book had been left open on a side table, ready to be taken up again, and a heap of laundry, back from the cleaner, waited for my mother's careful handling. A lead soldier waited on my brother's table to be painted out of its sad grayness. All this was now meaningless, futile, and worthless.

But at last, I was free.

CHAPTER 17

I never told anybody how I spent my years of exile in Rome. Even my best friend, Ernesto Coppa, never heard my story, and I always loved him for the way in which he accepted me as an old friend, despite all the time that had passed, without being curious or intrusive about my past. And I had gone through a lot before I knocked on his door in the early winter of '74.

I always thought it a design of fate that I should pick up the newspaper left on a dirty and worn-out armchair in the tiny lobby of the seedy Milan hotel that functioned as my temporary home, and see the advertisement calling for an investment in Ernesto's machine shop. It was destiny that we both independently found our professional interest in the same field. His name, printed at the bottom of the ad, brought a wave of childhood memories back to me, and I decided then and there that I had to see him.

Despite the money left me by Uncle Dan, which together with the respectable sum paid me by my parents' life insurance amounted to a small fortune, at least for a young man like me, I was drifting hopelessly and aimlessly. True, the diploma of practical mechanical engineer that I had in my pocket guaranteed that I would be able to make a living, but I had been thrown into a deep state of depression by my uncle's death, and I lacked the will to pull myself together and start a new life.

Since my arrival to Milan, three weeks before, I had slept a lot, I had walked around for hours every day trying to absorb the feeling of the city and reconnect with it, and I had chain-smoked over endless coffees. I used to sit outside and drink while watching the people who walked purposefully by me, like a faceless mass of untouchable strangers. I didn't seem to be able to stop slipping more every day, turning into a worthless wreck. The advertisement acted as a lifeline to pull me back into sanity.

I remember the moment I walked into Ernesto's shop as if it were yesterday. I resolved to go straight to him rather than phone because I didn't know what to say over the telephone, and I worried how he would react. Seeing him in person looked like a much better option, and I decided that if he showed any kind of reservation at seeing me after such a long time, I would walk away without telling him what I had come for. For a second, as I walked into his office, he looked like someone who'd seen a ghost, then his face lit up, and he said, "Is that really you?" When I nodded, he simply stepped forward and hugged me.

I was really moved by this reception, especially because we never hugged before, so I knew that Ernesto's reaction was spontaneous and true. The rest is history, and I have always been awed by how Ernesto used the little money I managed to invest and my humble and intermittent help to turn his small machine shop into the successful factory that he runs so well.

I would have liked to be able to tell Ernesto all about how life put me on a one-way street and left me without choices, but I couldn't find the courage. I have since realized that all the talk about "free will" that they gave us in school is a dirty lie. Everything is predestined, and we are mere playthings in the hands of fate. I have no other way to explain how every event in my life always turned out the opposite of what I hoped and worked for.

After my family's funeral, I moved in with Uncle Dan. The St. Anna was never mentioned again, and I simply assumed that my uncle took care of everything, including my personal belongings that waited for me at his apartment in Rome. We never discussed my immediate future and implicitly agreed that coming to live with him was the only option. Uncle Dan's apartment was cozy but small, and the only other room in the apartment was the one in which I had slept during my previous visits. I didn't mind that it was tiny; after a long time spent in a dormitory, I had learned to appreciate privacy above everything else.

A few weeks after the funeral, an envelope with officially-looking papers in it had arrived from the Ministry of Interiors, making Uncle Dan my official custodian until I reached the legal age of twenty-one. He showed them to me, but I merely glanced at them.

I tried to keep busy, helping in my uncle's shop, but some days I couldn't find the strength to get up in the morning. Uncle Dan understood and never tried to force me. He knew that I needed to mourn in my own way, which meant keeping a dry eye when other people were around and allowing tears only when I was alone and certain that nobody would hear. Morning times were the worst, particularly when I woke up from a beautiful and unreal dream, only to be reminded of the reality of my empty world.

I thought a lot about Alessandra, and once I even wrote a long letter to her, knowing that I would never post it. In the letter, I told her how much I loved her and how being separated from her had driven me insane; I told her in complete detail how I had sabotaged my father's car breaks in a surge of hatred brought about by our long separation, and how I was to be held responsible for my family's death. I made it sound like a great proof of my love for her—or so it seemed to me in my madness. I read and reread that letter several times before folding it and putting it in my leather document holder. Ironically, that was a present that my mother had given me a lifetime ago when I still had a childhood and a family. Reading my own words somehow trivialized my crime, making it easier to bear. That's probably why I kept the letter instead of destroying it. I know that it was a foolish thing to do, but with so many stupid acts on the "debits" column of my chart, who's counting?

Instead of the letter, I sent Alessandra a postcard with "Greetings from Rome" printed under a color photograph of the Coliseum. I wrote my uncle's home address on it but didn't sign my name, hoping that it would escape Alessandra's parents' censorship. I knew that she would recognize my handwriting and would have no doubts that I had sent her the postcard. But if it got through, it didn't elicit a response, and she never wrote me back. After a while, hope started to falter—not my love for her, that couldn't change— and although in the long waking nights I kept planning daring ways to get her back, all my schemes remained mere dreams.

My uncle was a good and wise man, and after a few weeks in which he left me alone to my mourning, he decided that time had come to move on. He walked into my room one morning when I felt particularly depressed and sat on my bed. "Get up, Roberto," he said in an undertone.

"I don't feel like it, Uncle," I answered weakly.

"You have to pull to yourself together and get on with your life," he said.

"Leave me alone, Uncle, please. I'm not up to that yet."

"You'll never be up to that if you let yourself go. Now it's time to go back to real life. Get up."

"You don't understand..." I started to say, but something stopped me in midsentence. It was the expression on Uncle Dan's face, one that I had never seen before.

"I don't, don't I? Don't you think that I understand about pain? Do you think you can imagine what it is like to lose your wife and your unborn child at the same time? Do you know the difference between the pain of someone like you who must start a new life and someone like me whose life ended a long time ago but is doomed to go on living? Don't tell me that I don't understand!"

"Uncle..." I started to say, but I couldn't go on. I didn't know what to say. His features softened, and he put his hand on my arm.

Something broke inside of me, and I felt tears surging like a tidal wave that I couldn't stop. I found myself sobbing in my uncle's arms, weeping like a child, and shaking uncontrollably. He patted my back and stroked it, murmuring, "There, there," in my ear.

When my sobs subsided, he released me from his embrace and looked at me. "It's good that you allowed yourself to cry. You needed it, and you'll feel better now."

I nodded, wiping my tears with the back of my hands.

"Now get up and get dressed," Uncle Dan ordered. "We have things to do."

I can't describe how much I loved him for being there for me. That's why I feel so bad about what came later.

CHAPTER 18

Uncle Dan and I decided that I wasn't ready to go back to a public school, so he found me a private, external school with a flexible program that allowed me to study most of the time at home. I wasn't inclined to being sociable at all and felt displaced in the company of other kids, so studying at home worked fine for me. The few frontal lessons that I had to attend were held in small rooms with no more than fifteen students at a time. The good news was that we had mixed-gender classes, which represented an interesting change for me. The bad news was that most of the kids in my class, like me, had some special problem, whether family or psychological or physical ones, so altogether, we were a sorry bunch.

We only had three girls in my class; the pretty one that I could have worked up an interest in always sat glued together with her boyfriend, taking every occasion when the teacher's back was turned to smooch. The second one was ugly, and the third one was potty. The potty one took an immediate interest in me, and, for a while, I went along with her advances and let her buy me sodas after school. I guess that I didn't want to seem entirely asocial, but I wasn't really attracted to her, and nothing she did was enough to arouse an interest in me. I kept my distance throughout, and after a while, I guess she gave me up as a bad investment. I can't even remember her name, so little she meant to me.

Despite my earlier lack of enthusiasm for school, I now put a lot of effort into my studies. For some reason, I felt that completing my high school exams would open a different life before me, one in which I might be able to forget the past and move on. I also read a lot and spent as much time as possible at my uncle's shop. Time passed quickly that way, and nothing notable happened for quite some time, which was a blessing that allowed me to gradually return to a renewed sense of normalcy, with a home and the best possible surrogate parent I could ask for. But, of course, it couldn't last; on the evening of the day I took my last exam Uncle Dan had his first heart attack. He had just come home from the shop and stood by the entrance door, smiling as I told him about the exam.

"It went well, Uncle. I feel so relieved you can't imagine."

"We must go out and celebrate. I'll go and change…" he said, and his face suddenly took on a pained look. His skin had turned ashen.

"What's the matter, Uncle?" I asked, starting to panic. His hand had gone up to clutch at his throat, and he seemed to have trouble breathing.

"I…don't…feel…well," he managed to say. He tried to take a step forward, and I reached for him and helped him to a nearby chair.

As he sat there, breathing heavily, I knew that something was terribly wrong with him. I ran to the phone and dialed the emergency number. An ambulance came mercifully quickly, and two paramedics put Uncle Dan on a stretcher without wasting time. I climbed into the ambulance with him, holding his hand, although he had lost consciousness. My mind was blank as I waited for a long time at the hospital for someone to tell me what had happened to him. I can't describe my relief when a doctor came out of the emergency room and said that Uncle Dan's conditions had stabilized. He wasn't going to die.

I spent that summer looking after him. I didn't mind missing the opportunity to go away on vacation. He had looked after me so well when I needed it that I was glad to be able to give something back to him. He slowly regained his strength, and we started making plans for my future. I still loved mechanics but felt that engineering studies at the university would be too much of an undertaking for me, so I enrolled in a school of practical engineering where I could pace my studies as it suited me, allowing me sufficient time to look after Uncle Dan's shop, which he was no longer able to manage on his own. That was a good choice because the second heart attack came two years later. It was less severe than the first one but forced him into a routine involving only a few working hours and a lot of rest. He had survived but was withering quickly before my eyes.

Uncle Dan always found ways to move me. On the evening of my 21st birthday, he came home with a thick envelope in his hand. "Here," he said, "take this. It's for you."

"What is this, Uncle?" I asked, scrutinizing the heavy envelope that he had handed to me without opening it.

"You know my friend, Pietro, the accountant," he said. "I've been talking with him a lot about inheritance taxes. You know what kind of leeches these tax people are. So, open it," he ordered.

I opened it, still not understanding what he was talking about. I took out a document, complete with red ribbon and stamps, titled "Deed of Ownership."

"What is this?" I asked again.

"This is the formal transfer of the ownership of this apartment to you. My present for your twenty-first birthday."

I looked at him incredulously. I hadn't expected anything like that, and his gesture had taken me entirely by surprise.

"I don't know what to say, Uncle. You shouldn't have done that. I'm grateful, but...your house..."

"Nonsense! I won't be around forever, you know, and why should you be paying taxes to get possession of something that I already want you to have? You're legally a man now, so that's how it's gonna be."

That was my Uncle Dan in a nutshell—warm, generous, and uncomplicated. But being a good person doesn't give you immunity from bad luck. Uncle Dan's health continued to falter, his arteries clogging up quickly, and he turned into an invalid who could barely walk without help. He kept an oxygen bottle by his bed at his doctor's suggestion, against any acute angina attack.

He still came to the shop every now and then but turned over the management to one of his old and loyal employees. I also helped, but I was happy that the responsibility for running the business hadn't been placed on my shoulders; I didn't feel ready for that.

A few weeks before my 22nd birthday, I came home early one afternoon, and as I unlocked the door just as the telephone started ringing. Uncle Dan had gone out for his afternoon stroll, which he took three times a week together with a nurse that came to look after his needs, now that he was becoming increasingly less self-sufficient.

I ran to the phone in the hall and picked up the receiver.

"Mr. Dan Buzzi?" an unfamiliar voice asked from the other side.

I answered "Yes" automatically, wondering who this stranger might be. I hadn't meant to mislead him into thinking that I was my uncle, but I had become so used to answering his phone calls for him at the shop, saying "Dan Buzzi's office," that answering in his stead had become second nature for me.

"I'm calling from the police station regarding the message you left this morning."

Had my uncle left a message with the police? That didn't make sense.

"Yes?" I asked inquisitively.

"Your message was unclear. You said something about a car accident and that your nephew was involved, but when the officer on duty asked whether you needed an ambulance, you said it had happened a long time ago. The note here says that you need a detective. Would you care to explain what it is that you wanted?"

Those words chilled me. Had Uncle Dan suddenly realized what I had been trying to say to that police officer on the day of my family's funeral, years before, back in Milan? Was he trying to get the blame for his sister's death properly assigned, and if so, why had he waited for years before doing it? And why hadn't he confronted me or asked me about it? Those were all tough questions that I had to answer, but right now, I needed to get rid of that policeman. To accomplish that, I had to think quickly.

"Mr. Buzzi..." came the impatient prompt from the other end of the line.

"Yes," I started, trying to make my voice sound as old as possible. It trembled with stress, so it wasn't so difficult to make it sound shaky. "My nephew and I saw a terrible accident two weeks ago, and my conscience has been tormenting me ever since for not reporting it. You see, this man in that red car ... simply drove over the poor dog, crushing him without mercy. The poor little thing didn't have a chance. I didn't report it because I wasn't quick enough to write down the license number, but my nephew thinks that perhaps you could investigate and find out the identity of the driver..."

"You called the police to report a hit-and-run accident in which *a dog* was killed?" The voice asked incredulously.

"Yes, but you see, it was a very vicious act, and the driver didn't even stop to look ..."

"Listen, Mr. Buzzi," the voice said, "the police are very busy dealing with real crime. We can't waste our time on a dog. Please don't call us again or we will have to file a complaint. Good day to you," he said and hung up.

I barely managed to replace the receiver on its cradle, so much my hands were shaking. I went to my room, closed the door behind me even though I was alone in the apartment, and sat heavily on the bed. My mind raced between different thoughts, and I had trouble focusing. One realization jerked me sitting up straight: the letter! The one that I had written to Alessandra years ago and had stupidly kept among my belongings, which amounted to a written and signed confession. If Uncle Dan had taken it, or if the police came and found it, I was done for. I opened the drawer in which I kept my private things and feverishly opened my document holder. That's where I got another shock: someone—obviously Uncle Dan—had gone through my documents. I knew that for sure because I always kept that letter carefully folded under a large photograph of Alessandra—the only one I had. But now, it lay in clear view above it. I couldn't imagine why Uncle Dan would be going through my papers, but in retrospect, I guess that he had been looking for something else and found my document holder by chance. Still, he shouldn't have read my correspondence; he should've known that no good could come from that.

I dropped the document holder on my bed, and then I took the letter with my hand that still shook badly and ran to the bathroom with it. I locked the door behind me and struck a match with which I set fire to the letter, holding it by a corner above the toilet bowl for as long as the heat let me, after which I dropped it into the bowl and flushed it. I opened the window to let the smell of smoke out, and then I lowered the toilet lid and sat on it, trying to regain my composure. I knew that I had to behave naturally while I figured out what to do. Uncle Dan could not be given any hint that I knew.

Uncle Dan came home late that afternoon, and the nurse helped him go straight to his bedroom before she left unobtrusively as she always did. I heard them coming in and hurried to greet him as usual. He stood in his room, his hand on the doorknob as if to keep me out.

"Good evening, Uncle. You're late today. Would you like some pasta? I've made a good sauce."

"No, thanks," he answered, feebly, without even looking at me. "I'm very tired, and I want to go straight to bed. Goodnight."

"Goodnight, Uncle. Call me if you need anything."

He nodded pensively and closed the door behind him.

I went to lie down but couldn't sleep. Different thoughts and memories kept me awake and weaved the fabric of my dilemma. Finally, when the clock struck 2 a.m., I got up and walked on the tips of my toes to Uncle Dan's room. I opened the door silently and gazed at him, in bed in the semi-darkness. He was lying on his back and his face, lit by the light that filtered through the blinds from the lampposts outside his window, was of a ghostly white complexion. He breathed small, quick breaths, letting out a faint whistling sound through his semi-opened lips.

I stood there for a long time, and looking at the man that I loved so much, I willed him to die, as if by concentrating on it, my mind could stop the meager flow of air that his ailing body barely managed to take in. But of course, his breathing went on with his chest almost imperceptibly moving. Finally, I could no longer bear it, and I got closer.

"Uncle," I cried softly.

He stirred in his sleep and then opened his eyes. When he realized that I was standing by his bed, I saw fear in his face. I resented it and rage mounted in me. He gazed at me without speaking.

"I wanted to talk to you, Uncle," I said. I spoke softly, trying to create a friendly atmosphere, but he said nothing, and I continued. "I think there may have been a misunderstanding..."

I left the sentence hanging in the air, hoping that he would take the hint and embark on a discussion with me, perhaps an argument, which would eventually put everything right between us. Instead, he tried to sit up, his eyes wide open, fighting for speech.

"You...you! Matricide! I...I," he said with hatred. He tried to go on speaking, but he had no air left in him.

"The oxygen...give me..." his hand tried to grab the mask that hung on the oxygen bottle, but I had moved it to get closer to the bed, and it was out of reach.

I took a step back, gazing at him in horror as he dropped back on his pillows. He tried again to sit up and to reach the oxygen bottle, but his old, frail body had no strength left in it, and after a short while, he stopped fighting. I stood there, unable to move or to take my gaze away from him. His right hand shot up in a final spasm that lasted no more than a few seconds. Then it was over.

I sank into a nearby chair. Now I could finally allow myself to cry and mourn for poor Uncle Dan.

You will think that I'm wicked, feeling sorry for myself because someone I loved just passed away when I had watched him die without helping him. But look at it from my point of view: what choice did I have? Obviously, Uncle Dan would have realized after a while that no one was calling him back from the police station and would have tried again. This time, perhaps, he would have gone there instead of phoning, and they would have listened to him. Be as it may, I had no doubt that our life together as a small family had come to an end. So I think it was God's will that he should die then and there; I simply didn't interfere with the natural course of events. Besides, he was old and sick; he had said that he didn't expect to live for long. I, in contrast, was young, with many years ahead of me to make amends for what I had done. Was I supposed to throw all that away? And hadn't life been hard enough on me already?

I had to wait till morning to make it seem like he died in his sleep without my knowing it, but I found it difficult to go back to bed with him in the apartment, so I sat in the kitchen, drinking coffee to keep myself awake. I picked up the phone at seven in the morning and called the emergency number I already knew by heart.

"Please, come quickly!" I cried into the phone. "My uncle isn't breathing. Please..."

The ambulance came in five minutes, but all they could do was to pronounce him dead.

"I'm sorry," the paramedic said. "There was nothing we could do. He's been dead for a while; he died in his sleep. Was he ill?"

"He had a heart condition. He'd suffered two heart attacks in the past," I said with a broken voice that I didn't need to fake.

A doctor came, spoke briefly with the paramedic, and went into Uncle Dan's room, from which he emerged less than a minute later handing me a death certificate. "I'm sorry," he said like a pro. He probably said it often.

They took him away, and I started to search the Yellow Pages for the nearest crematorium.

"My uncle's last wish was to be cremated," I said to the first establishment that answered the phone. "Could you please take care of that?"

"We're sorry for your loss," was the mechanical reply, given to me in a duly lugubrious tone. "We will take care of all the details. We are here to take those worries off your shoulders in this difficult time."

So Uncle Dan's body was cremated before anybody even thought that there was anything strange with his death. And why should they? He was old and sick, and I had nothing to profit from his death since I was his only relative and heir and already owned the apartment anyway. But when your conscience isn't clear, you have all kinds of thoughts ... So cremating him was the safe way, or so it seemed to me in my confused state.

Did I feel remorse for doing nothing to save him? Not really. Uncle Dan, or fate, or both had pushed me into a corner, and I had been left with no choice. You should never feel remorse for following the only course of action that was left open to you.

CHAPTER 19

As I said, remorse never worked for me. Perhaps that's some innate deficiency of mine, but I couldn't manage it. You have qualms when you did the wrong thing and realize that you could have acted differently—but I couldn't. I did feel terrible, though, because it was my fault that I had been left completely alone on this earth, and that threw me into a state of depression that I had never experienced before, even in my worst times—and God knows I've had a few. Only my work saved me from slipping into a mental state from which I might never have recovered; my work and Ernesto.

Teaming up with him, after I invested a good part of my small capital in his company, meant first of all that it made sense to find permanent quarters, and I was finally able to leave the depressing little hotel that had been my temporary home. I found a small apartment only fifteen minutes away from his shop—our shop, now—and threw myself into work. That kept me busy during the day, but I had the nights to deal with, and that wasn't easy. I kept dreaming of my parents and Uncle Dan, to the point that I was afraid to go to sleep some nights. Strangely, those weren't nightmares but rather dreams in which we had long conversations, mostly on neutral topics. For whatever reason, their smiling faces and pleasant manners scared me the most. I rarely dreamt of my brother, though, which was a relief.

On the first day of my return to Milan, I made a pilgrimage to the places of my youth. I stopped outside my elementary school, and then I walked back home, as I used to do after class. I had the notion that I should knock on the door of my old apartment and ask the current tenants to let me take a look around, but that was, of course, a stupid idea. All I could do was stand outside for a minute, gazing at the windows and remembering how it used to be before I felt uncomfortable and had to move on.

I had made the decision a long time before that I would not seek Alessandra out, although it had only taken me a few phone calls to acquaintances from the past, made from Rome, to learn that she was working in a department store in Piazza Duomo. I had almost gone there on my first day back in Milan, but then I had decided to keep my resolve to avoid her. She had obviously opted for a future that did not include me, and I was convinced that I would be better off keeping away from her. Nevertheless, my pilgrimage included a visit to Via Stampa, not to look for Alessandra but to revisit the places that had been so important to me in what now felt like another life. I approached Alessandra's building entrance, moving guardedly, afraid that I might be caught prowling around as if that were a crime. I checked the names on the intercom and felt relieved to see that the label next to her apartment number bore a different, unfamiliar name. She had moved, which meant that I could walk around in the neighborhood unnoticed, anonymous, and without fear of ridicule.

I strolled from her building to Piazza Vetra, taking in the familiar but now unfriendly place. Everything had remained as I remembered it, including "our" bench, but I couldn't bring myself to sit on it alone, so I simply walked away.

The weeks passed, and I got so immersed in my work that I neglected myself. On a Saturday morning in February, after some three months back in Milan, I realized that I had to go out and buy toiletries. I had been shaving for the last three days using the soap cake for lather because my shaving cream had run out, and my skin felt irritated and itchy all over. So I went to Piazza Duomo and the department store familiar to me from my childhood days. As a kid, I always enjoyed accompanying my mother for shopping there in early December, when the floors were all brightly decorated for Christmas. I always managed to talk her into buying some new decorations for our Christmas tree, even though we had a truckload of those already at home. I had good memories of that place, and then, I thought, the time has come for me to go out a bit for some window shopping and maybe to treat myself to a cappuccino at one of the nearby elegant coffee shops. I felt strangely excited at the thought and couldn't wait to get there. Of course, I knew that I might run into Alessandra, but I pushed the thought away, pretending she had nothing to do with my excitement.

I hopped on a tramcar at the stop near my apartment building and then walked the five minutes from its central stop to the Piazza, gazing at passersby with renewed pleasure. For a few brief minutes, I felt like a free-spirit teenager again. When I walked into the narrow space between the double doors at the entrance of the department store, I stood on the grate that blew hot air upwards, warming myself up and rejoicing in that long-forgotten childhood pleasure, and then, I walked into the store and took the escalator to all floors, one after the other, to familiarize myself with the current layout of the departments.

Although I had originally planned to get only some shaving

cream, I found myself buying other items. I bought two dress shirts and a tie to go with them, a frying pan that I wasn't sure I needed, and a set of kitchen knives that I knew I didn't. Toiletries and perfumes occupied the best part of the ground floor, so I took the escalator down and started looking around for my brand of shaving cream. I moved among the various stands for five minutes in an unsuccessful search for it, frustrated by the multitude of women's products on display.

I don't know what made me stop and stare at one of the girls behind a counter; I guess I had unconsciously been scanning the area for her, and as our eyes met and I saw the scared look on her face, I knew that it was Alessandra. Her hair was arranged differently, and she had grown thinner. She wore heavy make-up—something that she had always disliked as a teenager—but she was unquestionably my Alessandra. Her hand held the handle of a service door behind the counter, and she opened it. She dropped her gaze hurriedly and disappeared behind the door. I stood there, petrified, not knowing what to do. I had stopped in the passageway, and shoppers kept bumping into me, so I moved aside a little, keeping watch on the stand. Another girl worked there, serving customers; a white tag with golden letters, pinned to her shirt, said "Beauty Hostess." I watched her as she wrapped up a box for an old woman, and when the customer left, I approached the counter.

"Pardon me," I said, summoning my most charming smile, "I'm looking for your colleague. She helped me before."

"Alex? She just left. She didn't feel well. But I'm sure that I can help you. Were you looking for anything in particular?"

I hesitated. I didn't want to arouse suspicion, but I had to know more. "Actually...yes, she was being so helpful. I'd rather take this up with her because she said she had various ideas for me. You know, it's a gift I'm after," I hastened to add, hoping that it would sound right, "and it's very difficult...perhaps you can tell me when she will be back? When is her next shift?"

"I'm afraid that I can't tell you that. But I would be happy to help you instead. I'm sure that I can give you some ideas too..." she said. She sounded hopeful, and I was sorry to disappoint her.

"I'll think about it, thank you." I left before she could say anything else, feeling stupid and confused.

I went to another stand at the far-away end of the floor, and I approached another vendor. "I beg your pardon," I said, smiling as captivatingly as possible. "One of your colleagues told me to come back to pick up something I have ordered at her next shift, but I can't remember when you change shifts here."

"Oh, that's easy. The first shift is nine to three, and the second is three to nine. We open at half-past nine, and in the evening, we close at half-past eight. Did she tell you which shift she would be working?"

"No."

"Well, if you come a little before three, you either catch her in the first shift or have a short wait until the second one comes along," she said.

"Right. Thank you very much; that was a great help."

"My pleasure," she said. "Is there anything else I can do for you? Do you need anything from here?" she said. She made a sweeping motion with her hand, smiling invitingly.

I shook my head, smiled an apologetic smile, and left.

It was only when I got home with my shirts, tie, and kitchenware that I realized that I hadn't bought shaving cream, after all.

My decision to start stalking Alessandra was not one made lightly. That night I lay awake in bed, tossing from side to side, trying to find good, convincing arguments to forget all about her, but I knew I couldn't, now that she had reappeared into my life. I didn't kid myself that she wanted to see me; the way she fled when she saw me left no doubt about it. But I needed closure—I had to know if staying away from me had been her own decision.

I could barely wait until Monday, but that day she didn't show up for work. I walked by her stand perhaps a hundred times until people started to give me curious glances, but by then, I realized that she hadn't come. I was making myself conspicuous, though, and I had to find another way.

I walked around the building until I found the door marked "Employees Entrance" that I knew had to exist. The side street was a narrow one, and I parked myself next to a pillar that stood almost in front of the door, from which I could watch the entrance unseen. I waited there from 2 p.m. to 3 p.m. on Tuesday but didn't see her, so I came back at 8 p.m. and waited until everybody left the building. I repeated my watch on Wednesday with the same lack of success. I almost gave up. Her absence could mean that she had quit her job or was staying away because of me, but her colleague had said that she hadn't felt well, which could mean that she simply was at home, sick.

I decided to wait a few more days before drawing conclusions, and I came back the next Monday, just before closing time. I stood in the shade of the same pillar, in the freezing cold, until almost 9 p.m. and was about to leave, discouraged, when she appeared. Her thin body was bundled in a heavy overcoat, and she wore a wool hat and a scarf that hid her face, but I would have recognized her anywhere by the graceful way in which she moved and even by her eyes alone. I stepped out of the shadow and crossed the empty and silent street, finding myself right in front of her. I stopped and watched her, my head bare and my face straight in front of her eyes.

She stopped abruptly. She gazed at me but said nothing. It was as if everything around us had frozen, and we had been placed in a time capsule, isolated from the outside world.

"Alessandra..." I said when the silence became too heavy to bear.

She shook her head as if in disbelief. "What are you doing here, Roberto?" she whispered in a barely audible voice.

"I need to talk to you," I said. Talking to her like that felt unreal. For so long, I had dreamt of that meeting, painting it in so many different colors that I couldn't believe it was actually happening. But nothing was working like in my dreams; she wasn't throwing herself into my arms, and no happy ending was in sight. She addressed me like a stranger, and I stood out of reach, so tense that my muscles ached.

"It's not a good idea..." she said, whispering again.

"Why not? I just want to talk. Surely you can give me a few minutes," I added bitterly.

She hesitated for a moment and then said, "But not here."

"Right. It's cold here. Let's go and get a cup of coffee."

She nodded, and I started to walk in the direction of the nearby gallery. It felt strange to walk with her without touching, but I was afraid that any physical contact might scare her away. I walked quickly to shorten that surreal journey as much as possible.

In the café, I picked a corner table in a relatively quiet spot. The place was overheated, and the air was thick and heavy with cigarette smoke. We took off our overcoats, and I saw that she had changed from her salesperson's uniform into a light green, fluffy sweater that hid the contours of her breasts.

Once seated, I almost panicked, not knowing how to start a conversation. An efficient waiter saved the day by coming immediately to take our orders, giving me the time to adjust to

Alessandra's presence. I ordered cappuccinos for both of us, and he left. The time had inevitably come when I had to speak.

"So..." I said, hoping that she would pick the cue and start talking, but she merely kept gazing at me. I lit a cigarette, taking my time with the matches, hoping for a comment—anything—from her, but apparently, her mind was set on not helping me out of this embarrassing moment.

"You look good," I continued after a long pause. "Do you work regularly at the department store?" I added, mentally kicking myself for the shallowness of my conversation.

"Why are you here?" she asked, point-blank, instead of answering my question.

"I wanted to see you...to see how you are doing. I've missed you..." I said, choking on my words.

Alessandra had trouble speaking, too and, although she tried to hide it, her emotion was noticeable.

"It's been a long time. Everything's different now...I'm different. I must go," she added bluntly, getting up and grabbing her overcoat.

"You haven't drunk your cappuccino," I complained, standing up too, in the grip of a strong panic. I knew that if she left now, like that, I might never summon up the courage to seek her out again.

"I have to go home. Someone's waiting for me. Perhaps some other time..."

"When? Give me one hour, okay? Any time you want."

She hesitated, and I could see that she was debating with herself. She bit her lower lip, gazing at something in the distance above my shoulder. I kept silent, knowing that she shouldn't be hurried, until she said, "Wednesday evening. I don't work next Wednesday."

"Pizza okay?" I said, hoping to sound natural and not too eager.

"Pizza is fine," she said, smiling for the first time.

That made me smile too. She mentioned the name of a pizza house we both knew well from the past and added, "At seven sharp," in the same way she had always said that when calling for punctuality. That caused me a pang of nostalgia.

I watched her as she made her way through the maze of small, round tables in the café, and then I sat down again, feeling emptied of all energy. I lit another cigarette and finished my cappuccino. Alessandra's full cup stood on the table, resembling a staring, reproachful eye.

I didn't know what to expect from our meeting, but I made sure to get there in time. When I arrived around 6:30 p.m., the pizza house was still almost empty, and I picked a table from which I could see the entrance. Alessandra arrived ahead of time and came straight to my table.

"Hi," she said. She allowed the waiter to take her overcoat, and then she sat down. She looked more embarrassed than during our last meeting, and I wondered why.

"Would you like an aperitif?" the waiter inquired of us both.

"Only sparkling water, please," she said.

I simply shook my head. The waiter left menus with us and went. I studied the menu without really seeing it. I stole a few glances over the page and saw that Alessandra was reading it carefully, or maybe that's what she wanted me to think. Finally, when our in-depth study of the dishes became too ridiculous to keep up, I signaled the waiter, and we ordered—a Four Seasons pizza for me and a Margherita for her; our usual choices.

"I've gone through some pretty rough times, you know?" I

said when the waiter left. I had thought a lot during the last few days about the right way to pick up the threads and had come to the conclusion that my best card would be compassion. Surely hearing about all my troubles couldn't fail to elicit sympathy.

"I've heard about your parents...and your brother. I'm so sorry..."

"Yes, that was a blow. I hoped to hear from you after that..."

She seemed startled. She played with her forefinger, tracing the design of the tablecloth, and she now raised her head with a jerk and blushed a little.

"Everything was much more complicated than you would know," she said. She spoke sadly but didn't go on explaining.

Our pizzas came, starting a new phase of the conversation. We attacked it diligently, but after the first slice was gone, I laid down my fork and knife and looked at Alessandra. For the first time since my return, I had the opportunity to really watch her with leisure. She was even more beautiful than I remembered. Her face hadn't changed much but had taken on an expression of maturity that became her well. I watched as she chewed on her food, and to me, it was the most beautiful spectacle I had ever seen.

I was in love. Still. Again. Anything you care to call it. I had never fallen out of love with Alessandra; I understood that then. And I was scared; she obviously still had some feelings for me, but would she be able to love me again as she did before? I had to be careful not to hurry things, to avoid scaring her away at all costs.

"What?" she asked, smiling inquisitively.

"I didn't say anything."

"You were looking at me in a strange way."

"Sorry. I didn't mean to be rude. It's just that it is a little strange to watch you eating pizza after so long."

"I know what you mean," she said and then laughed a little

nervous laugh. "It *is* kind of weird...I mean, the two of us here, after so many years."

"So, how's the world been treating you?" I asked. I wanted her to talk and do as much as possible of the bridging over the lost years for both of us.

"It's okay now, but it has been tough for a while. After my father died two years ago, my mother and I didn't get on so well. I always was my father's girl, and I think that made her jealous. After his death, she kept finding all kinds of faults in me, and we fought constantly. Last year she decided to move back to the country, to go and live with her sister, who's also a widow. I don't see her much now, but we talk on the telephone every few weeks."

"So you no longer live in Via Stampa?" I asked, knowing only too well that she didn't. I really wanted her to believe that I hadn't checked on her, that I wasn't being obsessive about her or us; I wanted her to feel relaxed, to accept me back into her life.

"No. I live with my best friend now. Her name is Giorgia. She's fun; you would like her."

"I'd love to meet her," I said and immediately regretted it. I didn't want her to think that I was being pushy, so I changed the subject. "That's nice, sharing an apartment, I mean. I live alone," I said.

"And what did you do after you...went away?" she asked, out of context.

That was the cue that I'd been waiting for, and the story that I had carefully rehearsed in my mind came out, flowing naturally, with all the added pathos that came from the carefully studied emphasis on my various disgraces. As my tale unfolded and I recounted the hardship I had undergone at the St. Anna, I saw that her eyes were becoming damp. When I came to my family's burial and how I had expected her to show up and comfort me, her hand moved forward and patted mine, and she swallowed sadly. I thought that I was making progress.

"You know, you're the first to hear my whole story. I never felt like telling anybody but, somehow, I find it easy telling it to you."

"We always found it easy to talk to each other, didn't we?" she said, acknowledging the compliment. "Above anything else, we always were good friends."

"Yes, I've been missing that," I said, seizing the opportunity to turn the conversation to more personal tracks.

"We can still be friends, you know?"

"I'd like that," I said, not liking it a bit. The "let's be friends" position was not at all what I was after.

"Are you seeing anybody?" she asked, out of the blue.

"No. And you?" My heart was beating fast, not knowing what to expect but hoping for the right answer.

"I have a boyfriend."

My heart plummeted at hearing the words, and I averted my gaze, hoping that she wouldn't notice my emotion. After a brief pause, she continued.

"His name is Silvio. We've been going out for almost a year now. His father is from Brazil, and his mother was Italian. She's dead now, but his father still keeps an apartment in Milan for business. Silvio is in the diamond business, so he travels a lot. You'll like him."

I doubted very much that I would like him, but that wasn't the right time to say so. I nodded, and she continued.

"And since you're not seeing anybody, I'll introduce you to Giorgia. Who knows, if you two hit it off, perhaps we may go out together when Silvio is here." She giggled childishly at the thought, and I forced myself to smile.

Reclaiming my place in her life would require much more

work than I had budgeted for. A boyfriend was a much greater obstacle than the years that had formed a gap between us. But I was ready to tackle him.

CHAPTER 20

My date with Alessandra—or whatever you would like to call it—left me unsatisfied. I had got no answers to any of my questions; I simply couldn't find the appropriate moment to ask them. But we did exchange phone numbers and an undefined promise to keep in touch.

I felt pretty stupid when she left, refusing my offer to walk her home and softening her refusal with a polite kiss on the cheek. She'd had the upper hand in our unpronounced struggle to redefine our relationship, and as she left, she seemed more relaxed and contented than I had seen her until that moment. Unspoken rules had been made, and lines had been drawn, which could not be crossed. We were now officially "good friends," and our behavioral code had to follow that definition.

As I walked pensively away from the restaurant, I toyed with the idea of letting her go, of allowing my anger to take command and transform my frustration into hatred. I tried to imagine what she would do if, after a while, she realized that I wasn't going to call. But those were idle thoughts; I knew that I would never be able to give her up. Those few seconds during which her lips had touched my cheek had been enough to infuse me with an electrifying sensation of aching need for her.

Still, to regain some of my command over the situation, I decided to wait at least one week before I called her. Therefore, my surprise was complete when my phone rang only two days later, and I heard her voice.

"Hi, Roberto. How're you doing?"

"I'm fine," I answered guardedly. I hadn't expected this call, and I found it intriguing.

"I had a good time..."

"Me too," I said, holding back, still unwilling to be the one to take this conversation further.

A brief silence followed, perhaps signifying her puzzlement at the curtness of my replies, and then she said, "You remember that I spoke to you about Giorgia?"

"Yes?"

"I told her all about you, and she's dying to meet you. Are you free this week?"

"I could work it in..." I hesitated, not knowing what she was planning. "Is Silvio going to be there too?"

"No, I'm sorry. Silvio's leaving for a business trip to London tonight and won't be back for two weeks. I was thinking that perhaps you could come over for dinner, Saturday, to let you get acquainted with Giorgia and, maybe, you could take her out after dinner. How does that sound?"

"Saturday works for me," I said, trying not to sound enthusiastic. "I haven't gone out a lot lately."

"That's the plan, then. Don't expect a fancy dinner, though. I'm not a good cook, but I can make some decent spaghetti."

"Spaghetti sounds perfect to me. Saturday at what time?"

"Eightish. Oh, I'm so excited! And you'll need the address," she said and gave it to me.

So my true love was fixing me up with her best friend. Ironic, isn't it? But I would have agreed to be matched up with a gorilla if that meant an opportunity to get close to Alessandra.

As I got out of the taxi that Saturday evening, I found myself in an unfamiliar neighborhood that was far from what I had expected. The streets were narrow, and the façade of the long, impersonal building before which I found myself sorely needed a good coat of paint. The street was squalid, cold, and damp—an almost forgotten corner of the city. Obviously, Alessandra wasn't doing too well financially.

I checked the address to ensure that the dark entrance was the right one, then I tightened my grip on the bottle of Chianti that I had brought with me and climbed the badly-lit stone stairway to the third floor.

The door of the third-floor apartment had been hand-painted with a brown paint that was peeling away. It had no name on it, and I stopped there, uncertain, until I double-checked the address on the little piece of paper that I had brought with me. It said "third floor, brown door," so I knocked on it and waited. It took a few seconds before the door opened; I didn't know much about Giorgia, but the girl that stood at the door was nothing like anything I could have expected from Alessandra's description. She was petite, elflike, with short, red hair and the palest complexion I have ever seen. She looked up to me—she was almost a head shorter than I—with a questioning expression that immediately turned into a smile.

"You must be Roberto," she said, and I barely managed to nod before she turned her head and yelled, "Alex, Roberto is here!"

She then turned back to me with an apologetic smile, as if in a belated realization of the inappropriateness of her behavior. I smiled back, trying to put her at ease.

"And, surely, you're Giorgia," I said.

"Yes...come in. Alex is in the kitchen," she added, pointing in the direction of an open door behind her.

"Come in here," Alessandra's voice called from within.

I took off my overcoat and hung it on a peg near the door. Giorgia watched me without speaking and then silently motioned me to go into the kitchen. She then disappeared into another room as if to make it clear that she wasn't really involved in my being there.

In the kitchen, I found Alessandra working at the stove, wearing a colorful apron. Her face was flushed because of the heat, and that made her look amazingly beautiful. I stood at the door, gaping at her, and after a few seconds, I lifted the bottle of Chianti and showed it to her to ease my embarrassment.

"Oh, you shouldn't have! But since you did, here's the corkscrew," she said.

I took the corkscrew and put much more time and effort into cutting the foil and pulling the cork than the bottle really demanded, stealing quick, surreptitious glances at her during the process.

"So, where does that 'Alex' come from?" I asked.

"Giorgia started calling me that and, after a while, everybody else did, so I got used to it. It's cute, don't you think?"

"I like Alessandra better," I said.

"You can go on calling me that," she conceded, giving me a pensive look.

I simply nodded and fidgeted with the wine bottle some more. Alessandra got closer, her head next to mine, and for a moment, I wondered what that meant, but then she whispered to me, "How do you like Giorgia?" and I understood that she was simply being conspiratorial, working on her matchmaking.

"I've only seen her for a few seconds, but she looks nice."

"Let me go and see what *she* thinks," she whispered and disappeared.

I waited there, moodily, more self-conscious than ever. I felt like merchandise put up for auction and didn't like it.

Alessandra soon returned, looking radiant. She put a hand on my arm, which sent electricity up to my shoulder, and said, giggling like a little girl, "She thinks you're gorgeous! Here, help me with the spaghetti," she ordered, switching back to her practical self. "Giorgia! Grub is ready!" she then yelled, carrying a bowl of steaming pasta out of the kitchen and into a small living room that doubled as a dining room, with a small table barely big enough for four. Beside the table that got pushed aside after dinner, the room contained a little sofa, a tea table, and two comfortable armchairs. An old-fashioned, big black telephone stood on a small side table, and a glass shelf was crammed with audiotapes and books, scattered in no particular order on both sides of an antique and huge tape recorder. Unfamiliar mood music played as the big wheels of the tape recorder turned slowly. Pictures and nondescript decorations hung from the walls. The lighting was subdued, and the atmosphere was one of cozy homeliness.

I brought the wine with me, and Alessandra went back for the sauce. Giorgia and I stood in silence at opposite sides of the table, and I tried not to study her too openly. She was undeniably attractive, with small, rounded breasts that pushed against her white blouse, of fabric too flimsy for the cold temperature of the apartment. The cold was perhaps responsible for her pointed nipples showing in clear contour, but she certainly made no effort to hide them. Her trousers were made of a stretch fabric that left no doubt about her shapely legs. Her face was delicate, resembling that of a Venetian mask, with small but full lips of a strong natural red color, but if you watched it closely, you could see strength in it and the signs of a clear determination that had to come from a strong character. I took all that in with a quick glance, trying to avoid keeping my eyes fixed on any part of her for more than a split second. She, on the contrary, studied me openly, sizing me up without any sign of embarrassment until I realized that I had blushed.

The table had been set with two plates on one side, the one where I stood, and one on the other. Having completed her inspection of me, Giorgia sat down before the single plate and looked up. "Standing and sitting come at the same price, you know?" she said.

I sat down facing her. I tried hard to think of something to say, feeling somewhat stupid because I couldn't find a good repartee, but luckily Alessandra came to the rescue by bringing out the sauce. "I'm starved," she announced, starting to dish out liberal portions of spaghetti onto our plates.

I poured the wine, and dinner began, not a moment too soon.

The atmosphere during dinner warmed up and became more laid-back once the food was put on the plates. Alessandra prattled about this and that and functioned as an icebreaker. The conversation started to flow as soon as it moved to neutral topics. It was obvious that Alessandra was eager to make the dinner a success. On my part, I felt obliged to contribute to the conversation.

"Do you work with Alessandra?" I asked Giorgia.

"I'm a student," she answered and, before she could continue to explain, Alessandra intervened.

"Giorgia studies philosophy. She's so clever!"

"Pay no attention to Alex," said Giorgia, smiling a strangely coquettishly shy smile. "I'm doing all right, but I'm lucky that I don't have to hurry through my studies because my parents are paying for them, so I can do it at my own pace. Other students must work to support themselves, and at starvation wages too, so it's little wonder that I get good grades."

"And off she goes," said Alessandra, adding an amused little laugh. "We've got her started on '*Lotta Continua*'—'Perpetual Struggle'—so now we're in trouble."

"I don't like it when you make fun of the movement," Giorgia retorted with complete seriousness. Then she turned to me and asked, "Do you know anything about *Lotta Continua*?"

"It's some sort of Communist party, isn't it?" That was as far as my political knowledge went.

"It's much more than that. It's the only movement that is putting up a real fight against the bourgeoisie and the State, who exploit the worker shamelessly."

"Does that mean that you're a commie?" I asked, intrigued.

"I'm nothing of the sort!" she retorted angrily. "Our movement is about fairness. Do you think it's fair that the masses are overworked and underpaid while a small minority of privileged people live like parasites?"

"Well..." I said, "if you put it like that, of course, I don't think it's fair."

"I belong to the oppressed masses, and I am definitely underpaid, so you have my support. Carry on," said Alessandra. She spoke lightly, and I think she winked at me.

"But," I couldn't keep myself from asking, "from what you said about your parents paying for your studies, doesn't that make you a member of the bourgeoisie as well?"

"It makes *them* that, not me. I would prefer to work and

support myself through my studies, but then I wouldn't have time for the Movement, and someone has to take responsibility. I do."

I didn't know whether to be amused or concerned by what she was saying, but my master plan called for a close friendship with this girl if I wanted to get the run of the apartment, so I wasn't going to antagonize her. I could tell that this was her pet subject, and I decided to let her talk about it as much as she wanted. I was ready to be a sympathetic listener if it killed me.

"So, tell me, what does that involve? What do you do for the Movement?"

"I'll go get the dessert," said Alessandra. She put her hand on my arm, getting up, squeezing it quickly and surreptitiously, as if to tell me that I was doing well and should keep it up. I wished she wouldn't do that because it was torture to have her touch me in that casual and distanced way. Giorgia nodded, almost impatiently, waiting for her to get out of the way before she answered.

"There is a lot going on. We frequently have demonstrations against all kinds of things. That's the most dangerous part because we often get into real fights with the police or the neo-fascist movement, the MS. They are both as vicious as they come, and sometimes people get hurt really bad.

"Then we meet at headquarters to prepare flyers and to plan activities. We also have general meetings where we discuss matters of principle with newcomers and introduce them to our movement. You should come to one of those sometime; it's very interesting."

"I'd love to," I lied.

Her face lit up, and she smiled a broad smile. "Really? That's great. I'd be happy to take you to the next one if you want to come with me."

"Sure."

Alessandra walked into the dining room with a plate of non-appetizing dessert cakes that she had obviously bought cheap somewhere. "Where are you two going?" she hastened to ask.

"I was just telling Roberto that he should come to the next *Lotta Continua* meeting." Then, as in an afterthought, she addressed me. "You know, I'm meeting with some friends from the Movement tonight. You want to come and join us?"

I decided to play hard-to-get. I checked my watch and hesitated. "Oh, I don't know...it's getting late. Besides, I've never been involved in politics, and this is a bit sudden."

"I think you should go," said Alessandra, giving me a nasty look and kicking me under the table at the same time. I was obviously ruining her carefully laid-out plan. "I've been to these Saturday evenings with Giorgia, and they're fun."

"Will you be coming too?" I asked for the record.

"No. I have a splitting headache, and I'm going to bed."

How convenient it is for girls, that they can plead to be victims of headaches whenever they like, isn't it? If men did the same, they would be marked as liars; women, on the contrary, are simply exercising their rights.

"It *is* fun," Giorgia said. "It's not a political meeting. We meet at a wine bar near the university where they serve good cheese and Barbera at reasonable prices, and we talk. Some of the people are really clever, and the discussion often develops into a really exciting argument. If you've never been to one of those, you should come and see for yourself."

"All right, I'll make a deal with you. I'll come, but if the discussion gets too intellectual for me, we go somewhere else where I don't have to strain my brain."

"Deal!" said Giorgia without trying to hide her satisfaction.

Alessandra got up and beamed at us like a proud teacher at her pupils. "I'll make you coffee before you go," she announced in a no-nonsense fashion.

The wine bar was dimly lit, almost in darkness. It was located underground in the cellar of one of the ancient buildings surrounding the university. Tables of coarse wood filled the space, barely leaving walking room between them. Busy waiters had put bread, cheese plates, and wine carafes on the table, next to which they had placed coarsely-finished glasses. We stood at the bottom of the stairs that led into the cellar, allowing our eyes to adjust to the scarce light, and then Giorgia guided me to one of the tables. Six or seven youths were gathered around it, and a heated discussion was going on with one of the young men. Giorgia stopped a little behind him and listened to the argument. I stood beside her and gazed at the young man who Giorgia later introduced to me as Franco.

"Assuming for a moment—for a moment, I say—that Calabresi was the real person responsible for the murder of Pinelli, the question is whether there was a minuscule chance of bringing justice to this case by appealing to the establishment. Obviously, there was no chance in hell that anything would come of it," Franco argued.

"So you're saying that the comrades who terminated the commissary did the right thing?" asked one dark-haired girl with a dumb expression on her face.

"I'm not saying those were our comrades..." said Franco, conspiratorially, as if to hint that he knew more.

I looked at the young people around the table. Many of them wore turtle-necked sweaters that wanted to look worn out and proletarian, but which clearly came from Milan's more expensive boutiques. Although they differed in colors and style, they obviously adhered to an accepted dress code. The impression they conveyed was that of people in uniform.

"They are talking about the murder of commissary Calabresi, who was held responsible for the death of Giuseppe Pinelli, one of our comrades," Giorgia whispered to me.

I nodded. I had read about it in the papers a couple of years before, but I didn't know all the details, nor was I really interested.

Taking advantage of a lull in the discussion, she stepped forward and said "Hi," and then she introduced me to the others. We sat at the table with them, and I drank some wine and ate some pretty good cheese while Giorgia joined the other girls in their starry-eyed admiration of Franco's eloquence. On my part, I thought him pompous, verbose, and boring, and I let my attention wander, studying the people at the other tables around me.

It took Giorgia almost an hour to realize that I wasn't having fun. My silence, punctuated by a deep yawn, finally got across. "Do you want to leave?" she asked.

"I think I've had enough for the first time," I said, brightening up. "I don't mind if we do."

She smiled an embarrassed smile and nodded. We got up, and she said goodbye to everybody but only got a couple of "byes" in reply. The others were too engulfed in some futile argument to notice.

When we reached the top of the stairs, the cold air hit us, and we retreated back into the entrance of the wine bar. "It's freezing cold out there. Let's decide where we want to go before we get out," I said.

"Let's go somewhere you don't have to strain your brain," she said, smiling, mimicking my earlier statement.

"If you tell me that you found that interesting, I'll give up hope," I retorted vehemently.

"Honestly, that wasn't much fun, you're right. I'm sorry."

I smiled, noticing her embarrassment that was not in character with her forceful personality. "If I've got you to admit that, it was worth it. Now, I used to know a nightclub not too far from here that had decent music. Shall we check it out?"

"You lead," she said, so I lifted my arm, and she hooked on.

The nightclub was still where I remembered it, although the atmosphere felt different, but perhaps the real difference was that I had grown up. We took a quiet table in a corner, and I got us drinks. We didn't dance. I wasn't in the mood and didn't offer to, and she never mentioned it. We simply sat and talked.

"Who's that guy, Franco?" I inquired, keeping the conversation on neutral topics.

"He studies law and is one of the leaders of the student's group of our movement. He is very clever."

"Well, he's hiding his cleverness well," I said.

"Oh, don't say that! It's just that you're not used to our company. We're a nice bunch."

"You're nice," I said to lighten up the atmosphere. She smiled coyly.

By the time we finished our drinks, it was past 1 a.m., and I was ready to call it a day. I recalled the advice I once read on the train in a women's magazine that had been left by a previous occupant of my cabin. It said, "Never kiss on the first date if you want to keep your man's interest." I thought that was good advice for me too, so I kept my distance.

We managed to hail a taxi that dropped us at Giorgia's door. I didn't offer to walk her up the stairs, and she didn't invite me in.

"I enjoyed this evening ... in spite of your comrades," I said, smiling to emphasize that I really meant it.

"So did I," she said.

A few tense seconds of embarrassed silence followed, during

which she obviously waited for me to take the initiative. When I merely stood there, she gave me a quick peck on the cheek and whispered, "Good night."

"Good night," I answered, standing still, and after a brief hesitation, she turned and walked into her apartment building.

It seemed to me that I had made good progress. But, of course, that was only the beginning.

CHAPTER 21

Sunday started on the wrong foot, with the phone ringing too early in the morning. I picked up the receiver and was surprised to hear Alessandra's voice at the other end.

"How did it go?" she asked without even saying hello first.

"It's not even dawn yet, you know? How did what go?" I asked morosely.

"Don't be silly; it's ten o'clock already."

"That's what I meant."

"Don't make me beg, okay? I'm dying to hear what you think of Giorgia."

"I think she's very nice," I said. I wasn't sure about the right answer to that question and hadn't prepared myself for it.

"Hello, it's me, Alex! Stop being such a stiff..." When I failed to react, she continued in a more sober tone, "She thinks that you are gorgeous, funny, and intelligent. You really swept her off her feet; I can tell even if she doesn't say so. I know her well enough." Her voice sounded excited, like that of a little girl playing a game. That annoyed me. It was wrong; she should have been jealous, not pleased. But apparently, her mind was set on her matchmaking, and she continued, "So now come clean. What did you think of her?"

I hesitated, not knowing how she would react one way or the other, but I had little choice at that point; I had to play the game, and, besides, I did like Giorgia. "I'd like to get to know her better," I said. "I like her energy..." I hoped to come across as a serious person who was able to appreciate Giorgia's intellectual qualities and, at the same time, to make it plain that my heart was still free and there for Alessandra to pick up if she cared to. But, apparently, her mind was single-tracked.

"I knew it! She'll be so thrilled..."

"No way! You're not gonna tell her anything," I insisted, knowing too well that she would run to Giorgia to relate our conversation the moment she got off the phone.

"Oh, all right, if that's what you want," she said.

I confirmed that it was what I wanted and hung up. Alessandra's enthusiasm was a bit too much for me, but I had no choice if I wanted to win my way back to her heart. And, after all, I did find Giorgia attractive, and I hadn't been with a girl for quite a long time. Even though cultivating my relationship with her had become a clear necessity, I found myself looking forward to it.

The uncertainty factor plays a big role in building your position during courtship, so I decided to let Giorgia stew for a few days. Coming home from work on Wednesday evening, I reckoned that I had waited long enough, and I dialed her number. She answered at the third ring.

"Giorgia?" I asked.

"Roberto? Oh, hi..."

She sounded embarrassed, and I strangely enjoyed it. I had forgotten that courting games could be that fun.

"Hi. We haven't spoken for a while, and I was thinking..."

I left the sentence hanging there in the air until she felt compelled to say, "Yes?"

"Would you like to go to a movie or something?"

"Sure. When?"

"I was thinking perhaps tomorrow."

"Tomorrow's great."

"I'll pick you up at seven, so we can go to the first screening and maybe grab something to eat afterward."

"Great! I'll be ready."

"You haven't asked me which movie I plan to take you to."

"Oh, I'll trust you on that."

I felt a pang of disappointment. It's like shooting a sitting duck, I thought to myself.

When I picked Giorgia up, it was drizzling. March is a crazy month in Milan, and the sun had made a quick appearance that afternoon, making me forget my umbrella. She wore a wool coat with a collar of fake chinchilla, and her hair was topped with what seemed to be a Bohemian, badly knitted cap. We walked arm-in-arm to the underground station and jumped on the train that took us to the city center.

"I was planning to go and see a rerun of *Straw Dogs*. Have you seen it?" I asked once we got on the train.

"I haven't, but I've heard it's a good movie."

"It's a great movie. And Dustin Hoffman is great; he's the best. The plot is a bit strong, but it carries an important social message. So it's okay if we go?" I congratulated myself for the right mixture of intellectual talk and movie savvy performance that surely marked me for a man of the world.

"Sure," she said without hesitation.

The movie theater was almost empty, and we headed for a row in the middle. The previews were already screening, so we had to move in the darkness but finally decided on seats and sank into them.

The movie began and, as soon as the plot's tension mounted, she grabbed my left arm with her two hands and got closer. I put my left hand on her knee and left it there for a while. When she didn't complain, I started to massage it lightly with my fingers until she moved even closer and put her head on my shoulder. I could no longer wait; I lifted her chin with my right hand and kissed her. She returned the kiss with her eyes closed, moving her tongue quickly like that of a lizard until I forced her to slow down with the tip of my own tongue. Then our kissing became sensuous, no longer nervous or out of sync, which allowed me to analyze my sensations at leisure. I felt slightly hyperventilated—an inebriating sensation that I knew from experience meant real excitement. But the side of the hard seat got in the way of our caressing each other more, and I found that frustrating.

"You can watch the movie better with your eyes open," I whispered, at last, hoping that the words would carry my smile with them as well.

"Screw the movie," she whispered back without opening her eyes.

I kissed her moist lips lightly. "Let's go someplace more comfortable, then," I suggested.

"Your place," she said simply.

She had her eyes wide open now and was scrutinizing me so closely that I felt her breath on my face. That aroused me even further, so I merely nodded and got up.

Someone behind us shouted, "Sit down already," but we paid no attention to him and walked out.

I always took the tram car from the center of the city to my apartment building, but this time every second wasted on the way felt like a crime, so we hailed the first taxi we saw and rode in it, holding hands. Giorgia kept her eyes closed and put her head on my shoulder. We didn't speak, waiting impatiently for the chance to continue our intimacy uninterrupted. Ten minutes later, I opened the door of my apartment. As soon as I closed it behind us, she pushed me against it and tilted her head upwards for me to kiss her. I lifted her by the waist for the few centimeters missing, and then she wrapped her legs around me, kissing me savagely.

I walked from the entrance to my bedroom like some kind of strange animal, struggling to take off my coat and hers as I pirouetted, trying to keep my balance despite her weight that pushed our center of gravity to unbearable limits. She laughed out loud when I bumped into the wall but didn't stop kissing me. As she laughed, our teeth collided, and I felt a sharp pain in my lower lip where her front teeth had cut into the flesh. I tasted blood in my mouth, but she kissed me deeply and hungrily until her sweet taste took over.

At last, I managed to reach my bedroom and pulled her onto the bed with me, breathless. We struggled to take each other's clothes off clumsily because we couldn't stop kissing and feeling each other's bodies, even for the short time needed to undress. But eventually, all the layers came off. We hadn't spoken a word since the moment we had walked into the apartment, and we didn't speak as we made love, quietly and noiselessly as you do when you don't want to be heard by someone who sleeps in the room next to yours.

I was surprised to discover that it did feel like making love, not merely sex. I knew the difference well enough, believe me. I kept gazing at her pretty face as she lay satisfied, with her eyes closed, breathing almost imperceptibly through her beautiful, tiny nose.

She evoked tenderness in me and made me want to watch her more. Now that we lay motionless, I started to feel the cold, and I drew the coverlet above us. The warmth of her body under the cover came to me as a surprise and a reminder of other days, mixed with a pang of sorrow for the time lost.

Then, exhausted, we fell asleep in each other's arms. In the midst of sleep, I heard her mumble something that sounded like, "I really wanted to see *Straw Dogs*," but I may have been dreaming.

CHAPTER 22

At first, I found Silvio difficult to characterize. He was slightly taller than I and thin, almost in a sickly manner. He reminded me of pictures of tuberculosis patients I had seen in an old book, but perhaps that was caused by his chain-smoking and the frequent little dry cough with which he punctuated his speech. He grew his beard longer than was fashionable at the time, with an occasional white hair standing out among the corvine-black thick, tangled mass. Together with a host of little wrinkles at the corners of his eyes, his beard made him look much older than his declared age of twenty-nine. He didn't seem to be bothered by the crumbs and other miscellaneous food leftovers that nestled all the time in his beard and, along with his unkempt hair, made him look unclean. He wore designer clothes in an ostentatious manner that I found irritating and spoke with a heavy Portuguese accent. I caught him speaking properly a couple of times when he was tired or not paying attention, so I suspect he exaggerated that accent on purpose.

My initial reaction to him was shock; I couldn't understand what Alessandra saw in him. During the first ten minutes after she introduced Silvio to me, I watched him and listened to him speaking about his recent travel experience and wondered how she could be attracted to this shallow individual. Then I saw the eyes.

They were piercing, black and deep, and conveyed a strength that magnetized you. When he smiled at you, baring his nicotine-stained teeth, it was the eyes that you had to watch because they seldom seemed to follow the smile; they had a clear and constant message: I am in command, and you will do what I want you to do. He got his way pleasantly, and you appreciated it even more because you knew he didn't have to make an effort to be nice. All in all, he was a creepy individual.

The first time I met him, Giorgia and I had just returned from one of her afternoons of political work with which I had agreed to help. In the first weeks of our relationship, I found little I could refuse to do for her. I was still dazzled by the strength of my feelings toward her—I couldn't avoid calling that "love" even though it felt completely different from what I had experienced with Alessandra. That confused me too because I had never thought that loving two women simultaneously, although with different intensities, would be possible.

Silvio kissed her on the cheek, and then he shook my hand, slapping me on the back at the same time. He had a strong, manly handshake, but I found his back-slapping routine too damn familiar and annoying. That was before I got used to him and his manners. After a while, you stopped being bothered by his unconventional ways.

"Let's make some spaghetti. I'm famished!" he said to Alessandra after half an hour of chitchat, to which I contributed little.

"I'm too tired. Why don't you go for a pizza?" she answered.

"Oh, c'mon! You don't have to work. Come, Roberto," he said, getting up from the couch, "let's show these girls how men cook real spaghetti."

Apparently, the thought that I might not oblige never crossed his mind because he walked quickly to the kitchen without looking back. I gave Alessandra an apologetic look, and then I got up.

"Let me show you where everything is," said Giorgia. She seemed amused, while Alessandra didn't seem to care one way or the other, so I decided to play along.

Spaghetti was prepared in record time, with me contributing the sauce. Luckily, Silvio kept chatting, saving me the need to think of topics of conversation. Then, the four of us sat down at the small dining table to eat.

"This is good, Silvio," said Giorgia appreciatively after she swallowed a forkful of spaghetti. It always amazed me what huge portions her petite body was capable of handling.

"Don't look at me," said Silvio. "The sauce is Roberto's."

"You never told me that you can cook," Giorgia complained jokingly.

"I have many hidden qualities. The sauce is one of them."

"But not the most important to you, Giorgia, I'm sure," intervened Silvio, smiling meaningfully. Then, addressing Alessandra, he added, "don't you like our spaghetti? You haven't eaten anything."

"I'm not hungry," she said, and for the first time, I noticed that she wasn't smiling. "I'm not feeling well. I'll go to bed now."

"A touch of the flu," I offered, wishing to make myself useful.

"Go and lie down, Alex," said Giorgia, getting up. "I'll make some tea for you."

After that, the conversation languished, and when Giorgia returned to the sitting room to tell me that she would stay at home to look after Alessandra, I politely turned down Silvio's offer to go together to the bar for coffee and headed moodily home. In that brief time, I had realized that when Silvio was in the room, he monopolized everybody's attention, and, as a result, I stopped existing for Alessandra. On the other hand, I missed Giorgia the minute I crossed the threshold, so perhaps I needed to find the strength to forget about Alessandra and concentrate on Giorgia and me. I had never been so confused in my life, but much worse times awaited me ahead.

One thing was indisputable: Silvio wasn't bluffing about having money. He drove a brand-new Alfa Romeo 1750, a dream car, and a very expensive one, particularly when fully equipped with all the accessories as his was, which included a hi-fi, top-of-the-line stereo system with those huge pre-recorded cassettes that, at the time, cost a fortune. His car became the subject of conversation two weeks after our first meeting and, again, during an afternoon of idle talk at the girls' apartment.

"I'm going to the country tomorrow morning. I'd invite you guys to come, but I'm going to visit my grandmother, and that's no great fun. I guess I'll take the seventeen-fifty."

"You own a seventeen-fifty and didn't tell me?" I said in awe.

"Do you like it?"

"I'd say that 'like it' is an understatement. When I buy a car, that's the one I'll get."

"Want to go for a test drive?" he asked.

"I'd love it!" I said. I jumped enthusiastically to my feet.

"Come on, then. It's parked just across the street."

Giorgia, who had followed these exchanges silently, got up too. "I'm coming along. I want to see how Roberto drives."

To my surprise, Silvio lifted a restraining hand and shook his head. "This is a guys' thing, honey. Some other time, okay?"

Giorgia was hot-blooded and quick-tempered, and I fully expected her to blow her top. I gazed at her, hoping that she would understand how much I wanted to go and, at the same time, that I didn't want her to be offended. To my surprise, she shrugged it off. "Yes, you go," she said, and I couldn't tell if she was speaking to him or to me.

Alessandra was sitting on the couch. She had one of her moody spells that always culminated in her feeling unwell and going to bed. She hadn't spoken much up to that point and didn't seem to be taking an interest now, so I grabbed my jacket, and we left.

The car was everything I had expected of it, and I drove around in a state of ecstasy, grateful that Silvio wasn't damping my enthusiasm for the accelerator. He didn't seem concerned either for his own or the car's safety and didn't ask me to slow down even once. When, after more than half an hour, we returned to the same parking space, I switched off the engine and turned gratefully to Silvio. "That was amazing; thanks a lot!"

I turned to open the door, but Silvio's hand on my arm stopped me.

"There was something I wanted to ask you if you have a minute," he said. He sounded serious and looked more so than I had ever seen him.

"Sure..." I said.

"You're a smart boy. I know that. I could use some help from a smart one like you in my business if you're interested. I can always use good people."

"I really appreciate it," I said. He had taken me by surprise, and I didn't know what to make of it. "But, as you know, I have my own business..."

"Ah, yes, the mechanic shop...but you don't have to give that up. You see, I deal in diamonds, and they need to be carried by reliable people. And sometimes other merchandise as well. We have ways of carrying it through different countries, but the courier must be reliable and intelligent. Aside from that, we look after all the details, and you get full instructions for each trip. It's really light work if you do it right. You only need to make a few trips every year to get rich. I'm sure you can find the time for *that*..." he added, smiling at his own joke.

"I really don't know what to say. I never thought of anything like that..."

"You don't have to give me an answer now. Think about it. I'm leaving the day after tomorrow for a business trip to Brazil and will be away for three weeks. You can give me an answer when I return. Okay?"

"Okay," I said.

"And, of course, you understand that this offer is confidential. You shouldn't talk about it with anybody. It would be...unwise to discuss it."

I nodded and swallowed. I wasn't planning to talk about it or to consider it. I wasn't sure what it all meant, but it certainly put Silvio in a different light.

"Of course," I said.

"Good boy," said Silvio. He sounded damn paternalistic.

In the excitement of the drive, I had forgotten for a moment that I didn't like him. Now, as I watched his shark-like smile, I had no trouble loathing him.

CHAPTER 23

I know it sounds childish, but I started to enjoy the political activities to which Giorgia took me. The atmosphere was one of camaraderie, and everybody was so purposeful that, in some way, their enthusiasm was contagious. I even struck up a friendship with Franco, who turned out to be fun to be with, despite my first negative impression of him. Once he knew you and no longer felt he needed to impress you with his intelligence, he became more interesting. Giorgia was ecstatic when she saw that we hit it off and, after an initial "I told you so," never mentioned my venomous comments about him again.

I think that many of the students who had signed up with the Movement did that for the sex and were as clueless as I was regarding the aims of *Lotta Continua*. But because, at least allegedly, everybody was in it for "The Cause" (whatever that was), everything else became subordinate to it. The atmosphere was one of permissiveness and promiscuity as I had never seen anywhere else. The air was at all times tangibly charged with hormones, and couples were created and dissolved at a speed that defied the eye.

The *Lotta Continua* headquarters consisted of one large central room and several smaller ones. You had to be very careful not to step on a couple of comrades making out when you walked into any room.

Although nothing was ever said to me, it was clear that, before my time, Giorgia had also played by the non-rules. On my second visit to headquarters, I witnessed an argument between her and a pimpled young man who walked around with an air of self-importance.

"Stop it!" Giorgia hissed.

I was reading a pamphlet, and I turned my head to see what the matter was. This pimpled person was standing next to Giorgia, rubbing himself against her.

"C'mon, give me a break," he said, without budging.

"Take your hand off my ass, or I'll kick your balls," Giorgia said. She spoke dangerously and without smiling.

The pimpled individual, clearly taken aback, took a step away and eyed her malevolently.

"You weren't so prudish last time I saw you," he threw at her.

"Well, I am now, so keep your hands in your pockets," she retorted.

Feeling that I had to do something, I took a step forward and said, "Giorgia..."

"It's okay, Roberto," she said, "he's leaving."

The young man gave her another look and then left without arguing.

"What was that?" I asked. The incident had troubled me.

"Nothing. Just a jerk."

"But..." I tried to say.

"Just a jerk," she repeated, and that was all she would say.

Franco was of a different kind. He spent a lot of time and

effort trying to draw me to the cause, undeterred by my candid statement that I had no interest in politics and only hung around for the sake of Giorgia.

"Oh, well ... as long as you help the cause, I don't really mind why you do it, but I bet that I will turn you into a convinced comrade in the end," he concluded after one of our endless discussions.

He sat in a chair before me, leaning purposefully forward as he always did and continuously pushing back the long tuft of hair that kept falling before his eyes and obscuring his view. His sweater came from the latest Gucci spring collection, and as such, it created a strange contrast with his emphatic proletarian speech. I shook my head, perhaps for the tenth time that day.

"Sorry, no can do. I have nothing against your ideas, but I also don't have anything for them. I simply don't care about politics," I pointed out.

"You should work harder on him," he complained, half-seriously.

The latter remark was meant for Giorgia, who had dropped the crayons with which she had been coloring a white cardboard sheet and now stood behind me with her hands on my shoulders.

"Believe me, I do," she said, "in many ways."

I turned my head and gazed at her. She smiled naughtily at me. And I understood what she meant. So did Franco.

"You can keep your sexual innuendos to yourself, my dear. We're not impressed," he said and stormed out of the room.

"What's biting him?" I asked. His behavior surprised me.

"Oh, nothing. Pay no attention to him."

"You know what I think? I think he's jealous ..."

Giorgia laughed.

"Don't laugh. I'm starting to be jealous myself. I see that you two have a special relationship, and, frankly, I don't like it."

"You don't?" she asked mockingly. She was still smiling with amusement.

"No, I don't. For instance, do you have to hug him every time you see him? And he touches you way too much on every occasion. I wish ..."

"Roberto ..."

"No, let me finish. I wish you would keep some distance from him. I'm not unreasonable or bigoted, but it really annoys me."

"Roberto," she said again and waited.

"Yes?"

"Franco is gay."

"What?" I almost shouted incredulously.

"He's gay. G-a-y. We've known each other since kindergarten, and I love him like a brother, but he's no competition for you, so calm down, okay?"

I felt stupid and relieved. More stupid, though.

As I sat there, mulling on my stupidity, the door opened, and a youth, whose name I can't recall, rushed in.

"Have you heard? The murder ..." He panted as he spoke.

"What murder?" asked Giorgia, jumping to her feet.

"The fascists killed a boy, one of ours. Varalli is his name. They shot him in Piazza Cavour."

His eyes sparkled with excitement, and he trembled a little, either because he had run up the stairs or because of overexcitement. He took a few deep breaths and continued, "We are going to march tomorrow to protest the killing. Get ready. I've got to go and tell the others. Pass the word to everybody. We meet here."

He rushed out, leaving us prey to contrasting emotions. All this action was exciting, but a killing was no joking matter. I wasn't sure that I wanted to get involved in it, and then I remembered something else: tomorrow was Giorgia's birthday, the 17th of April. I had planned a quiet dinner in a nice restaurant, not a protest march. So, obviously, that was our way out.

"It's a pity that we won't be able to participate," I pointed out.

"What do you mean 'we won't be able'? I wouldn't miss it for anything in the world."

"But, tomorrow is your birthday," I protested.

"And what a birthday present that is for me—a real protest, at last, for something worthwhile."

I gazed at her. Her face was flushed with excitement, and her eyes were brilliant. I realized that attempting to talk her out of it would be futile.

"I'll make it up for you on Saturday, then," I said, resigning to the inevitable.

"Thank you," she said, hugging me and tipping her face to invite a kiss. "You'll march with me, right?" she asked after we kissed.

I had had no intention to get involved in this protest that was no concern of mine, but of course, after this, I had no choice but to say, "Certainly."

At that moment, Franco walked in with a serious expression.

"Have you heard?" he inquired.

"Yes, and Roberto and I will march tomorrow," Giorgia said proudly.

"This is bad, very bad," said Franco and sighed.

"But at least it gives us an opportunity to make our voice heard," Giorgia pointed out.

"I wish it were an altogether different opportunity. It will be a protest march, unlike any other, tomorrow."

I was surprised by the sobriety of Franco's words. Surprised and pleased to see how reasonable he was.

"We will be there with you, Franco," said Giorgia.

"Yes, we will," I added to satisfy a strange need I felt to strengthen him.

"Thank you, guys," he said simply.

Giorgia hugged him, and then we left. This time the hug no longer annoyed me.

Back at my apartment, I brewed us coffee, and then we sat on the couch, drinking in silence.

"Do you think that it will be dangerous tomorrow?" she asked in a low voice.

"Why would it be? We're not going to confront the neofascists; we are merely protesting the ineptitude of the police. It's a protest march, not a battle."

"Still, the fascists may be provoked, and we've seen today what they're capable of. Poor boy...they said he was only seventeen..."

Something in her voice made me turn my gaze and look at her. I saw tears in her eyes; she was biting her upper lip to keep herself from crying, but it wasn't working. I hastened to put my coffee cup on the table and, without a word, I took her in my arms and held her.

That night we made love tenderly and very quietly; perhaps she really feared that something bad might happen but was too proud to back off from her commitment. I went to sleep with those thoughts and woke up with them. They made me nervous, extremely nervous.

It is an exhilarating experience to be part of a crowd, particularly a noisy one in motion. If you add to it the rhythmic sound made by several hundred marching pairs of feet and the loud chanting of simple mantras, yelled in unison, you can understand the high level of excitement, mixed with what you might call "noise dementia," in which I and everybody else around me had been thrown by an adrenaline rush in the first five minutes of the protest march. We shouted "Lotta Continua" and "No, no, the fascists will not pass!" and similar slogans as we walked.

We marched arm in arm in long lines, often without being at all acquainted with the ones who linked their arms with ours. I had never seen the one on my right, a middle-aged man who behaved like a possessed soul and shouted so loudly that I barely managed to hear my own words; I had Giorgia on my left, and she, in turn, had linked her left arm with Franco's. Every now and then—I never knew when this was going to happen and was always ill-prepared for it—the lines would stop to allow us to disengage from our neighbors and to stand, shaking our fists as we shouted a string of slogans. Then, the march would resume as spontaneously as it had stopped.

Our protest took us to a street much narrower than the one in which we had walked at the start, made even more crowded by a long line of cars parked on the right side. Our line broke to readjust to the new terrain, and with much surprise, I found myself at the forefront of the protest, with only one line of noisy comrades before me. The march stopped, and, to my horror, I saw that the first row was standing face-to-face with a compact wall of well-equipped policemen. We stood there, and probably everybody felt as uncertain as I was as to what we should do until a loud roar came from behind us, and then the lines of protesters began to waver. Before I knew what was happening to me, the man on my right propelled himself forward, pulling me after him and pushing the first line of men into the wall of policemen. I let go of Giorgia's hand, and soon, more bodies pushed from behind, thrusting me into the police grounds.

In the confusion of the moment, all I wanted to do was to keep my balance and try not to fall into the huge mass of retreating policemen. I somehow managed to stay erect, but that might have been a mistake because I then found I was standing before a young policeman at the exact moment when a shower of cobblestones, water pipes, and other hard objects was thrown from behind us onto the police line. I gazed at him, hoping that he would understand that I had nothing to do with it and meant no harm, and I saw fear in his eyes, which turned into anger when a cobblestone hit his shoulder. He lifted his club—the police used rubber-coated clubs back then—and then I felt a sharp pain on the side of my head.

I have no recollection of the next few moments or of how I got there, but the first thing I remember is that I was sitting between two parked cars, holding my right hand to my temple to keep a sticky liquid, which later turned out to be my blood, from running freely on my shirt. Giorgia's face hovered above me, but I couldn't see her clearly, partly because of the dim light of the late afternoon and partly because my vision was blurred. She was speaking to me, but all I could hear was a whooshing sound in my ears and the faint echo of a loud noise coming from the mass of protesters that now looked like a battlefield.

Slowly I got on my knees, and then, fighting nausea, I managed to stand up. Although I couldn't hear her clearly, Giorgia's body language made it plain that she was urging me to move. She put her arm around my waist, mindless of the blood that stained her clothes, and by gentle pressure, she pushed me to move through the parked vehicles and across the narrow pavement. I felt so weak that I had to lean on her, but even in my confused state, I worried that she might not bear the load of my heavy body. As I gave my back to the crowd, I thought I heard gunshots, and the fear that they generated infused some strength in my weak legs.

I don't know how we managed to get that far. It seems to me that I lost consciousness at times even when I was walking. Still, after a while, the noise of the clashes became distant, and I realized that we had reached a narrow and empty secondary street. Giorgia guided me toward the hood of a parked car, and I leaned on it, feeling emptied of all strength. She gently pulled the hand that I held to the side of my head, and I saw that she was crying.

"Don't cry; it's all right," I managed to say. I even tried to smile, but it hurt too much.

"It's not all right. It's *not* all right. It's all my fault," she cried. Then she pulled herself together, wiped the tears from her eyes, and took off her cardigan. "Here, use this to stop the bleeding," she said, handing it to me. "Stay put, don't move. I'll go and find a taxi."

She didn't wait for me to agree and ran away toward a nearby intersection. I couldn't have moved in any case, and it was all I could do not to fall off the hood while she was gone. My consciousness drifted a bit, and I was recalled to reality by the grinding noise of a vehicle's brakes. Giorgia walked quickly to me and helped me get up and navigate the short distance to the taxi. The driver opened his window and looked at me with curiosity.

"What's the matter with him?" he asked. "You said your friend wasn't feeling well, but he's bleeding."

"He doesn't feel well; he slipped and cut his head on the pavement," said Giorgia as she pulled the door after her.

"We go to the hospital, then?"

"No, it's no big deal." She gave him the address of her apartment, and the driver made a U-turn without further comment.

We drove very fast, which was good because I felt that I would be sick any moment. The driver probably feared the same and wanted to get rid of me as soon as possible. Luckily, we managed to reach the apartment without me throwing up. I think that climbing those stairs was one of the most difficult endeavors of my life, but with Giorgia pushing from behind and me clutching at the handrail and moaning with every step, we finally got to her door.

Giorgia's hand trembled as she fumbled with the apartment keys. She still kept her left arm around my waist, and I think she was afraid that I would fall if she let go. She was probably right. At last, she opened the door, and we got in. Exhausted, I pushed the door closed with my back and then fell into a sitting position on the floor. Giorgia dropped down beside me, and then, finally relieved of the tension that had given her the strength to get me home, she was no longer able to contain her tears. She cried and sobbed, holding my hands so hard that it hurt. Amid my confusion, the one clear thought I had was that it was good that she was letting it out.

CHAPTER 24

"Oh, my God! What happened to you?"

I opened my eyes and saw Alessandra's worried face above me. I tried to speak, but I was too weak, so I raised my right hand and made what I hoped was a dismissive gesture.

"It's my fault. All my fault," said Giorgia, between tears.

"He's hurt. We must take him to the hospital."

"No, no," I mumbled. My head wasn't clear, and I couldn't think straight, but somehow I knew that going to the hospital was a bad idea.

"We can't take him to the hospital," said Giorgia. "They'll arrest him if we take him there. You don't know what it was like..."

Giorgia paused, overwhelmed by emotion, and sobbed—or perhaps she took three quick breaths, I don't know which. Alessandra continued to stare at her, and she went on.

"I don't know what happened, really...we were marching peacefully, shouting slogans against violence, and then I heard a noise and the police charged...I think I heard shots..."

"You can tell me about it later. Now we need to take care of

Roberto," said Alessandra, cutting her short. She got down on one knee and waited.

Giorgia nodded, biting her lower lip. She imitated Alessandra's stance, and they both reached under my armpits and helped me up.

"I can walk by myself," I said. I spoke hoarsely while they propelled me slowly toward the bathroom.

"Shhh, don't be a hero," Alessandra admonished me gently.

I felt very shaky on my feet, so I didn't try to quicken the slow pace at which they walked me. When we got into the bathroom, Alessandra grabbed a small plastic stool and placed it before the sink.

"Sit here," she ordered.

I was glad that I could finally sit because I started to feel nausea rising again in my throat. Giorgia tightened her grip on my arm, and I tilted my head a little to gaze at her, although it hurt me to do so. Her face was wet with tears, and, for some reason, that made me want to cry too. To prevent both of us from crying, I knew that I needed to reassure her and stop the flow of her tears.

"I'm fine, really. I'm actually having fun," I said, trying to sound cheerful.

I don't know why, but instead of cheering her up, that made her break down in more tears. She collapsed to a seating position on the edge of the bathtub and took her face in her hands, sobbing uncontrollably. She kept sobbing for a minute or so until Alessandra called her name.

"I need your help," she said. "We need to wash the wound, but we must take off his shirt first. I can't do it all by myself." She spoke softly, almost motherly.

Giorgia raised her head and nodded. She wiped the tears from her eyes quickly with the back of her hands and came to stand beside me again. She and Alessandra gently unbuttoned my shirt and then carefully rolled up my undershirt. The strange feeling of detachment, as if all this were happening to somebody else, made me wonder. The blood had caked on my clothes, making them stick to my skin, but the undershirt finally came off. What irony, I thought: the two girls I like best in the world are undressing me, and I am in no state to really enjoy it. I toyed with the idea of telling the joke out loud to lighten up the atmosphere, but speaking was a difficult endeavor, so I gave it up, which was probably all for the best.

Alessandra filled the washbasin with lukewarm water and then dropped a large sponge in it. "Can you bring your head above the basin?" she asked.

Despite the pain, I did my best to oblige, positioning my left cheek parallel to the water, and Alessandra took the sponge and squeezed it above me. Little streams of reddened water dripped from my head into the basin, and I felt a sharp pain running all the way down to my throat from the wound above my right temple, which until then had manifested itself mainly with a dull, thudding ache. Water also wetted my neck and chest, but I ignored it.

"Ouch!" I cried despite my wish to appear heroic.

"I can see it now," said Alessandra. "It's not as bad as I feared, but it may need stitching...I don't know."

"What should we do?" asked Giorgia with anguish. She kept twisting her hands, and the anxiety resounded in her voice.

"First of all, we'll finish cleaning it and put some disinfectant on, then we'll bandage it and see. If the bleeding stops as it seems it has, maybe that will be sufficient," said Alessandra.

"I have a friend at the university who volunteers as a paramedic at the Green Cross. I'll call him afterward and ask him if he thinks that we should do anything else. He has experience in trauma; I trust him."

"Good. Now let's get this done," said Alessandra.

She sounded practical and in control. I wondered how she managed to be so coolheaded and deal with my wounds and blood so confidently; perhaps she didn't care about me and was unconcerned—or perhaps quite the opposite, she found the strength to dress my wound because she cared. You get all kinds of incongruous ideas after they hit you on the head...

When the ordeal of washing and dressing my wound was over, they took me to Giorgia's bedroom. Alessandra gave me some silky pajamas, too big to be hers, and I put them on without asking questions. I did so with Giorgia's help, slowly and at times painfully. When I took off my dirty and wet trousers, Alessandra modestly turned her face to the wall until she heard that I was ready, and then she gazed at me as I lay on the bed facing the ceiling in the only position in which the pain was bearable.

"How do you feel?" she asked. She sat on the edge of the bed, facing me, and peered into my eyes. "How's your vision? Your pupils are slightly dilated."

"I'm fine now. I only feel like shit," I tried to joke.

"I know...but you should feel better soon. The painkiller we gave you is strong and should kick in now."

Giorgia came back into the room. I hadn't noticed that she had gone, and I wondered if that meant that my senses had been damaged by the blow. I seemed to be able to concentrate only on my immediate surroundings. Much as I tried, I couldn't think about the future or cast my mind back even to the immediate past.

"I spoke with my friend," she said, "and he was emphatic that we shouldn't let Roberto sleep for at least the next four hours. He said that he may have a concussion, and if symptoms develop ... if he starts to behave strangely...we must take him to the hospital, no matter what. But if he goes to sleep, we won't be able to notice. So I must sit by him, but oh ..."

Tears again started to flow on Giorgia's tormented face, and she shook her head in a hopeless gesture.

"I am so worried about Franco," she said, by way of explaining the renewed tears. "I don't know what happened to him. I lost sight of him for a moment when I rushed to you," she was now talking directly to me, which she had avoided until then, "but when I looked up before we ran away, I couldn't see him anywhere and I'm afraid he may have fallen down. I don't know what to do. If it weren't for this situation, I would go and look for him."

Obviously, I was "the situation," so she needed absolution from me. I should have been annoyed that she had time to think about Franco in such a moment, but I cared for him too, and I wanted to be reassured that he was okay.

"It's all right, you can go. I feel fine now. I'll be okay."

"If you're worried, you should go and look for him," said Alessandra. "I'll keep watch over Roberto. Just give me a few minutes to shower, and then you can go."

Without waiting for an answer, she got up and left, and Giorgia sat on the bed beside me and took my hand.

"You really don't mind?" she asked, and when I managed a smile, and an almost imperceptible head shake, she relaxed and spoke more calmly. "I feel so guilty, you know?"

"Don't," was all I had the strength to say. The painkillers had kicked in, so the wound didn't hurt that bad anymore, but I felt queasy and faint.

She leaned over me, kissed my lips gently, and then she pressed her cheek to mine. Her tears wetted the side of my face, but it was pleasant to feel her so close, and I didn't mind. I summoned the strength to lift my hand and stroke her gently on the back. We remained in that position for a while, without speaking, until I felt that I was drifting away a bit, but the warmth of her body passed a life-giving feeling onto my own body and seemed to carry optimism and strength with it.

Alessandra returned, clad in two-piece pajamas with Disney characters, making her look like a child. The vision allowed me to forget for a moment that too many years had passed and that the woman who stood before me was no longer my teenage love. Giorgia kissed my lips again and stroked the side of my face gently with her fingers.

"I'll go now, then," she whispered. "I'll be back soon."

"I'll be fine, don't worry," I whispered back, simply because I didn't have the strength to raise my voice and impart conviction to that statement.

With a final squeeze of my hand, she got up and left. The room was in semi-darkness, in deference to my migraine-inducing light phobia, which I hoped was a temporary condition caused by the blow to my head. Alessandra's silhouette against the light coming through the door put the finishing touch to what my brain perceived as the most surrealistic picture I had ever seen.

"I'm cold," I complained.

I felt Alessandra's warm hand on my forehead and, with an effort, I opened my eyes.

"You're okay. You don't have a fever," was her verdict.

"I...feel cold," I insisted.

"Here, let me cover you. You'll feel better."

She spread a blanket over me, and then she sat on the bed and watched with a worried expression as I struggled to speak. I wondered if her expression meant that I looked as bad as I felt. I had trouble keeping my thoughts on track as quick, disjointed ones popped up in my head, but I tried to focus on what, at the moment, seemed to me to be the vital issue.

"Listen, I need to tell you. You know how I feel ..."

I took her hand and gazed into her eyes. Her expression vacillated between startled and amused, but she didn't try to take her hand away.

"You're delirious. I'll go and get you an aspirin," she said.

She got up, but I didn't let go of her hand, and she stood there, patiently waiting for me to release her.

"No, please ... I need you to listen. If I die, I need you to know ..."

"You are not going to die, don't be stupid! You got your head banged, and you're talking nonsense."

I wasn't going to give in, so I pulled on her hand, and she sat down again.

"Now listen to me, please," I pleaded. "When you stopped writing, you broke my heart, but I always loved you—God knows how much I tried not to, but I always did, and I still do."

She looked at me in the semi-darkness, sitting still without speaking. I waited for her to say something, but when she didn't, I went on.

"There, now you know. And if you tell me that you don't care at all about me, I'll go away, right now, and you'll never see me again. I wasn't planning to come back into your life, I swear. I meant to respect your decision to stay away from me, but when I saw you in the store, I could no longer bear it."

I spoke quickly for fear that she might say something that would stop me from baring my heart; I couldn't stand her saying something that would make me feel stupid. My mouth had dried up, and my throat felt like sandpaper, but I had to keep talking.

"So you just say the word, and I'm gone. Say it!"

I expected confusion, maybe anger or mockery, but she was

smiling. It was only a hint of a smile as if she was trying to hide it, but it was unmistakably there.

"You're not going anywhere, the state you are in. Why, you wouldn't make it to the door."

She paused for a moment, her face animated by visible emotion as if she were debating about what to say. Finally, she smiled her strange, intriguing smile again before turning frighteningly serious.

"I've been thinking about you, too," she said.

"And?" I prompted her.

"And what's the point of talking about it now?"

"I deserve to know, right?"

She considered my question for a moment, and then she nodded gravely.

"I believe you do. But it's so complicated ... with Silvio and Giorgia ..."

"This is not about them; it's about us. We need to air it, or we will never have peace. I will never have peace. You can't imagine what I've gone through all these years ..."

"Me too ..."

Her voice broke, and tears appeared in her eyes. She chewed her lower lip. I could no longer contain myself. My pain, the wound, everything was forgotten, suppressed by too strong an emotion. I pulled her toward me, and she didn't resist. Her head came to rest on my right shoulder. I started to massage her back with my left hand, first above her pajamas. Then, when she didn't show signs of resistance, I lifted the edge of her camise and gently caressed her lower back.

I was in ecstasy. Being able to touch her again, to feel her soft skin, was a dream come true. I had to pinch myself to make sure that I wasn't dreaming. In those moments, I did think briefly about

Giorgia. The thought of how she would react had she known what I was doing crossed my mind for a second and then was gone. Much as I cared about Giorgia, those moments of intimacy with Alessandra were a God-sent gift, and refusing or questioning it in any way would have been a sacrilege. I had no question in my mind that the protest march, the police, and my wound were all part of a divine design meant to bring us together again.

"I'm not the good girl you think I am," she said as if confessing to me. "I've done things in the past ... things that I'm not proud of."

"I don't care," I said. "I love you."

"Don't say that," she said, her voice muffled by the pillow in which she had buried her face.

"I've said it, and I'll say it again until you believe me," I responded stubbornly.

She lifted her face from the pillow and moved away from my shoulder to gaze into my face from a short distance. Her eyes were dry and her countenance serious.

"Do you really mean it?" she questioned.

I had no doubt about what should come next. I applied a token pressure to her back—I couldn't do more than that, the shape I was in—and then I moved my hand up to the back of her neck. She kissed me gently, and I kissed her back, mindless of the pain that the slightest movement shot through my skull. She pulled back and kept gazing at me without speaking. My head was light, and my heart was beating fast. She leaned down and gave me a peck on the side of my mouth, and then she sat up and smiled broadly.

"You kiss like an invalid," she teased me.

"I *am* an invalid, but not for long," I said, and then a shiver belied my bold statement. I felt cold again.

"Move aside a little," she ordered. When I did so, she lifted the blanket and lay beside me. "I'll keep you warm," she promised.

She put her right arm around my chest, and then she lifted it and ran her hand along my body, caressing me gently. I was in heaven; I didn't want to speak or move for fear of breaking the spell. But I had too many questions regarding the past and the immediate future, which I had to ask, so I broke the silence after a while.

"What I don't understand is ..." I started, but she cut me short.

"Shhh ... Don't speak now," she whispered.

"But ..." I tried to protest, but she silenced me by kissing me again, this time lusciously.

I stopped arguing and simply allowed myself the luxury of being led without the need to plan, think or worry. I felt her hand touching my body everywhere, as if in a quick reconnaissance of the terrain of which she was taking possession, and I closed my eyes to enjoy the intimacy for which I had been longing for years.

Then, of course, the telephone rang. Alessandra kicked the blanket away, and with a quick "I'll be right back," she jumped to her feet and ran to the living room. When she returned after a short while, her expression was inscrutable.

"That was Giorgia. They found Franco, and he's okay ... sort of. He broke his arm, and they are taking him out of town to where his grandmother lives. It's about two hours from here, but they have a doctor friend of theirs there, who will put him in a cast without asking too many questions. She's staying the night there and will be back sometime tomorrow."

Knowing that Giorgia would not be returning soon came as a great relief. I was given some more time to put together the pieces of the puzzle that Alessandra had become to me. The announcement didn't seem to call for comments, so I said nothing. She came to the bed, lifted the blanket, and gave me a naughty smile.

"She made me promise that I would look after you, and I intend to keep my promise."

Then she pulled the blanket over her head and kept it.

CHAPTER 25

For the first time in years, I woke up the next morning feeling blessed. The window was open, and mixed spring scents came through it, arousing long-forgotten feelings of renewal and well-being. From another direction, through the door, came the inviting smell of freshly-brewed coffee. I lay in bed, a prey to a laziness of the kind you can afford only when you are away from home on vacation and have no real reason to get up; I let the cool air coming through the window play on my face, relishing its caress. My head didn't hurt as badly as the previous night, and I felt my old self again. I was also hungry, and I realized that I hadn't eaten since the morning before. Noises came from the kitchen, and I tentatively sat on the edge of the bed, preparing to get up. I remained seated for a minute, waiting for a slight dizziness to pass, and as I prepared to get on my feet, the phone rang. I heard Alessandra's quick steps and then her voice.

"Yes. Where are you?" A long pause ensued, and then the unidirectional conversation continued. "When are you coming back? Aha. I understand ... I'll see if he's up. He looked okay to me when I checked on him this morning. Wait a second."

After a moment, Alessandra's head popped around the door.

"Oh, you're up ... Feeling okay? It's Giorgia. Can you come to the phone?"

I nodded—a mistake because that sent a spike of pain through my brain—and got up slowly. She watched me struggle but didn't try to help. I guess she was through humiliating me with her Mother Theresa approach. Careful not to slip or trip over a rug, I walked to the sitting room and picked up the receiver that Alessandra had placed beside the phone.

"Hi," I said, and I was surprised at how hoarse I sounded.

"Honey ... how do you feel?" Giorgia's voice seemed both concerned and guilty.

"My head feels twice its size, and I'm kind of weak, but the bottom line is I think I'll survive."

"I was so worried, but I called last night, and Alessandra said you were all right ... otherwise, I would've come home; you know that."

"I know, don't worry. When are you coming back?"

"Tomorrow. Franco has a multiple and splintered fracture and is having a bad time. We're in his grandmother's house, but she's a hundred or so and can't take care of him, so I have to wait until a friend comes to relieve me tomorrow morning. Oh, I'm so sorry ..."

She choked over the last words and then remained silent.

"Don't worry. Alex is taking good care of me," I said, and I gazed at Alessandra, who curtsied mockingly and smiled a wicked smile.

"I know, she's so great ... I have to go now, love. I'll try to phone again later. I'm calling from the grocery, and my last token just dropped."

Right then, the line went dead, and I put the receiver back on its cradle.

"Here, take this," Alessandra said, handing me something in a plastic wrap.

"What's that?"

"A brand-new toothbrush. Go brush your teeth, and then I'll give you breakfast. Come back here and sit on the sofa."

"Yes, Mother," I said. I hated being ordered around, but I took the toothbrush and went into the bathroom.

From a variety of used and twisted tubes that adorned the shelf, I picked a brand of toothpaste that I had used before. Tiny red clots of caked blood still showed at the bottom of the sink, and I ran hot water to wash them away before I brushed my teeth. I felt refreshed but weak, so I returned to the living room and sank on the sofa. Alessandra brought coffee and a basket with brioches in it. She sat beside me and put a newspaper before my eyes.

"I went out while you slept and got you a newspaper. It was quite a mess you got yourself into. Look here," she added, pointing to the headlines, "one student dead, killed by a police jeep, and at least fifty wounded. Are you nuts, getting involved in that kind of thing?"

The anger in her voice surprised me, and I responded meekly.

"I had no idea, honestly. Stupid me."

"Stupid is right. I hope you'll be more careful ... I can't call in sick every time you get thrashed." She smiled coquettishly and quickly picked up her cup and drank to hide it.

"So you're not going to work today ... you know what? That reminds me that Ernesto must be worried sick. He doesn't know where I am and hasn't seen me for two days. Let me call him."

I grabbed the phone from the table next to me, put it on my lap, and dialed the shop's number. The familiar voice of Marina, our secretary, accountant, and *factotum,* said, "Ecorluc, good morning." Ecorluc was the new name of our joint company, coined from a blend of our names, Ernesto Coppa and Roberto Lucci.

"Hi, Marina. Has Ernesto arrived yet?"

"Roberto! My God, where are you? Things have been crazy here, and Ernesto is really worried."

"Nothing to worry about. I'm fine, but I've taken a bad fall, so I have to remain in bed for one or two more days." I smiled roguishly at Alessandra as I said that, and she met my gaze without blushing.

"But, you see, we've had a police inspector here, asking questions about you, and Ernesto doesn't know what to say. He had to go with him."

I felt a shiver along my spine. The newspaper said that thirty thousand people took part in the protest march yesterday. Why of all those people was I so important to be noticed by the police?

"A police inspector? What did he want?" I blurted out.

Alessandra gave me an inquisitive look, but I signaled her to wait.

"He asked a lot of questions about the accident ... you know, your family's. He wanted to know if Ernesto knew anything about it if he had been talking to you before and after it ... questions like those. Ernesto told him that at that time, you were away at a boarding school, and you two were not in touch, but the inspector didn't seem satisfied and asked him to come to the station to give a statement. What's the matter, Roberto? What does he want?"

"Nothing. Just a state employee wasting taxpayers' money on an old accident. Listen, Marina. I need the rest so I'm staying with my friends and I won't tell you where I am. We never spoke today, okay? Tell Ernesto that I'll be okay, but I need to stay in bed, so I'm not going to any police station. The inquest—if that's what it is— has waited for years, and it can wait a few more days. Do you understand what I'm saying?"

"How can I? I never spoke to you," said Marina and hung up. A good kid, that's who she was.

I sat, pensive, with the phone on my lap, until Alessandra took it away and then sat down facing me.

"Do you care to tell me what that was all about?"

"A policeman came to ask questions about my family's accident after all these years. If this is the speed with which the police works ..."

"It bothers you, right? I can tell."

"It's just that it brought back memories ... things I prefer not to think about ..."

"You were talking in your sleep, you know?" she said, turning serious.

"I hope I wasn't saying anything stupid," I said, smiling, trying to lighten up the atmosphere.

"You talked about your family. You mentioned the accident, and then it was as if you were talking to your parents. At one point, you sounded so worked up that I almost shook you awake."

"I can imagine. I dream of them all the time. I miss them so much, despite everything..."

My expression must have been really sad because her eyes filled with compassion, and she caressed my cheek with her fingers in a motherly gesture.

"You should put the past behind you," she said.

"I wish I could...I try so hard not to think of them all the time, but so many things remind me of them."

"Then let me help you forget," she said, speaking softly, and then she kissed my neck.

"I like the forgetting bit," I said when she stopped for a moment, "but we need to talk. All this is so confusing to me, and there are so many things I need to ask you ..."

"We can talk later," she said.

The tone of her voice left no room for argument.

I expected that talking to Giorgia upon her return would be awkward. For the first time since I met her, I didn't know how she would react, and besides, I had my guilt to deal with. She had returned the next morning, and as soon as she had checked on me and given me a quick kiss, Alessandra had immediately taken her to her room "for a talk." I knew exactly what the talk was about because Alessandra had explained to me how things worked between Giorgia and her, but I couldn't say that her explanation has made me any less nervous. It looked like my scheme had worked, and I had won Alessandra back, but something else had gone wrong: on the way to doing that, I had developed real feelings for Giorgia.

"What shall we do?" I had despaired, realizing that our bubble world, in which the two of us had lived since the day before, would burst with Giorgia's return.

"It depends..."

We were lying on the couch where we had made love gently, unhurriedly. Alessandra wasn't forgetting that my wound still hurt, and I hadn't gotten my full strength back yet.

"On what?"

"On how you feel about Giorgia and me sharing you," she had said.

I hadn't seen that coming. She had spoken seraphically, without any embarrassment. I gave out a nervous laugh. "What do you mean...the three of us?"

"I mean that you can spend time with Giorgia and time with me. It's not mutually exclusive. So long as the way it works is clear and agreed, it should keep us all happy."

"But why do you think that she'll be okay with it?"

I was amazed by the new Alessandra that I was discovering. She discussed all this unabashedly as if sharing her best friend's boyfriend was the most natural thing in the world. I had never been a puritan, but I think that I may have blushed at that point.

"We have shared a boyfriend in the past, before Silvio's time. That one was *my* boyfriend, so she owes me," she said, making it sound like an entirely reasonable thing.

"Oh, I don't know...won't she be mad at me? I'm sure she'll feel betrayed. And perhaps it will hurt your friendship too."

You'll think me crazy; what she was proposing must be every healthy male's dream, so what was I being difficult for? But I really felt bad. I had let my love for Alessandra be an excuse for ignoring Giorgia's feelings, and I had cheated on her—I knew of no other way to put it.

"Let me handle it. I know how to talk to Giorgia," she had said.

Since the alternative was to confess to Giorgia that I was a cheat or to lose Alessandra again, I had no choice but to let her have it her way. But I wasn't happy or relaxed as she seemed to be.

"One more thing, though," she cautioned me. "Silvio must never know."

"I'm certainly not going to tell him. Where is he, anyway? He should've been back by now."

"He's been detained. He called and said that he had to stay longer. He got involved in some political struggle in Brazil—I don't know the details, but it's something that has to do with a friend of his father's—and they confiscated his passport. But he said that it's a matter of days before he is allowed to leave."

A thought that I had been repressing now inevitably surfaced. "Do you love him?" I asked, fearing the answer.

She only hesitated for a moment, and then she said, "I like him. He's fun, let's leave it at that. But he must never know," she repeated. She spoke gravely, making it crystal clear that the point really concerned her.

She wasn't telling me everything about her relationship with Silvio, I was sure of that, but I saw no point in probing further, at least for the time being. I needed to concentrate my thoughts on the next day and what I would tell Giorgia if, after all, she didn't take it well. I realized how much she meant to me and how I didn't want to lose her for the first time.

I had been sitting on the bed in Giorgia's room, nervously waiting for the girls' talk to end. When Giorgia came in, closing the door behind her, I jumped to my feet and waited for the painful scene for which I had been bracing myself. Instead, she walked up to me, took my two hands in hers, and kissed me gently on the lips, reaching up on the tip of her toes.

"Don't you want to hit me?" I asked, trying to ease the tension with levity.

"I should, but I'm so glad that you and Alessandra have become close again that I won't break your neck ... this time," she said.

"I'm confused," I confessed. "I thought you would be mad at me, and I wouldn't blame you if you were."

"I'm not mad at you. Well...perhaps a little," she conceded. "But I can't be mad at Alex. She and I are twin souls; we're like one person; we share everything. Girls sometimes are like that; I don't know if you can understand. And besides, are you going to love me less on account of her?"

"I'll love you more if that's possible," I said, and I meant it.

"See?" she said, smiling radiantly.

She hugged me with all her strength. I put my arm behind her shoulders and, slowly, I walked backward until my legs met the bed. Still entwined, we sat on it, and then we lay down and cuddled together. All I wanted now was to hold her in my arms and let the warmth of my body tell her how grateful I was.

I found Giorgia's outlook on life difficult to understand. She took everything lightly and in a simplistic manner, and I could never predict when something that seemed unimportant would turn out to be vital to her—and vice versa. I often felt that our relationship moved on thin ice because of that. Alessandra, on the other hand, had become a complete mystery to me. At times I felt as if she had outgrown me in experience, but mostly I was mystified by the changes that had taken place in her character. It was strange and confusing because I thought I knew her so well, but I often felt that I was talking to a different person, to a stranger.

After our lovemaking the day before Giorgia's return and once my confusing dualism involving her and Giorgia was set aside by Alessandra's shameless bigamist proposition, I felt that the time had come to clear up our past.

"You haven't told me yet, why you stopped writing to me."

She didn't answer right away, as if she was looking for something to say, but after her silence had lasted too long to keep up, she spoke flatly and distantly.

"It was really hard to find what to say. I tried, you know that, but my letters gradually became meaningless, and yours became shorter, soulless. I knew that I had to keep writing to help you through the tough times, so I wrote to you, but one day I read the letter I had just written and realized that the separation had already estranged us to the point that it sounded farcical. I never mailed that letter; I decided that I'd wait for a real letter from you, one to rekindle the feelings that I knew I still had inside me, but your letters stopped coming altogether."

"I did write to you, and I poured my heart into those letters. You don't know what I was going through…"

"I know that now. I found out, much later, that my mother had been intercepting your letters and destroying them, so I never got them. But I found out about it too late; too much had happened, and I had changed."

"But you could have gotten in touch with me. I tried every way; when I couldn't reach you I phoned Alice…"

"Alice, that bitch! You know that she bragged to me that she had shielded me from you. Shielded me! She had kept your phone call from me for months. When she told me about it, I got so angry that I slapped her and told her that I'd never speak with her again."

"I wonder what could have been…" I said. I felt a pang at the thought of all the lost time.

"I'm no good at the 'if' game," said Alessandra. "Our life is what we have now, and nobody's promising a tomorrow for us. Anyway, I don't want to think about it. I'm hungry; looking after you, War Invalid, is a tough job. I need food and so do you. I still have plans for you today," she said. "Let's go and make some spaghetti."

We ate spaghetti from the same plate, sitting side-by-side on the sofa, and drank Chianti wine from a rounded bottle. If that doesn't sound like much to you, you're wrong: it was the closest thing to paradise that I could imagine.

CHAPTER 26

As I woke up from a refreshing sleep, I saw that Giorgia was standing by the bed, holding a bag in her hands; the bag looked familiar.

"I went to your apartment to pick up a few clean clothes. The ones you wore are a total loss," she said, handing the bag to me. "Alex is at work, but I figured that it would be safe to leave you alone for a short while."

"What time is it?" I asked.

"It's three in the afternoon already."

"I need a shower," I said. I felt sticky all over.

"I'll make some coffee first, okay?"

I nodded eagerly, and off she went, returning five minutes later with a hot cup from which I drank avidly. I threw my legs out of bed and sat gingerly at the edge.

"I'll be back in ten minutes," I said, grabbing the bag.

"Where do you think you're going?"

"To the shower, where else?"

"The blow on your head must have screwed up your brain,"

she said. "You don't think that you can take a shower all by yourself, do you? What am I supposed to do if you lose your balance and break your neck?"

"I'm okay; you shouldn't be fussing," I tried to argue, but, in reality, I did feel a little shaky in the legs.

"No way. I'm coming in with you."

"I can see no objection to that," I said and smiled. Getting whacked on the head apparently may also have its advantages.

The process of getting me into the shower turned out to be far from simple. First of all, we had to remove the bandage that, seen in the mirror, looked like some kind of dirty turban. However, the lint had stuck to the wound, and it took some cautious but nonetheless painful pulling on Giorgia's part, accompanied by careful wetting with lukewarm water, to make it come off. About midway through the pulling exercise, she applied a little too much strength. For the first time in my life, I literally saw the stars.

"Ouch!" I cried. Tears of pain formed at the corners of my eyes.

"Oh, I'm so sorry, baby! I'll be more careful," Giorgia exclaimed. I stole a quick glance in the mirror and saw how contorted my expression was. With an effort, I relaxed my facial muscles.

"You can make it up to me in the shower," I joked to ease the tension, but Giorgia only nodded seriously.

Without the turban, I felt much better and touched the side of my head guardedly. The place felt stiff and rough, and when I looked at my fingers, I saw a little coagulated blood on them, but, overall, it didn't look too bad in the mirror. I took off my clothes slowly while Giorgia fumbled with the faucets.

"The water is not too hot. Try to keep your head away from the strongest jet in the middle."

I stepped hesitantly into the shower, letting the warm water welcome me in gradually until my full body was under the jet that hit my shoulders below the wound level. Giorgia undressed quickly, stepped in, and joined me under the jet. She held a large, natural sponge in her hand.

"Close your eyes and let me pamper you," she ordered.

She surely was serious about pampering, and I had no business interfering, so I let her. But all good things eventually came to an end, so we got to the point where she had to clean the wound.

"Easy!" I half cried, and a half cautioned when she poured on my head a foul-smelling liquid that burned like blazes. "What is this, anyway?"

"It's a disinfectant. We need to wash the wound. I know it hurts, I'm sorry, but my paramedic friend who gave this to me said it's the best and that the others hurt much more. We need to clean your wound three times a day with it; I'm sorry."

I gazed into her face and tried to guess whether the drops trickling from her eyes were water from the shower or tears. Judging by the look on her face, she hurt more than I.

"It's all right; it's not a big deal. I can handle it," I said. I felt very brave.

She hugged me without saying a word, and I hugged her back. Her wet skin against mine had a silky feeling to it, and I closed my eyes, enjoying the simple pleasure of the close contact with another beating heart.

With a long shower behind me and dressed in clean clothes, I felt like a new man. Giorgia had done a great job with my new wound dressing, which was now small and, although still quite conspicuous, no longer made me look like a soldier fresh out of a front-line battle. All of a sudden, I felt the urge to go out and feel alive again.

"I need to go for a breath of fresh air," I said.

"I'll come with you," said Giorgia stubbornly.

"No, you won't. Stop treating me like an invalid. I'll only go as far as the café to buy some cigarettes and a newspaper and maybe drink an espresso."

I hadn't expected her to give in easily, but she apparently saw my point.

"Okay, but promise me that you won't go far."

"Scout's word," I said, smiling with relief.

The world outside looked different, although I wouldn't have known how if asked to describe the difference. It was a subjective feeling brought about, no doubt, by the change in my biological rhythm after a long stay in bed. Be as it may, the sheer delight of walking to the tobacconists was incredible. I was in such a good mood that I decided to invest in an expensive box of Marlborough Gold, and I lit the first one before I left the shop, walking smartly with a rolled-up newspaper under my arm. Then I sat in the nearby café by the window to watch the people walking by outside. I drank coffee, smoked, and skimmed through my newspaper, feeling alive and well. The world seemed a perfect place to me, and right then, I couldn't have thought of any way to improve upon it.

Although I wouldn't have admitted it to Giorgia, my brief outing had left me quite exhausted, particularly because of the need to climb too many stairs, so I was happy when she and Alessandra, who meanwhile had returned from work, decided to fix us a special dinner in honor of my "return from the dead." While they were busy doing that, I sat in peace on the sofa, my body relaxed, gazing thankfully into nothingness.

Dinner was delicious, but I had trouble chewing the T-bone steak because of a pulsating pain in my temple, which attacked me each time I tried to work with my teeth. The girls gave me curious looks when I winced, and I had to explain.

"We could chew it for you," said Alessandra and giggled. "You know, Indian squaws used to do that for their warrior husbands who had no teeth left."

"Or we could put your steak in the blender and then straw-feed you," added Giorgia mockingly.

"You're both very funny, thank you very much!" I said. "May I remind you that it's not really my fault if I'm barely alive?"

"Oh, don't be so serious all the time!" Alessandra complained. She got up and circled the table to my chair, and then she hugged me from behind and planted a kiss on my cheek. "We are trying to give you a good time. Lighten up, will you?"

She remained behind me, massaging my shoulders lightly while I slowly finished my steak. Giorgia, who sat beside me, put her hand on my knee and caressed my thigh. I nodded but said nothing. I had no intention of breaking the spell.

As soon as dinner was over and the dishes were washed, Alessandra tactfully disappeared into her room. Leonard Cohen was singing to us about the Sisters of Mercy from the tape recorder that, although ancient, was the only modern thing in the living room. The song sounded strangely fitting for my dazzling and not yet fully comprehensible double liaison. Giorgia took my chin in her hand and gently pulled my head toward her, then she kissed me slowly, deeply, and possessively.

"I was so scared of losing you...and felt so guilty..."

"It wasn't your fault," I tried to comfort her, seeing that she was crying again.

"Yes, it was. I love you so much..."

"I love you too," I said, and I meant it.

"Promise me that you will always be here for me...that you will always love me as much as I love you."

"You know I love you," I said, speaking hoarsely.

"No, promise me!" she demanded.

"I promise," I said. I meant that too.

Later, as we lay intertwined in bed, naked and happy after our tender lovemaking, the door of Giorgia's room squeaked open. I looked in the direction of the noise and saw that Alessandra had come in, dressed in her childish pajamas. She approached the bed, and I gazed at Giorgia to gauge her reaction. She smiled smugly, a barely hinted but satiated smile, and looked up at Alessandra.

"I can't sleep. I had a bad dream," Alessandra whispered, and once again, the little girl surfaced in her. "Can I come and sleep with you?"

Giorgia raised her right hand and took Alessandra's. "But of course, doll. Hop in," she said, pulling her toward us.

Without a word, Alessandra climbed into bed and lay down on my other side. I made room for her, and she nestled in the hollow of my shoulder. She extended her left hand over me and gently caressed Giorgia's shoulder.

"Thank you," she whispered.

Giorgia responded with a smile.

But I bet that my smile was the fullest.

CHAPTER 27

Much as I enjoyed sleeping over at the girls' apartment, the time had come to resume a normal life, and the first step was to move back to my apartment. Giorgia insisted on accompanying me. I was fretful, partly because I hadn't been there since the protest march, but also because it was time for me to go back to work. Alessandra had left early for her shift, and Giorgia and I had eaten a late breakfast without her. I wanted to take the tramcar, but Giorgia insisted on a taxi. I gave in easily because I was still embarrassed to be seen in public with my head bandage, and I also enjoyed feeling and acting lazy, as a convalescing patient should.

I unlocked my door, but before we could step into the apartment, a figure appeared out of the shade of the corridor and approached us. He had been standing in a niche, and we hadn't noticed him before. I was startled by this sudden appearance, and my surprise grew when he spoke my name.

"Mr. Lucci?" he inquired.

I sized him up. He was small and stocky, with an almost completely bald head. He looked unimpressive, dressed in a badly creased gray suit, and my first thought was that he had to be some kind of peddler, although he carried no bag or briefcase. However, he didn't seem dangerous to me, so I let Giorgia walk past me through the door and turned inquisitively to him.

"Yes?" I said. I spoke uninvitingly; I wasn't in the mood to buy anything.

He took his time walking towards me and then stood at a short distance.

"I'd like to speak with you, Mr. Lucci. My name is Police Inspector Bellini, of the criminal division. It's about your parents."

"What about them?" A cold shiver ran along my spine, and I felt cold sweat on my forehead. I kept myself from wiping it because I knew that the act would have made me look nervous.

"May I come inside? I don't think that we want to discuss it here."

"I'd like to see some credentials, please. I don't know you," I said, still hoping that he would turn out not to be a real policeman. He fished for a wallet in his inner pocket and showed his badge to me. "Come in," I said after a brief glance at it. I had no choice but to resign to the intrusion.

Once inside, I waited in silence as Bellini pointedly scanned the room with his eyes. Giorgia stood by me, clearly at a loss to understand what was going on, and after a few seconds, her red-headed temper had the better of her, and she erupted.

"What is this? Who the hell are you? What do you want?" Then, she asked me, "Why did you let him in?"

"This is Inspector Bellini," I explained, trying to sound unruffled. "I gather that he is investigating my parents' accident. Is that right?" I added, addressing him.

"Uh-huh," he said, nodding briefly.

"Now? It's ancient history! You took your sweet time about it, so why bother me now?"

"We do what we can do when we have to do it," he said. "And who are you, miss?"

"I'm Roberto's girlfriend. What business is that of yours?"

"In my line of work, everything is my business," he said. "I may want to speak with you separately. Kindly write your name, address, and phone number here," he added, handing her a little notebook.

She gazed at him and then at me, and when I said nothing, she took the notebook ungraciously from his hand and scribbled in it before giving it back to him.

"I would like to speak with you privately, Mr. Lucci," he finally said.

Whatever he wanted to discuss, I really didn't need Giorgia to be a part of it, so I motioned him to my kitchen and invited him to sit at the small Formica table.

"Wait a second, please," I said and went back to Giorgia, who waited, seething and tapping her feet.

"I would kick him out if I were you. What a cheek, barging in like this after all these years!"

"I know, I know. But that's how they work; what can I do? This may take some time; you'll better go back to the apartment."

"I have some things to take care of. I'll call you when I get home."

She gave me a hurried kiss and left. I went back to the kitchen, where Bellini waited patiently at the table.

"Some coffee?" I asked to ease the tension.

"No, thank you. Later, perhaps. Now, tell me: what is that bandage on your head?"

"I slipped and fell on the pavement. A bad blow, but nothing that a little rest won't cure. I stayed in bed for the past two days."

"I know. I've been trying to reach you. That's why I came here this morning, hoping to find you at home. You will ask me what's the hurry after all these years. Still, the truth is that we have a visiting colleague from Rome, who's investigating a related matter. He's quite anxious to go back home. So I'll have to ask you to accompany me to the station where we can take your statement."

"I don't understand," I said, a prey to sudden fear. "Why is it my problem that you have a colleague visiting from Rome? I can't spare the time right now. You know I've been sick, and I have to go back to work. They need me there."

"Mr. Lucci, I'm trying to do this the easy way, and I'm asking you politely. Please don't force me to use other options to get you there because I will."

His voice was calm but flat and hard, and I realized he was no person to play games with.

"All right, if you need my help, I certainly want to give it to you. I'll call my partner at work and tell him that I won't come in today either."

"You do that," said Bellini encouragingly.

He turned his gaze to the table as if to say that the matter was closed, and I went to my bedroom to phone Ernesto. He was truly pissed with me and kept ticking me off for disappearing on him like that, for making him worry indescribably, for not making the little effort to pick up the phone and let him know what was going on with me—and all I had to say to him was how right he was, and how sorry I was. I don't know if I managed to quench his concern about the police snooping around the shop—we never discussed that again, and I have always been grateful and will always be that he never pried into my private affairs.

When I emerged from my room, feeling pensive and not knowing what I was heading for, Inspector Bellini stood by the apartment door, which made me wonder whether he feared that I might try to escape.

"Will it take long? I asked.

"That depends very much on you. If you cooperate, it may be a short thing. If I were you, I would want to unburden," he added as I locked the door behind me.

He didn't explain what he meant by that, and I knew better than to ask. His car waited at the curb—a plain, blue police car with no external signs—and he opened the passenger's door for me. He drove slowly through the traffic, and I sat in silence, concentrating my thoughts on what lay ahead. One thing I knew for sure: my life and happiness hung on my ability to remain calm.

The interrogation room to which Inspector Bellini led me instantly brought back memories of a similar one in which I had been kept many years before. The police station was much more impressive and bigger than the one to which the finance police had taken me, and the interrogation room was more modern and in better repair, but the smell of fear was the same. I was still looking around and getting used to the surroundings when the door opened to admit a tall, lean man of about fifty.

"Superintendent Paci," said Bellini, unceremoniously, pointing a thumb at the newcomer.

"Of the Rome police," added the newcomer. He didn't offer to shake hands; instead, he sat down, and so did Bellini, taking the chair beside him. I felt stupid, standing, so I took the only remaining chair at the other side of the table and sat down too, facing them.

"So, Mr. Lucci," said Paci. He gazed at me as if waiting for an answer, and when I said nothing, he continued. "You used to live with your uncle in Rome, correct?"

"Yes, of course."

"We are taping this," said Paci, pointing with his forefinger to a box with wires that led to a microphone positioned on the table.

"Wait a second," intervened Bellini. "We do things properly here, in Milan. Today is the twentieth of April, the time is half-past twelve, and we are interviewing Mr. Roberto Lucci. Present are Inspector Bellini and Superintendent Paci," he recited pointedly to the microphone.

Paci watched him with a sarcastic smile on his lips. I could sense a tension between the two officers. When it was evident that Bellini had finished, Paci continued.

"Please tell me about your uncle's death."

"There isn't much to say. Uncle Dan had been sick for a long time—a heart condition, you know—and one night, he passed away in his sleep."

"Why did you have him cremated?"

"That was his wish. That's what he told me, and I wanted to honor his will."

"That's not what his friends told me. They said quite the opposite that he was against cremation. Look here, Mr. Lucci—why don't you confess and put an end to all this? You'll feel better after you unburden your conscience."

I got up on my feet, truly enraged, feeling waves of heat in my face that, surely, was flushed. I found myself shouting at Paci and shaking my fist at him.

"How dare you! Who do you think you're talking to? What is this idiotic nonsense about my conscience?"

"Yes, you ask a suspect to confess, and it's 'case solved.' So that's how it's done in Rome," Bellini murmured sardonically almost to himself, causing Paci to blush. Then he spoke firmly and ordered, "Sit down, Mr. Lucci!"

Not knowing what else to do, I sat down and gazed at Bellini, avoiding eye contact with Paci. Bellini studied me meditatively, and after a few seconds, he addressed me again.

"Who's Alessandra?" he asked.

I composed myself, knowing that I had to come across as a cooperative person. "The only Alessandra I know was my girlfriend many years ago. Why do you ask?"

"If you don't mind, I'll ask the questions for now. At the time of the accident that caused the death of your family, was she with you?"

"What do you mean by 'at the time of the accident'?"

"I mean, on the day of the accident."

"I think you've got your facts crossed. At the time of the accident, I was away at a boarding school, the St. Anna. I had been away for a year then, and Alessandra hadn't been in touch with me for quite some time."

"So why did you brag with her that you had killed your family?" Paci asked point-blank, eliciting a pained look from Bellini.

"You know, I think you're delusional," I said. I was angry and no longer cared about trying to ingratiate myself with him. "I don't know where you're getting those crazy notions from."

"From this letter, among other things," said Paci, handing me a piece of paper.

I took the paper trying to keep my hands from trembling, because at that moment I was sure that, somehow, the police had got hold of a copy of my letter to Alessandra. Perhaps Uncle Dan had made a Xerox copy before returning it to my document holder. So my relief was immense when I saw that it was another letter. It was written in Uncle Dan's neat handwriting, dated two days before his death, and it was short but hurtful. I remember it by heart. Here is what it said:

"*Respectable Commissary of Police, Rome,*

I have reasons to believe that my nephew's son, Roberto Lucci, whom I have always loved as my own son, has murdered his entire family, including my beloved nephew, his mother.

Roberto has confessed his crime to his girlfriend, Alessandra, and there is no doubt in my heart that he is guilty of such mortal sin. I will give you further details when you see fit to interview me.

I beg you to take this letter as seriously as this serious matter requires."

Uncle Dan's signature followed, along with his address and telephone number. I read and reread the letter, using the time to regain composure.

"We received this letter a few days after your uncle's death but, as you know, we are very busy, so it didn't get the attention it deserved until a few weeks ago," said Paci.

He paused and gazed at me.

"I don't know what to say. This is pure nonsense," I said, trying to steady my voice as much as possible. "As I told you, I was nowhere near my family when the accident occurred, and I hadn't visited home for a long time."

It was Bellini's turn to speak now. "So why would your uncle come up with such a wild story if there was no foundation to it?"

"I don't know. He was a very sick man, and he was on medications. Perhaps that made him lose his reason. I have heard that old people often lose contact with reality and become paranoid."

"I don't believe a word you're saying!" said Paci, banging his fist on the table. "Do you want me to tell you what I think? I think," he continued, without waiting for my answer, "that you murdered your family, and then you killed your uncle, probably poisoning him, and that's why you cremated him in a hurry. We are running laboratory tests on the ashes and will soon know what poison you used. You may as well confess now and save us all the trouble."

I decided to ignore him and addressed Bellini. "Inspector," I said, "I shouldn't even bother to respond to such wild accusations. My uncle died of natural causes, and you can play with his ashes as much as you want, but you won't find anything. Still, you strike me as a reasonable person, so if I give you the means to verify that my uncle's letter is pure imagination, will you leave me in peace? Being reminded of my tragedy is hard enough as it is."

Paci started to say something, but Bellini silenced him with a dismissive gesture. "I'm listening," he said.

"Alessandra, the one to whom we've been referring here, is easy to get in touch with. She lives in the same apartment with my girlfriend, whom you met this morning. You can go and ask her if I ever said anything to her about my parents' accident—anything at all, except sharing my grief with her." I then glared at Paci, "Bragging, you said. The letter doesn't say that. You should be ashamed of yourself!"

Again, Paci seemed to be about to speak, but Bellini checked him with an imperious motion of his hand. They both got up, and Bellini spoke decisively.

"We will go and interview this Alessandra of yours. Meanwhile, you'll have to wait here. I'll make sure that you get some food. A sandwich, perhaps. Do you have any special dietary requirements?"

"I'm not hungry," I said, shaking my head.

"You've got to eat," said Bellini matter-of-factly. "You may have to stay here for a while."

Bellini made good on his word, and a young, uniformed policeman came in carrying a tray with a sandwich and a Coke on it. Then I was left alone. Three hours later, I opened the door and poked my head out. The corridor was full of people, many in uniform, walking to and fro. I stopped a young officer who walked in my direction with a newspaper.

"Would you mind lending me your newspaper? I've been waiting for hours, and I'm bored," I asked courteously.

If he was surprised, he didn't show it. He handed me the newspaper with a nod, and I retreated into the interrogation room, where I sat down to read it from end to end.

A while later, I felt the urge to go to the bathroom, so I got out, located the nearest WC sign, and returned to the interrogation room and my newspaper. For a murder suspect, I wasn't being kept under too tight a surveillance.

It was late afternoon by the time that Bellini returned. He came alone and walked a couple of paces into the room. I stood up and waited.

"We've had a long talk with your girlfriend, Alessandra. Most of what you said checks out. Personally, I think you're off the hook, but Paci has different views. He's sure that the analysis of the ashes will find poison, so we're not closing the investigation yet. You're free to go now, but make yourself available, okay?"

"Okay," I said, and then I couldn't help myself adding, "This Paci is a jerk."

"Don't tell anybody, but I agree with you. I have no jurisdiction, though. That's Rome," said Bellini, making a vulgar gesture.

I could have almost brought myself to like him.

CHAPTER 28

Emerging from the police station into the cool, late afternoon, I walked to the street corner and stopped to consider what to do next. I wanted to go straight to the girls' apartment, partly because I was eager to listen to an account of their interview with the police, but also because I knew that they had to be worried about me. But I was sure that questions would be asked, and I had to have all my answers figured out for them. For that, I needed time to think, so I walked until I found a quiet café where I could sit in a corner with a cup of coffee and a sandwich and think quietly.

I finished eating and sat there, chain-smoking and running that afternoon's interview again in my head. The fresh air and the food did much to restore my composure, so after half an hour, I paid my bill and left.

It was dark by the time I got to the girls' apartment. I let myself in with the key that Giorgia had given me the day before and closed the door quietly behind me. The apartment was silent, as if nobody was there, but when I walked into the living room, I saw Alessandra sitting on the sofa and Giorgia in an armchair facing her. As they saw me, they both jumped to their feet and stood there, gazing at me. I had expected them to welcome me back from my ordeal and pamper me the way they knew how; I had anticipated that Giorgia would fling herself into my arms and that perhaps Alessandra would follow suit. I certainly hadn't expected them to stand, staring at me without a word of welcome, and that made me speechless for a moment. Then, knowing that I had to say something, I took a step in Giorgia's direction and said, "I'm back, honey."

It was a lame line, I know, but it was the best I could think of. And then she did the most extraordinary thing—she raised her right hand in a halting motion and shook her head. "Don't..." she said, and I stopped in my stride.

"What's going on?" I asked.

Giorgia didn't answer and turned her gaze to Alessandra, so I did the same and waited for her to speak. She swallowed quickly, twisting her fingers at the same time, and then she spoke in a low, toneless voice.

"The police were here. They spoke with us for two hours," she said.

"I know. I sent them to you, so what's the big deal? I know it's unpleasant to be interviewed by the police—believe me, I've been there—but that's no reason to be mad at me. I had no choice—they had some strange notion that I was somehow involved in my family's accident, and I had to prove to them that I wasn't even around when that happened. So why the long faces?"

"They showed us the letter," said Giorgia, speaking hollowly. She now stood to my left, so I had to turn my head to see her, and when I did, the expression on her face scared me. I tried being nonchalant.

"Oh, that stupid thing," I said, ending my sentence with a little laugh.

"I...we didn't find it funny. That policeman thinks that your uncle has been murdered, and they're running tests to prove it."

"Oh, c'mon, don't be ridiculous! I'm here, right? They let me go because they don't believe that stupid theory either." I started to panic when I saw the hard, cold stare that Giorgia was giving me. I stole a quick glance at Alessandra; her gaze was softer, and she looked more embarrassed than angry. "I can't believe that you're even considering it," I retorted, gazing straight at Giorgia.

I didn't need to fake the anger in my voice—I *was* angry. At that moment, I needed support more than anything else, and instead of supporting me, she was being judgmental. But the blow surprisingly came from Alessandra; speaking with her soft, compassionate voice, she took the three of us to the point of no return.

"When I read your uncle's letter, all of a sudden I understood the things you said."

"Things I said? What things?"

"You had a fever, and I thought you were delirious. You kept saying, 'I didn't mean it to happen that way, Mom. Can you forgive me?' And things like that. Then you spoke to a Mr. Paolini—I think you were dreaming then—and you explained to him what you did with your father's car brakes. I didn't understand much of it because you mumbled technical terms, but what I heard was enough to get the gist."

"Alessandra..." I tried to say to stop the flow of her speech, but she continued in that frighteningly quiet voice.

"Later, when you woke up, I asked you about your dream, remember? And you said that you had a nightmare about your family and the accident that killed them."

"I don't believe that this is happening to me," I said, shaking my head in disbelief. "You're accusing me...you accuse me...and all because of a bad dream I had? How insane can that get?"

Alessandra was crying now, silent, big and slow tears, and the pain was in her voice too.

"How can you explain all that? Suddenly it all comes together...the letter, your words...I'm so confused...I haven't told the police about your dream. I didn't want to make it harder for you. But I torture myself that, much as I love you, perhaps I should've told them."

Giorgia remained silent, but her presence in the room, that of a hardheaded woman who hasn't said her final words yet, loomed large. Every now and then, I stole a glance at her to make sure that she wasn't about to explode before I got a chance to explain myself.

"But I always dream about my family. Wouldn't you be dreaming about yours under the same circumstances? And since their death, I have tortured myself a thousand times, trying to think of how the accident could have occurred. The police didn't know or didn't bother to find out, and left with the uncertainty, I have explored so many possibilities, both while awake and in my dreams. That's all there is to it, so am I to be blamed for my tragedy?"

"But there is the letter. You can't discount that," Giorgia said in her flat, cold voice.

"The letter is nothing more than the result of senile paranoia. Here, you can tell by yourself: the letter says that I have told Alessandra about my presumed crime—but I haven't told Alessandra anything, have I? Here, ask her! Have I ever told you anything as stupid as that?"

"What if there is another Alessandra, one we don't know about?" asked Giorgia.

My heart felt heavy because I knew by this question that Giorgia had crossed a line that would irreparably divide us—the line of distrust. I moved my gaze from Giorgia to Alessandra, who was still crying silently. I saw no tears in Giorgia's eyes, only a hard, cold, and unsympathetic stare. I knew then that I had lost my battle.

"So what happens now?" I asked, feeling and sounding resigned to the inevitable answer.

"We need to take a break until we can figure all this out," said Giorgia, speaking more softly now that it was clear that my resistance had been broken.

"You broke my heart, you know that. But I still love you both—you know that too," I said, for the first time feeling tears of rage rising in my eyes. I wiped them off quickly with my hand, hoping they wouldn't show, but new ones immediately took their place.

"We love you too," said Alessandra. She sniffed and dabbed at her eyes with a handkerchief.

So I asked Giorgia, "Do you love me too?"

Her face showed the signs of an inner struggle, but only for a second.

"The key, Roberto," she said, without looking me in the eyes.

I dropped the key on the coffee table and walked out, dragging after me the shattered remains of my dignity.

CHAPTER 29

I was lucky to have my work, or I would've gone mad. That was always what kept me going during hard times, and I don't know how I would have managed during the months following my break-up with Giorgia and Alessandra without my work at the shop. I immersed myself in it, starting early in the morning and working late so as to come home exhausted, which was the only way that I could manage an occasional dreamless sleep. I lost weight too because I often forgot to eat and sometimes during the weekend I had no food in the apartment. But I didn't care. I carried a dull ache with me, which dominated my day and sapped my strength. Sometimes I think I might have done better seeing a shrink, as Ernesto suggested, but I was too depressed to help myself.

Three months after the painful scene at the girls' apartment, I woke up one day unable to bear the separation anymore. As a last resort, I went to the *Lotta Continua* headquarters and sought Franco out. He was there, as active as always, except that his arm hadn't healed well, and his elbow was frozen in an arched, awkward position. He told me about it when I asked him how he was doing, and then he waited for me to speak. We stood at the door to the main room, and other people, some of whom I knew, kept bumping into us. I had to whisper to keep our conversation private.

"I miss her, Franco," I said straight out.

"I know. She told me all about it...I don't want to judge. I'm sure it's hard on her too."

"Could you talk to her?"

"What good would that do?" he asked after a brief hesitation.

"I need her to know that I love her, that I miss her. I can't believe she's keeping this up for so long."

"You know how hardheaded she is..." said Franco.

"Will you tell her that I want to talk to her, to meet her?"

"Frankly, I don't know...she was so definite about staying away from you," said Franco, shaking his head sadly.

"But will you? For me..." I insisted.

"I'll see what I can do," he finally said without enthusiasm. "If she changes her mind, I'll call you."

I thanked him warmly and left. He never called, but I should have known that he wouldn't; he never asked for my phone number. So I resigned to never hearing from the girls again.

Then Giorgia called.

I hadn't heard her voice in seven months, but I recognized her as soon as she said, "Roberto?" I had thought of calling her many times after my talk with Franco, and more than once, I had sat by the phone with the receiver in my hand, trying to find the courage to dial her number. I never did—I knew that she wouldn't speak to me. Hope is hard to die, so at first, I had hoped that a phone call would come after a cooling-off period, but I had always expected Alessandra to be the one to make it.

"Yes?" I said, instinctively unwilling to admit recognition or eagerness.

"It's Giorgia ... how are you?" she added after a pause.

"I'm fine. I'm doing okay ... except that I miss you."

"I didn't call for myself," she hastened to point out. "It's Alessandra who asked me to call you."

"Why didn't she call herself? She doesn't need intermediaries."

"Roberto ... she is not well. She's in the hospital."

"What happened to her? Did she have an accident? How is she?"

I started to panic and felt a painful knot in my stomach.

"No, no accident. She's ill, and she would like to see you ... if you're not too mad at her, that is."

"Mad? I'm not mad. I miss you, and I miss her. I miss you both, dammit. But what does she have? What's the matter with her?"

"It's better if you talk to her. If you hurry, you can get there in time for the last visiting hour today. Write down the details; it's a big place."

I found a pen and wrote the details that Giorgia dictated to me on the back of my hand. She made me read them back to her, and once I did, she said, "Go see her, Roberto," and then she hung up.

The Polyclinic Hospital is a huge building dating back some two hundred years and, even with the indications that Giorgia gave me, finding Alessandra's ward took me twenty minutes and several bad turns in the maze of corridors. At last, I found her room, a large one with ten beds, seven of which were occupied. Nobody seemed to have visitors, and the woman in the first bed by the door—an old woman with an uncannily wrinkled face—was fast asleep, so I tiptoed quietly toward the last bed by the window, which the ward nurse had told me was Alessandra's.

It was no fancy room, but rather one reserved for public health service patients, and all that was available for privacy were thin, green curtains surrounding the bed. The one by Alessandra's bed was drawn, and I quickly crossed it where the ends met, near the head of the bed. I then looked down at Alessandra. She was asleep and beautiful despite the oxygen mask that covered her nose and mouth. She was thinner, though, and her cheekbones stood out and made her look strange, different. I kept watching her, uncertain whether to wake her up, but she sensed my presence and opened her eyes.

"Roberto..." she said. She smiled invitingly, and I took her hand.

"I hear that you're giving us problems, baby," I said, smiling back and trying to lighten up the atmosphere.

"You came," she whispered, taking off her oxygen mask.

"Of course I came. You couldn't have kept me away if you tried. So now, tell me, what's the matter with you?"

She hesitated, closed her eyes for a moment, and swallowed before responding.

"You remember that I was going to see a doctor, that I was always tired and wasn't feeling well? He made me take some tests, and the results weren't good. They call it 'congestive heart failure,' and it gets worse with time."

I patted her hand reassuringly.

"It's good that they found the problem. I hear that this is a good hospital, and I'm sure that you'll be back on your feet in no time."

I had no idea what the medical term meant, but sure as hell, I was there to encourage her and see her through it. I squeezed her hand to emphasize my support, but rather than having encouraged her, I saw that her eyes had filled with tears.

"Don't cry, my love, or I'll cry too," I threatened, jokingly.

She didn't speak right away, and I waited patiently for her to react.

"There is no cure ...," she said after a few seconds of silence. "It ... it only gets worse ... and I feel so bad."

I don't think that her words actually sank in, then I rejected the notion that she might not get well altogether.

"Don't say that," I admonished her. "If they don't have a cure here, I'm sure that we can find a specialist somewhere else who knows how to deal with it."

"Oh, yes. There is a private Swiss hospital in Geneva where they use a new technique, an experimental one. But it's very expensive, and I had to raise the money first. But don't worry—Silvio is paying for it. He's rich and is making arrangements to get me there. So you see, everything's going to be all right."

"I want to help too. I can help; I have some money. Why didn't you call me?"

"I can manage, but thanks ..."

"Don't thank me. You should've called me before. I'm here for you, you know that."

"I know that ..."

She choked on her words and coughed. Her hand went to the oxygen mask, and she put it back on her mouth and nose and breathed avidly. After a few seconds, she took it off again.

"I'm sorry," she said, "that ... I doubted you. I ..."

"Don't tire yourself speaking. Apologies can wait."

"No. I wanted to see you and tell you, you know, in case that ... if I ... if I ..."

Her voice broke, and I stooped over her and placed my cheek to her wet face, then I whispered in her ear, "It's going to be all right. You'll get well, and I love you, and let's forget about the bad things in the past, okay?"

"Okay," she whispered back submissively.

A hand tapped my shoulder, and I got up. The nurse who had directed me to Alessandra's bed stood behind me.

"You must go now, sir. Visiting hour is over."

"One more minute, okay?"

She nodded and said, "But please, be quick," and then she left.

"I'll be back tomorrow. Wait for me," I said.

She nodded faintly, and I kissed her lightly on the lips.

"Don't go anywhere," I added, hoping to extract a smile from her. She didn't manage one, and I pressed her hand once again, hoping to pass on some strength to her, and left.

Outside, I let the cold air into my lungs and allowed it to freeze my ungloved hands, as in an act of penance. I eyed with hate the Christmas decorations that already hung in the streets. How dare anybody plan to be merry, I wondered, when my Alessandra lay in that cold building?.

CHAPTER 30

As soon as I got home, I dialed Giorgia's number. I needed her cooperation in getting things moving faster. Alessandra didn't look well to me, and I thought that the sooner we got her to the Geneva hospital, the better. Most of my money was invested in non-liquid capital funds, but I was sure that the bank would let me borrow cash on those. And money was of no importance—I would have given it all to get Alessandra quickly and safely into the hands of the right doctors.

I let the phone ring for two long minutes before giving up. Apparently, Giorgia was not at home. I kept trying every half hour until, frustrated by the lack of response, at midnight, I gave up.

I went to bed and lay there awake, thinking of how grateful Alessandra would be for my stepping in and helping out with her cure. I fantasized about our future together and imagined myself strolling with her on the beautiful grounds of a Swiss clinic. I finally fell asleep feeling optimistic and looking forward to my next visit to her in the morning.

I woke up feeling cold and alert. I had left a window ajar, and the room was frozen. By my bedside clock, the time was a few minutes past seven a.m., late enough to try Giorgia again. Without wasting time brushing my teeth, I went to the phone and dialed her number once more. This time she answered after a few rings.

"Yes?" she said. She sounded sleepy.

"It's me, Roberto. Listen, Giorgia, I need Silvio's phone number."

"Silvio's? What for?" she asked, now sounding more alert.

"You know, you should've called me sooner. I know that Silvio is raising the money for Alessandra's treatment, but I want to contribute too, and I want to speak with him and help to get her to Switzerland faster." I knew that I sounded reproachful, and I meant to. It seemed to me that Giorgia didn't understand that treating health problems should never be postponed.

"Roberto ..." she hesitated for so long that I thought the line had gone dead, but then she spoke again. "Silvio isn't raising any money," she said in a low voice.

"What do you mean? Perhaps you're not up to date. That's what he is doing. Alessandra told me so yesterday."

"That was four months ago. He promised to come up with the money within two weeks, and then he disappeared. His phone is disconnected, and his father's apartment is locked. The pig is probably in Brazil now and won't show his face around here for a long time."

"But...but then it's even more important that I get involved. You know I have some money, and I will use it right away. Do you know the name of the clinic in Switzerland and who I should be talking to?"

"Roberto," she said, and her voice was frighteningly soft. "It's too late. The clinic wouldn't take her at this stage. She's missed the train."

"I ... I don't understand." I felt weak at the knees and had to sit down. "Then why did she say that she was going to Switzerland? And if Silvio disappeared four months ago, why didn't you call me right away? You should have, Giorgia. You should have called me!" My last words came out as a strangled sound as I tried to choke back my tears.

"I wanted to," she answered, now speaking with sadness in her voice, "but she wouldn't let me."

"Well, she did let you, yesterday, that's the important thing. Better now than never."

She remained silent for quite a while, then continued hesitantly.

"The doctors ... they told her that she only has a few more days ... That's why she asked me to call you. I'm sorry. That's also why the hospital let me stay with her until late at night. Yesterday I kept her company until after midnight, and I only left when I was sure she was fast asleep. I've been doing that every night for the last week."

"I don't believe you. It can't be!" I panicked. "I want to speak with her doctor. What's his name? Give me his name. I'll go and talk to him immediately."

"It's no use. They've done all they can for her..."

"Give me his name!" I shouted.

"Professor Margoni, but..."

"Thank you," I said coldly and hung up.

I didn't make time for coffee or food. I dressed in haste, brushed my teeth perfunctorily, and rushed out of the apartment. In the street, I jumped into a taxi that took me to the hospital. Once inside, I ran like a madman through the corridors, shouting requests for directions at passing nurses and doctors, until I reached a door with a sign on it that read "Professor A. Margoni, Internal Medicine." I knocked on the door and turned the handle without waiting for an answer. Inside, a middle-aged secretary looked at me superciliously above her horn-rimmed spectacles.

"This is not reception time, sir. And do you have an appointment?" she inquired with the air of someone knowing that obviously, I didn't have one.

"No, please," I said, panting, "this is a matter of life or death. I must speak with Professor Margoni right away."

"What about?"

"It's about one of his patients, Alessandra…"

"Are you her husband?"

"No, I'm her boyfriend. But you see, it's about paying for her transfer to a Swiss clinic; that's what I'm here for."

"I'm sorry, but even if I could let you in—and I have clear instructions against it—the professor would not speak with you about a patient unless you are a blood relative." Her voice had softened now, and she seemed friendlier.

"But I'm telling you that this is a matter of life or death," I insisted desperately.

"It always is," she said, shaking her head sympathetically. "The professor doesn't treat simple cases. But I'll tell you what to do; here, take this form," she said, handing me a piece of paper and a pen. "It is a written consent form that says that the medical staff can talk to you about the patient's conditions. Take it and have the patient sign it, then come back here, and I'll sneak you in between two appointments. Come back in half an hour."

"Thank you. Thank you!" I said, hoping she would understand how grateful I was.

"Sure," she simply said and got back to the papers on her desk.

Alessandra's room was not far from the professor's office, and

I arrived two minutes later. But as soon as I walked into the room, I saw that something was wrong. Only four patients were in the room, and Alessandra's bed, the one by the window that she had occupied the day before, was empty. A bare mattress gave the metal frame of the bed a detached, sterile look, and the tubes of the oxygen mask were neatly coiled on top of the small cabinet next to the bed. As I stood there, gaping at it, a nurse came in, and I grabbed her by the sleeve of her uniform.

"Where did you move Alessandra? What are you doing to her?" I almost yelled at her.

"I'm sorry, I just began my shift," she said, admirably patiently, gently pulling her sleeve away from my grip. "The patient in this bed, you mean?"

"Yes, this one," I emphasized, patting the mattress.

She studied a chart on the board in her hands and looked up at me.

"Please, sit down," she said, pointing to an armchair near Alessandra's bed.

"I don't want to sit down. Please just tell me where she is, and I'll go there."

"Sit down," she ordered, pushing me lightly but firmly on my shoulder.

I took a step back and sank into the armchair. I guess I already knew what was coming then, but my brain rejected the thought. She stooped to bring her face close to my eye level, and then she spoke my life sentence.

"I'm very sorry. She passed away early this morning. I'm really very sorry," she repeated.

The world around me became a blur, and when I raised my head that I had buried in my hands and reopened my eyes, she was no longer there. I guess this must've been routine for her.

Routine—what ill-conceived word for an event that meant the end of a world worth living in for me.

Know that Death is watching you
rejoice in the fields or between white walls,
like a peasant who tends the growing wheat
until it is ripe for the scythe.

Sappiate che la morte vi sorveglia
gioir nei prati o fra i muri di calce,
come crescere il gran guarda il villano
finché non sia maturo per la falce.

Fabrizio De André, Recitativo - 1968

EPILOGUE

"Dad! Are you still listening to those tapes? You've been at it all weekend ..."

Ernesto Coppa's teenage daughter charged into the sitting room, looking and acting annoyed. Seeing her father's haggard face, she stopped, and her tone turned to worried.

"Da-ad! What's the matter? Are you feeling well?"

Ernesto sat up, emerging from the emotional state in which the last tape had thrown him, and realized that his face was wet with tears. He hastened to wipe them with the palms of his hands and managed a forced smile.

"I'm fine, don't worry. It's just ... I've been listening to Roberto's tapes, as he asked me, see?" he added, handing her a note.

The note, written in Roberto's unmistakably neat and oblique handwriting, read, "I beg you to listen to these tapes."

"What ... what does he say in his tapes?" she asked.

"Oh, plenty." Ernesto sighed. "But now I've come to the worst part, I think. The last tape was still in the recorder that we found next to Roberto's body, and it must have recorded his last moments. I don't really *want* to listen to it, but I have to ..."

"Do you want me to sit with you while you listen to it?"

Ernesto gazed at her and what he saw in her resolute expression was a mature young woman who meant what she said.

"I'd like you to," he said.

Without another word, she sat on his lap, put her arm around his shoulder, and cocked her head to touch his own.

Ernesto put the last tape in the recorder, rewound it for a few seconds, and then hit the play button. Roberto's anguished, canned voice made him shiver...

So you see, my dear Ernesto, this is where my story ends—or at least the part of it that it makes any sense telling. You know the rest. You're familiar with the long, grey years that I spent at work, dragging myself on without any passion or expectation from life, and you will agree with me that they harbor nothing more of interest, nothing that merits being told to the public.

I am sitting outside on the porch now, and I can feel the cold, but it's not the frosty wind blowing from the fields; it's the cold within that freezes my heart. I look through the lines of cypresses and imagine that I can almost see the golden statue of the Virgin Mary, the Madonnina, on top of the Duomo—although, of course, it's too far from here, and it's only my imagination playing tricks on me. My brain has been toying with me a lot lately; sometimes, I imagine that I see my father walking toward the trees and waving to me, as I remember him from childhood...or perhaps as I want to remember him. And I see many others whom I had forgotten, and sometimes they speak to me. I suspect that my medicines are responsible for that. But of all my hallucinations, I like the Madonnina best. Imagining her helps me feel the heart of Milan beating inside me, as it did when we were boys together. Then my mind can go back freely to those times...

I never heard from the police again. They could have had the decency of sending me a note confirming that the case had been closed, but they didn't bother. On my part, I decided against phoning Bellini and asking him; no sense calling the bear from the wood.

I never spoke with Giorgia again. After the funeral, I only saw her once, about ten years ago. I almost bumped into her in the street, but I don't think she noticed. I don't know if she married, and, frankly, I don't care.

I visited Alessandra's grave at least every week, often more frequently, and while I was there, I sometimes went to put flowers on my family's grave. Every visit to Alessandra's resting place was a renewed meeting with her. I could sense her presence, and I truly believe that she sensed mine. But it wasn't the same with my family. They remained distant, aloof, making me feel unwelcome as if I were disturbing their rest, so I always cut my visits short.

My relationships with women, if you can call them that, were always brief and marked by indifference. I have had many of them— I guess I kept deluding myself that I might find passion and love again—but they always turned out to be nothing more than the unsatisfying fulfillment of a sexual need. You know that my memory is good still, but I couldn't tell you the names of more than a handful of them, and their faces are only a blur to me.

Here, I've said it all ... at least, all that counts.

You are undoubtedly asking yourself what purpose it may serve to bare my secrets before one and all, both as the recipient and the administrator of bad luck and misery. I don't have a good answer to that question besides telling you that I feel it is my duty and right to share the truth with the world. Maybe, and so I hope, learning from my mistakes and those of others will help generations to come to do the right thing. Perhaps fathers will learn to judge their sons with greater leniency, talk to them more, and learn about their inner world to enjoy a relationship based on unconditional love. And one can hope *that sons will find ways to establish a real dialogue with their parents and understand what really matters to them, so they will learn to respect them. And then again, perhaps lovers will find the strength to let go of hopeless loves instead of turning them into the center of a miserable life.*

And if any of that happens as a result of reading about my mistakes, even only to one person, then my effort—your effort—won't have been in vain.

And now, my dearest friend, allow me to give you a few instructions ... nay, I shouldn't presume to instruct ... I merely wish to tell you how I think these memories of mine—or rather I should say, this confession of mine—should be presented.

Wait. I'm tired, and I must rest now. I'll go on recording later...

The tape resumed with the sound of panting, and then Roberto's voice was heard again.

I was resting, and I heard voices calling. I'm on the porch now. Can you hear them, Ernesto? I can't figure where they come from.

Wait a moment ... I see something ... Yes, I wish you could see the line of cypresses in front of me. It's dark already, but the Madonnina shines brightly above it against the dark sky. I wonder how that can be ... I know I'm too far away from the center of Milan to see her, but still, I can make out her distinctive features as clearly as I see my hand ...

Oh, yes ... yes! It is my family coming from behind the tree-line; I can see my father's face distinctly and my mother's. And it's my brother who waves to me. Now my father speaks ... can you hear him in the recording? No, I guess his voice is too faint and far away for the tape to pick up. He says that he has missed me; would you believe that?

He has never said anything like that to me before ... that he missed me. It ... it feels good—I don't know how to explain.

I can't see clearly what my brother is signaling to me because my eyes are filled with tears, and you know what? They're tears of happiness; I'm sure you can hear that in my voice. I have missed my family so much and for so long ...

They just stand there. But why did they stop? I want them to come over and talk to me. To me and to the tape; I need them to tell you and everybody that it wasn't my fault ...

Oh, I see now what was keeping them. They were waiting for Alessandra. Here she comes. How beautiful she is!

I hope you can hear me, Ernesto. Speaking is difficult now, and I have to save my breath for Alessandra, so I can't speak too much.

"Come over here, Alessandra!"

It's getting darker, and I can't see too well, but I can tell that she's encouraging me to come to her. I wish I could, but the cypresses are too far from where I sit, and I'm too weak ... I don't think that I can make it.

But I have to try ...

She needs me; she's waiting for me. They all need me ...

The sound of a chair being pushed back was clearly heard in the tape, and then Roberto's voice became farther and fainter.

I'll tell you what she said when I come back, Ernesto, okay? Hold on a minute ...

"I'm coming, my love. Wait for me ..."

The recording ended with an indistinct sound that could be steps and then a few more distant words, the last ones on the tape.

"I'm sorry, father. I never meant to ..."

Then it was only the wind, blowing into the microphone for long minutes until the tape stopped with a sad click.

Meet the Author

Kfir Luzzatto is the author of twelve novels, several short stories, and seven non-fiction books. Kfir was born and raised in Italy and moved to Israel as a teenager. He acquired the love for the English language from his father, a former U.S. soldier, a voracious reader, and a prolific writer. Kfir has a Ph.D. in chemical engineering and works as a patent attorney. He lives in Omer, Israel, with his full-time partner, Esther, and their four children, Michal, Lilach, Tamar, and Yonatan.

In pursuit of his interest in the mind-body connection, Kfir was certified as a Clinical Hypnotherapist by the Anglo European

College of Therapeutic Hypnosis.

Kfir has published extensively in the professional and general press over the years. For almost four years, he wrote a weekly "Patents" column in Globes (Israel's financial newspaper). His popular guide, *FUN WITH PATENTS—The Irreverent Guide for the Investor, the Entrepreneur, and the Inventor*, was published in 2016. He is an HWA (Horror Writers Association) and ITW (International Thriller Writers) member.

You can visit Kfir's website and read his blog at www.kfirluzzatto.com. Follow him on Twitter (@KfirLuzzatto) and friend him on Facebook (https://www.facebook.com/ KfirLuzzattoAuthor.